ENCHANTED
A Tale of Remembrance

by

Leia Marie

ENCHANTED A Tale of Remembrance by Leia Marie

Published by In-Awe Press

P.O. Box 148, La Veta, CO 81055

www.in-awe.net

Copyright © 2023 by Leia Marie

All rights reserved. No portion of this book may be reproduced in any form without permission from the publisher, except as permitted by U.S. copyright law.

Heartfelt appreciation for permission to quote from the following sources:
Where The Wild Things Are, by Maurice Sendak ©1963, Harper Collins Publishers
The Great Forest...And Beyond by Leia Marie ©2023, In-Awe Press
Overstory, by Richard Powers ©2018, W.W. Norton & Company
Brown Bear, Brown Bear, What Do You See? by Bill Martin, Macmillan Publishers

Cover and Page Design by Mel McCann

Author Photo by Cindy Stegmeier
www.femininenaturephotography.com

ISBN: 979-8-9869997-0-8

For my sweet husband,
the steady ground beneath my feet
lifting me to the stars

Table of Contents

Preamble... 1

The Amble Begins... 3
    A Tale Is Told 6
    An Invitation Is Offered 8
    Lana 10
    Jack 13
    Jessica 17
    Ella 22
    A Pause 24

The Amble Resumes... 27
    Ann 31
    Eric 35
    Phil 42
    Pausing Again 48

Ambling On... 51
    Emma 56
    Richard 65
    Meghan 70
    Pausing Anew 74

Ambling Again 77
    Kayla 82
    Mia 91
    Antonio 95
    Sister Constance-Marie 100
    Pausing Once More 106

The Amble Continues... 109
    Aingeal 115
    Sakiya 121
    James 128
    Pausing Yet Again 134

Rambling Onward...137
    Nikki 141
    Chloë 147
    Hunter 151
    Re-Pause 154

Re-Ramble... 157
    Maliq 162
    Sarah 166
    Mandi 170
    Jacob 175
    Another Pause 180

Ambling Anew... 183
    Henry 188
    Selva 192
    Másání 195
    One Last Pause 200

A Final Amble... 203
    The Holy Ones 207
    Widening The Aperture 211
    Leave-Taking 217

Post-Amble... 223

A Few Parting Words From Leia 225
    Gratitudes 229
    The Great Forest...and Beyond 231

About the Author 237

Preamble...

Welcome, my friend. As I sit to write, sunlight pours through south-facing windows, and though the chill of this February morning can still be felt, my writing space has warmed sufficiently to bring comfort. Today is Imbolc, an ancient Celtic festival celebrating the expansion of Light as Winter turns toward Spring. The word itself comes from the Old Gaelic meaning "in the belly," and refers to the time when new life begins to stir, though it is not yet visible to the outer world. An auspicious time to begin a book, yes?

So on this Imbolc and in my cozy writing space, my fingers tap-tap-tap away, lacing words together. And this is what seems true to me in this moment: that which presses to come through me yearns just as strongly to be received by you. I find this an astonishing process. Magical, really. Images and concepts transform into words on the page. You receive those words, breathe life into them, make them your own. But the magic does not stop there. As in some sort of cosmic relay race—though perhaps cosmic relay dance gets at my meaning more precisely—you will carry what is offered here into the next leg of your own journey. As you make real these ideas in your own life—playing with them, grappling with them, dismissing some and further developing others, while weaving them through your own truths—the magic will continue in ways both direct and circuitous, as you then share that magic with others...and as they share with others still. For this is how it ever is, in this cosmic relay dance that is unending.

Yes, together we will create something magical that will expand in ever-widening circles. I am delighted you have joined me in this process. I am enchanted.

The Amble Begins...

Imagine this...A vast space in which all is dark and silent. This is not the dark silence of emptiness, but of a fullness gathering itself together, pausing to sense how best to make itself known to you. You're not sure how you know this, or why you trust that you are safely held here. It is simply so, and a kindling reverence takes hold as you await the unfolding that will soon come.

As we pause for a moment here, sweet reader—and be assured we shall not linger long—I ask that you offer yourself to the mystery of this place. I appeal to the capacity for make-believe that surely you exhibited in the yesterdays of your childhood. It is a talent that just as surely lives on to this day, albeit perhaps buried beneath the numerous facts and the dogged reasonableness of the adult you have become. Rekindle it now so that you might enter this world not as reader alone, but as the wonder-filled, imaginative child that resides still inside you. Critique my words later if you're so inclined, but for now give yourself to the delight of pretend-play, even as I suggest images for your eyes and place words upon your tongue.

As promised, our respite has been brief. Yet even as we tarried for those few moments, a subtle change has occurred. You notice the darkness has become a bit less inky, less all-pervasive. Shades of gray swirl within it now, sparkling with other hues as does mist at the riverbed in dawn's first light. You feel yourself moving forward, though this movement has not come from volition of bone, muscle, mind or heart. You are being *pulled*. It is as though the gathering that fills this place has made a decision and gathers you now as well. And still you are unafraid.

There is light ahead, a flickering that radiates warmth though you are still a distance away. As you move closer you realize it is flames you see, flames that reach and sway in a dance as old as fire itself. And now some portion of the darkness resolves into a hearth, the kind you may not have seen in this lifetime, but have always known—an opening deep and wide, stones worn smooth by time and fitted precisely one to another. A mantel of darkened wood stretches above, holding a jumble of dishes and pots. You are close enough now to feel the fire's heat, to hear its pop and sizzle. You also hear the wind's keening wail. Recognizing the sound of ice pinging against panes, you turn your head to see a casement of old wood looking out onto a night as black as pitch.

"It be quite a storm, indeed," she says, in a whisper-soft voice laced with age. You are not startled, though you were unaware that someone was near. You turn toward the oldest woman you have ever seen, sitting in a low rocker but a few feet away. A gown of sparkling sapphire drapes her slender frame and spills onto the floor. Hair, thin and fanned around a deeply furrowed face, is as white as a swan's back in moonlight. Her eyes are the vivid blue of a mountain sky, but as they hold yours, you know them to be portals opening onto an immense depth.

"Good God," you think, "we're just one spinning wheel away from a full archetype here!" And she throws back her head and guffaws, a surprisingly full-bodied sound for someone you took to be quite frail.

"Well, I guess you could say that," she comments moments later in a voice you had mistaken for fragility, but realize now is rather musical, even shimmery, "though we were hoping that, to use your phrasing, we'd succeeded in reaching the full archetype." With speech strangely though pleasantly accented, she continues. "We chose outer forms that would best convey that which we wish to impart. We hope they please you, and that seeing me as an old woman come to tell you a tale will make you feel at ease. You may call me Zosia. Please sit."

You turn toward the chair she indicates, a sturdy thing crafted of well-worn wood and covered with thick cushions of bright, though slightly faded, fabric. Noticing a level of anticipation bordering on the jitters, you sit and remind yourself that you feel no threat here.

Knowing your thoughts once more though you have yet to speak, Zosia nods. "No harm shall come to you in this place, child. Allow your body to be at rest while my story unfolds."

As she gestures to the hearth, you find your chair has turned to face its flames. They grow strangely vivid for several moments, swirling and twirling and leaping about. Soon, though, they settle as images form in their light, images Zosia's words bring into being...

A Tale Is Told

"Once upon a time, in a land far, far away and as near as your own heart, there lived a people who had lost their way. They had become enamored of things that did not serve nor aid in realizing the promise of their birth. Precious time was given to pursuits that did not feed souls. They called things important that were inconsequential. And those exceptional minds, capable of creating beauty and ingenious designs, too often forged discord instead.

Something had to be done, for they now careened all too near a precipice that could very well claim them. The Guardians, for all folk have them, watched and debated among themselves the level of intervention possible. There are, you see, clear rules as to the intercession allowed, for along with elegant minds, the people had been gifted the ability to choose, to determine for themselves how best to proceed in any given situation.

This, as with all gifts, was sacred and could not be overruled. The statutes were quite clear on this point, allowing for soft incursions only. And so, prophets and teachers had been sent, myths generated and passed down, and ream upon ream of sacred writings amassed. The people were indeed moved by the messages of the Wise Ones, but often forgot or never let those words root deeply into the soil of their being. And purest wisdom not deeply anchored and well-tended swirls away with the first rising wind.

So it came to pass that another Council of Guardians was called, though those words are but a poor attempt to convey such a meeting in that time out of time, in a place that lies beyond human understanding of locale.

What transpired cannot, of course, be fully shared, nor would you be able to wholly grasp the meaning of the words spoken there. I can, though, tell you this much. The gravity of the situation led the Guardians to find a new way to step forward in loving support of those endearing, but oh so young, souls. Free will could not be taken away, it was true. But an enchantment could be devised that would offer respite from all the busyness, allowing this bevy of souls the chance to choose with greater clarity.

And so the Guardians joined their considerable power into a potent incantation that cast a hush over this world, one that brought an outer stillness to encourage an inner one. In one household representative of them all, this is what occurred.

Silence fell and clocks paused in mid-tick. Lana could move freely, though all activity around her ceased. Her partner sat rooted in place, and their son's arm was poised in midair, action figure grasped in unmoving fingers. Their young daughter napped on, snuggled with her favorite stuffed animal. You might think the woman would be alarmed by the immobility of her loved ones, but she was not, for the magic was laced with calm. All was as a dream, sparkling with a vibrancy that soothed even as it buoyed and invigorated. And the power of this spell was such that the son saw his parents stilled, though he was not. Likewise for her partner. And when the girl child awoke, she found herself deeply rested, the house as quiet as a moonbeam, and her family hushed and at peace.

And across the land, in hamlet, village and city alike, it was the same. This conjuring was such that no one thought of doing mischief or frittering away this dream that was no dream. Like a bee to the fragrant nectar of a blooming flower, each was lured to the unique spark that was heart and soul. All attuned to who they could be, who they already were in their innermost selves. And for the duration of the enchantment, which felt like minutes to some and days to others, they remembered."

An Invitation Is Offered

Zosia falls silent. The fire hisses and crackles, though images no longer form in its flames. Wind continues to howl, but the sound seems quite distant now, cocooned as you are with this old woman. Long moments pass.

"Have you any thoughts?" she asks at last.

You notice that you are facing one another now, though you have no memory of movement. There is also a steaming mug in your hand, and you spare nary a thought as to how it came to be there. Recognizing there is no need to rush, you take several sips of the unfamiliar but aromatic beverage as you allow your answer to rise up.

"Thoughts, no," you say, the first words you have spoken in this place. You breathe deeply, take another sip. "I find this uncanny, this being here with you, seeing all you spoke of coming to life in the fire of an ancient hearth. Yet while it is strange to me, it is also captivating. I feel touched in some place deep inside, a place that lies beneath thoughts or the words to express them."

"Ah," she smiles, "I thought it might be so. Would you like to be taken deeper still? You have already seen much, and perhaps that is sufficient for your needs. Perhaps there is no desire to know more."

"No," you shake your head adamantly, as certain as you have ever been. "I definitely want to know more. I have *always* wanted to know more."

With a quick nod, one that suggests a confirmation of what was already known, Zosia gestures to the hearth, which you find yourself facing once again.

"Then that wish shall be granted. As you have already seen, this hearth is no simple structure for the containment of flame. And yet, just as any noble hearth funnels smoke up its chimney that we may remain clear-eyed, this one is likewise designed to promote clarity of vision. It is a window opening unto other worlds, one that will carry you into the lives of others. Though you will not be able to move in body there, you will be gifted the ability to perceive each life as though it were your own. So please sit back and be content as you travel forth. We shall begin by entering the home of the family mentioned in my tale."

And with that, the fire bursts into a brighter, more lively dance before calming once again. Lives begin to unfold in its flames and, bright-eyed and eager, you join with them there.

Lana

It is the silence she notices first. Quiet is a rare thing indeed in this house that is home to a fiendishly active boychild of seven, an imaginative and increasingly willful 4-year-old girl, two adult women, and a bouncy little mutt of a dog prone to excited yips and wholehearted immersion in whatever kid madness is going on.

But the quiet that has settled over the house this day is like nothing Lana has ever experienced. It isn't just that clocks have stopped or news no longer spews from Jessica's laptop as she sits immobile on the couch, feet propped on the coffee table, Mugsy stilled in sphynx pose beside her. It isn't even that Jack has quieted in mid-roar, arm extended with his Dino X-Ray action figure—whom he'd cleverly named Dino X-Ray—poised to destroy the Lego tower he'd been working on for the better part of an hour.

What strikes Lana most strongly is something she cannot name. This quieting seems to go deeper than cessation of sound or lack of movement. And when she considers that perhaps she oughta be worried at the distant look in the eyes of her wife and son, she finds she isn't. She knows there is nothing to fear here. How could there be when the air itself feels so lovely, so invigoratingly *good*?

She does, though, think it wise to check on Ella who, after they'd begun *The Great Forest...and Beyond* for the third time, had just drifted into an increasingly rare afternoon nap. She finds their youngest sleeping soundly, curled around her stuffed orangutan.

Lana stretches out beside her daughter, drifts off for a time herself, and wakes looking into the nighttime sky she'd painted on Ella's ceiling. Stars and planets sweep across an expanse of deep blue, with the ceiling light standing in for a full moon. Her eyes drop to the scene she'd begun on the one windowless wall. It was to be an autumn meadow leading to the outer edge of a forest thick with trees, with a scattering of wildlife throughout. Life being what it is, though, she'd gotten sidetracked before she was done. The forest was finished, but the foreground field remained mostly empty, with only a fox, three tumbling kits, one patch of butterfly weed, and a stand of tall amber grass. As Lana walks to the kitchen, she wonders again if she'll ever finish that wall, though just yesterday Ella had been quite adamant that she loved it *exactly* as it was. Just as well, since there was enough to do without insisting on unnecessary projects.

Lana makes tea, absorbs the quiet as she lets it steep. "It's as though I myself am steeping," she whispers and feels tears rise. As she watches the steam swirl into the welcoming air, those tears flow silently, effortlessly, wondrously down her cheeks. These are not the messengers of painful emotion. They are not accompanied by wrenching sobs. Lana recognizes the quiet tears of simple release, ignited as she drops down into herself. "How long has it been?" she asks aloud.

When both tea and tears are spent, she feels more steeping is in order. And so she draws a bath. As the tub fills, she walks back to Ella's room, stands before that unfinished wall, entranced by the blank space where nothing yet exists. That emptiness stays with her as she lowers herself into the hot-hot water. It remains as she makes herself dinner. It hangs on as she curls into the huge bed she and Jessica bought the year they knew themselves ready to make a family.

And in the way of dreams, it stays with her in an altered form throughout that long night. For in the dark hours, she gives that blank space what it longs for. Lana paints again. Not mice in a field or autumn-gold aspen on a child's wall. No. She paints now for herself. Images leap onto canvas, strokes bold, color vivid. She has painted a dozen when that night is done.

And when she wakes to sunlight streaming through the window, she knows it is time. She loved painting Ella's room, and had delighted in helping both children put color to paper for their own creations. But it is time now to paint for herself once more. Of this she is certain.

Lana dresses in old clothing, and descends the basement stairs to reclaim what has been stored away since their move to town 8 years ago. From the back of the deepest closet she hauls out the easel and the boxes that hold her precious supplies. She bypasses a pre-stretched canvas for a roll of linen, takes one of the four empty frames. Three trips are needed to carry it all upstairs.

She writes a note to Jessica in case life resumes its hectic pace before she returns. Running a hand over Jack's head as she walks by, she places the note on Jessica's keyboard, leaning over to place a kiss on her sweet wife's head. Lana then lugs her supplies out to the small room off the garage, her intended studio space that has somehow become a jumble of gardening supplies, old bikes, and assorted junk.

And within this dream that is no dream, Lana brings her studio to life. Not fully, for that will take more time than she wants to give now and trips to the dump and the secondhand store. Yet when she turns off the shop vac an hour or so later, a good section of the room is hers and she can imagine the rest as it will one day be.

Lana sets the easel so the light hits just right. Lays out tubes of oil paint, pallet and knife, her cherished brushes, mineral spirits, linseed oil, gesso. Using the worktable that runs along the back wall, she cuts, stretches and staples a canvas to its frame, feeling again the rising excitement she recognizes as foreplay to the main event. And as she primes the canvas, she knows that she also is being primed. As each layer of gesso dries, Lana walks the backyard or simply sits as images rise from wherever such images come from.

And as she stands finally before the emptiness of that waiting canvas, Lana feels the familiar thrill-fear filling her as the flow beckons. She reaches for the palette, squeezing onto it ultramarine, phthalo blue and titanium white. She opens the window to the late morning air and pours linseed into a jar. She chooses a brush and holds it lightly as she dabs oil onto the ultramarine, stirs it about. She pauses, feeling the current swirling around her now. And then Lana touches brush to canvas and steps fully into that flow, letting it carry her away.

Jack

"*Graarrrrr*," Jack growls as Dino X-Ray crashes into the tower. "*Bam!! Crash!!!*" he hollers as his own foot assists in the demolition, sending Legos flying.

As his voice continues to rise, in some corner of his mind he registers it odd that no one tells him to settle down. But it is only when Ender the Dragon breaks apart after crashing into the wall that Jack gets that something strange is going on.

He looks over at Mommy. She's sitting on the couch staring at her laptop, like she hasn't heard a thing. And Mugsy is asleep beside her, which just doesn't make any sense at all. He should be barking and dashing in to grab the flying blocks.

"Mommy?" he says as he walks over. "Are you asleep, too?" But no, her eyes are open. He gently touches her cheek, but she doesn't move. And neither does Mugsy when he strokes his furry head.

"This is weird. Very, *very* weird!" he says as he walks off to look for Ella and Mama. His sister is asleep too, the normal kind, but she doesn't move when he nudges her. He finds Mama staring at nothing in the den, and she doesn't react either when he gently squeezes her arm.

Yep, this is definitely weird, but Jack isn't scared. In fact, he feels happy. But when it occurs to him that he can now make as much noise as he wants and no one will yell at him to use his stupid inside voice, his happy turns into very excited.

"I can scream!" he says in a slightly raised voice. When neither of his moms says anything, his voice grows louder still.

"I CAN SCREAM!!!" he hollers and waits. When the silence continues, so does he. "I CAN SCREAM. AND I CAN USE MY OUTSIDE VOICE INSIDE THIS HOUSE! AND NO ONE IS GOING TO STOP ME!!!"

Gosh it feels good, he thinks, as he ratchets the volume up even more. "I CAN YELL. I *MUST* YELLLLL!!! "he shouts. And then he is Max from *Where The Wild Things Are*, stomping and marching through the house. "I WILL ROAR MY TERRIBLE ROARS AND GNASH MY TERRIBLE TEETH! AND YOU...CAN'T...STOP...MEEEEEE!!!"

But after a while of no one stopping him, he gets a little bored. And the truth is, yelling is kind of hurting his own ears.

"I think I need to yell outside," he says in a normal inside voice. "This place is just too small. It traps my shouts. They need *room*!"

So Jack opens the backdoor, dashes across the porch, shoves through its door, and runs down the steps, screaming once again. Then he marches around the backyard, shouting and yelling until his throat begins to hurt. And then he sits on the grass and wonders what to do next.

And that's when he hears it. It's a squeaky sort of sound, which he finally tracks down to the big tree in the corner. And sure enough, something is flopping around in the grass beneath it.

Walking closer, Jack sees it's a bird, though it doesn't look much like one. It's mostly pink because it has hardly any feathers, and he can see its skinny legs and little wing bones popping out. Its eyes are open which he knows is a good thing, but he also knows this bird isn't old enough to survive on its own. It needs help.

Good thing Jack loves nature shows, because he knows exactly what to do. First, he looks up into the tree. He knows there must be a nest up there somewhere, but it's way too high to see. No way is he gonna be able to put the little bird back, and there's no way its parents can either.

"Don't be afraid, little bird," Jack croons as he kneels on the ground near the cheeping little creature. "I'm not gonna hurt you, but I gotta get ya someplace safe, cuz a little bird like you could get hurt out here on the ground all by himself."

No one has to tell Jack to use his inside voice, even though he's outside. No one has to tell him to be gentle either. He knows how not to scare little things. Slowly, he reaches out and scoots his palms under the tiny bird, who is surprised into silence.

"I've got you, birdy," he says as he carefully lifts it. And this boy who so recently stomped about while roaring terrible roars and gnashing terrible teeth, walks very slowly back to the porch, climbs the steps, pushes the door open with his shoulder, and puts the bird down on the rug inside.

"Aw, don't worry," Jack says when the bird starts to cry again. He shuts the door tight. "I'll come back, but I gotta make you a new nest."

Once he gets into the kitchen, he's not quiet anymore. He races into the living room and past his sleeping Mommy, talking excitedly all the while.

"I found a baby bird!" he hollers as he runs up the stairs. "It fell out of its nest, and I rescued it, and now I have to keep it safe."

Jack rushes into his bedroom, grabs one of the shoeboxes from his shelf, dumps its cool things onto the floor, and races back out. He snatches two towels and a roll of toilet paper from the bathroom, and runs back down the stairs. He slows his steps, though, as he reaches the porch.

"See, I came back," he says softly to the bird. "Don't cry. I'm here and I'm gonna make you a safe place to stay until my Moms wake up. Then we'll call the Nature Center and see what we should do."

Jack folds one of the towels into the shoebox, and scrunches toilet paper into a nest-like shape, talking in a soothing voice all the while. "You're such a tiny bird that you might have to stay at the Nature Center for a little while. We went there once and they take real good care of birds like you. There!" Jack says, putting the nest into the box. "I hope this'll make you feel at home, little bird. Now I'm gonna pick you up again and put you in there, so don't be scared, okay? Here goes."

And once again he scoops the bird into his hands, but he uses the towel this time. He knows he should have used one before, but he didn't have a choice. He couldn't leave the bird out there by itself while he went to get a dumb towel. No tellin' what mighta happened!

Again, the bird stops crying when he picks it up, and starts its frantic peeping again when he places it carefully in the toilet paper nest.

"Don't you like it?" Jack asks, disappointed. But when the bird keeps crying, another thought pops into his head. "Maybe you just want me to hold you. Is that it?"

And sure enough, the bird stops crying as Jack gently picks it up. And remembering that he himself always feels better when someone holds him when he's scared, he moves over to the chair, carefully sits down, and puts the bird in his lap, keeping his hands under the towel for warmth. And even when the bird starts crying a few seconds later, Jack is still sure it feels better being with him than all by itself in a box.

That's when Jack notices a feeling inside. It doesn't hurt exactly. Well, it kinda does, but it isn't a bad hurt. It's a hurt that makes him want to take care of the baby bird and make it feel better. Later Mommy said that feeling sounded to her like a special kind of love, a mix of wonder and tenderness and a fierce kind of protectiveness. She said that's the way she felt when he was a baby, like she'd do anything to protect him and keep him safe.

And when she said that, Jack knew she was right. But sitting on the porch on this very weird day that turned out to be a very wonderful day, he knows only that he doesn't want to scream or stomp or roar terrible roars. He wants nothing but to sit here with this baby bird, watching it stretch out its neck, or try to stand on its skinny legs, and giggling at how cute it is when it flops over. And he feels very proud when it gets up to try again.

"You're a very brave little bird," Jack whispers, "and I promise to keep you safe until your wings are strong. And if you do have to go to the Nature Center, I'll come and visit you every day 'til you're big enough to fly away."

And even though saying that makes his chest hurt worse, though still in a good kinda way, Jack knows that is exactly what he will do.

Jessica

At first she thinks the internet's crapped out again. She'd been wondering if changing companies had been the right move, but they liked the idea of thumbing a nose at the Big Boys, and had decided to give the newly formed and locally owned start-up a chance.

Rousing Mugsy from what she guessed was rabbit chase ecstasy, she gets up to check the router. And sees Jack. Their son is never still, certainly not when engaged in acts of mass destruction and surely not with an arm outstretched at such a strange angle.

"Hey, buddy, what's going on?" she asks, aware in some part of her brain that she isn't concerned in the least by his lack of response. Her breath does catch, though, when she sees Lana in the double rocker in the den, still as stone, book opened on her lap, eyes glazed. Well, not exactly glazed, Jessica sees as she steps closer. More dream-like. Not at all like last time.

With Mugsy at her heels, she checks on Ella, finds her curled around Wangtang and sleeping soundly, which calms her some. Yet Jessica is still antsy, even though she knows without a doubt that all is well.

"Looks like it's just you and me," she says to Mugsy, who yips and promptly trots to the door, tail wagging, an endearingly hopeful mutt face turned her way.

"Good idea, boy!" she responds, somehow knowing it's safe to leave the kids at home. "Let's take us a walk." When Mugsy's mad circling calms enough to attach the leash, they step out into a world subtly though profoundly altered.

Leaves rustle as usual in the light breeze. Large birds soar and smaller ones flit and twitter about in the bushes that line the drive. But all sounds of human activity have ceased. Car engines no longer rumble, and there are no shouts across backyards. In the next block, they pass a bearded man frozen in place, back bent, the electric whine of the hedge trimmer he holds silenced. On the main road, cars are anchored in place, human occupants immobilized.

"Well, this is pretty darn weird, isn't it, Mr. Mugster?" Yet Jessica is aware that despite the strangeness of it all, she remains not the least bit alarmed. In fact, she feels enlivened now. Free. All edginess gone.

"What the hell, Mugsy. What do ya say we lose this leash and take a run?" she asks as she bends to unhook him. "It's been a while, but I think we remember how, don't you?"

And indeed they do. They cross the street at an easy lope, turn onto the trail a block farther on. Following its snaking path through the woods, they arc around humans stopped in mid-stride and inert cyclists who somehow haven't toppled to the ground. And while the occasional chittering squirrel awakens the predator lodged deep in his fierce canine soul, Mugsy is perplexed by a dog they pass who stands as unmoving as her human.

"Methinks I smell magic, Muggins," Jessica says in a lousy British accent, while also realizing it all feels quite natural at the same time. And ultimately, it must have felt the same to Mugsy who, after a few sniffs, dashes ahead of his own human once again.

Twenty minutes later, they exit the trail near the college and sprint to the lawn that stretches beside the parking lot. Jessica stops then, hands on knees, letting her heartrate settle, while Mugsy throws himself onto the grass, panting with tongue lolling.

"I'm with ya, Mugsy Boy!", she says as she flops down beside him and stretches onto her back. "Shit, I think we've gone soft if a little jog like that can do us in."

As her breathing gradually calms, she stares up into the vast expanse of blue sky dotted with a few cumulous clouds. And Lana's face appears before her again. Not the Lana in the rocker this afternoon, but the Lana she'd found on that other afternoon, 37 days after Jack's birth.

Gawd, it was awful! It had begun during Lana's last trimester, which was why Jack's room hadn't gotten finished before his birth. While he was still sleeping in the open-sided bassinet next to their bed, Jessica had finally slapped some paint onto the walls herself, covering over one half-formed tree and a sorry-looking squirrel. She'd finished stripping and staining the bureau, and had arranged the cloth diapers, stuffed animals, and all those adorable little onesies and infant outfits that had been amassing themselves in boxes and bags around the house.

Still neither of them had been overly concerned, thinking Lana's shifting moods were just the baby blues. And she'd seemed better during those first weeks after Jack's birth when they were both home and delighting in their baby boy. But when Jessica returned to work, her once competent and take-charge woman began to sink, coming undone at the least little thing, crying for no reason either of them could figure out.

Guilt slams into Jessica again now. How could she have been so stupid? How could she not have known?!! Sure, she got that postpartum depression was a thing, and she knew that interrupted sleep wasn't helping at all. She just didn't get that it was *that* serious.

Nothing had prepared her for walking into the house that day after work. Jack's wails met her at the door, not alarming in itself as already their boy knew his mind and made sure everyone else did too. But when she found his bassinet in the living room and him in it with no Lana nearby trying to soothe, she knew something was wrong, very wrong.

"What's the matter, little man?" she'd crooned as she scooped him up, jiggling him as she walked through the house looking for Lana. She found her huddled on the floor of the laundry room, staring straight ahead and whispering, "I can't. I can't."

"It's okay, sweetie," Jessica soothed, sitting down beside her. "I'm here now. I've got him and I've got you."

With one arm holding their baby, the other holding the only woman she'd ever love, Jessica waited. And though Lana said no more, she did lean into Jessica. A good sign, but it made it that much harder to do what needed doing for Jack. His tiny body was shaking with what she chose to believe was indignation, though she knew it had to be way past feeding time as well.

"I'm sorry, Lannie, but I gotta take care of our Jack, okay?," she said softly as she leaned Lana back against the dryer. "I'm gonna go heat some milk for our boy, and I'll be right back. You stay right here, okay? I'll be right back. Just as soon as I can."

As she walked to the kitchen, got a bottle of breastmilk from the fridge and heated it on the stove, she kept that bouncy thing going with Jack, speaking softly to him while also calling out her movements to Lana. And in her mind she formed a mental to-do list: call the doctor, get hold of Lana's parents, figure out how to take more time off.

It was horrible, though thankfully that had been the worst of it. Lana's mom came to stay with them for a month or so, and it was sweet luck that the first antidepressant worked so well, though it did take a few weeks and the dose had to be tweaked twice. Jessica's boss was kind, allowing her to work from home, which everyone knew was mostly a joke. She just couldn't focus, and felt the need to be with Jack all the time, which she suspected was why they had such a tight bond to this day.

Slowly Lana rose from that dark hole and became herself once again. She was able to gradually discontinue the medication a year later, once her hormones had settled back down. And though they were watchful throughout her pregnancy with Ella and in the months after her birth, any symptoms Lana had were mild and managed easily. She'd resumed sessions with her therapist, and they made sure she was surrounded by the good friends they had not yet made when Jack was born.

"Well, Mr Muggerly," Jessica says now as she gets to her feet, the dog following suit, "that's enough of a sashay down memory lane for one day." But as she wipes tears from her face, she realizes she feels only the echo of the guilt and fear that had hit hard a few minutes earlier. "Another strange thing about this strange day," she whispers.

They cross the lawn and come onto the rise that looks down on the athletic field, where the women's soccer team had obviously come to a screeching halt mid-practice. Around the field's edges, a few women are caught in lunges, banded lateral squats and other cruel strength-building exercises.

"Shit," she winces, "makes my quads burn just lookin' at 'em, Mugster. Hope their muscles get some of whatever magic we got going on here."

Cones are arranged at intervals down the center of the field, where other women, though statue-still now, had clearly been practicing technical skills, alone or in various combinations of players.

"Let's go on down, Mugsy," she says, starting to jog down the hill.

She walks among the women then, hoping she isn't being intrusive or overriding some magic protocol she doesn't know anything about. While a part of her mind registers the superb form of those engaged in juggling, shielding, volleying, heading and various passing drills, what calls to her most are the faces.

The fierce determination of a woman doing a plank series, though caught now with her weight on one arm, the other frozen while pushing the ball in a wide arc. The expectation in the face of a player in a group of five knowing the next pass is coming to her. And the triumph of this woman here who has finally executed the perfect move for which she'd trained so hard.

And Jessica remembers. Oh, how she loves this game! Any game, really. Aerobics and weights are just things you do to stay in shape, and watching sports on TV can be an enjoyable way to pass the day if anyone has the time. But being part of a game—the wild action, play turning on a dime, the sheer unpredictability of it—well, talk about being in the moment!

She'd never say this to anyone of course, but it feels almost holy. No, not almost. It *is* holy, a way of being fully alive in the here and now, of being part of something bigger than yourself. Great practice, she thinks now, for inhabiting life, being solidly present, connected with your pals, and ready for whatever comes at you. God, she misses it!

And yet, though Lana'd encouraged her to sign up with one of the rec teams, she'd dragged her feet. Of course it had been out of the question at first, what with setting up the house, getting used to a new job, and the colossal joys and fears of those first few months after Jack's birth. Even when things improved, though, it just didn't feel right to leave Lana alone any more than she already did. But Jessica knew now that it hadn't been worry for Lana that had her making excuses, or at least that wasn't the largest part of it. It was the memory of her own fear that made her uneasy whenever she was away from home.

"So, Mugsy, do ya think we might be able to let that one go, after 7 friggin' years?" she asks now. Though in saying it, she knows she already has.

She taps one of the balls with her foot, begins weaving it around the cones and frozen women, while guarding the ball from Mugsy, who yip-yip-yips merrily, canine heart delighted that something long-clenched in his human has finally let loose.

Ella

Ella's eyes open. Wangtang's do, too. The house is very quiet. They get out of bed and walk to the living room. Mommy is sitting on the couch, looking at her computer with Mugsy asleep beside her. Jack stands like a statue.

"Hi, Mommy," Ella says as she pats her arm.

"Hi, Mugsy," Ella says, as she rubs his head.

They don't answer.

"Whatcha doing, Jack?" she asks, walking over and tugging on his Dino X-Ray arm. She thinks it's a little bit strange that he doesn't tell her to stop bugging him, but she doesn't think too much about it. She walks off to look for Mama.

"Are you asleep, too?" she asks Mama, as she climbs up in the rocker and rests her head against Mama's arm.

"I guess they're all sound asleep," she says to Wangtang when Mama doesn't answer either. "And it's soooo quiet. Isn't it *wonderful!*"

Hopping from the chair, she and Wangtang skip back to the bedroom. Ella likes skipping, especially now that she's getting good at it.

"Hey, Wangtang! Wanna go to the Forest with the kids?" she asks in an excited voice. Even though everyone else is quiet today, she can hear Wangtang talking in her head just like always. He's excited, too.

"So we start this way," she reminds him as they climb onto the bed. "You sit right next to me like this, and I put the magic book on my lap like this," she says, making sure everything is *exactly* like it needs to be for the magic to happen. "And I start reading, even though Jack says I can't, but I can too!"

Running her fingers under the words on the front cover, just like Mama does when she teaches her, Ella reads, " '*The Great Forest And Beyond.*' And all these words here, Wangtang," Ella explains as she flips the pages, "are telling us about how the kids are playing in the field when the giant red bird—though it says it's a giant *ruby* bird, but Mama says that's just a very pretty kind of red—drops them this Invitation," she says, pointing to the words on the next page."

It doesn't matter that some of those words are very big or that Ella's finger runs under them faster than she can say them, because she knows them by heart. "*Needed: Three Adventurous Children For An Undertaking Of Great Importance. Must Be Kind. Must Be Curious. Must Be Brave. All Interested Children Meet At The Edge Of The Great Forest At Dawn Tomorrow Ready To Travel Far.*"

"And so now the kids are getting all their things ready," Ella explains as she flips a few more pages, "and the grown ups are making their magical presents, but they don't tell us what they are because it's a secret. And this page is where the kids start walking on the path into the Great Forest." And here Ella closes the book and Wangtang climbs onto her lap.

"So now, Wangtang," she continues, putting an arm around her hairy friend, "we have to look at Mama's wall, at that place where the trees start. You can't see the path there, but that's because it's magic and magic paths are usually invisible, but it's still there. And so we close our eyes until we see Ginger, Lily, and Rio right next to us."

Usually, Ella and Wangtang have to stay real quiet for a long time. Not today, though. Almost as soon as they shut their eyes, they see the kids beside them and the trees in front of them. They all hold hands then, and step onto the Forest path together.

And they walk through the magical trees. They ride on dolphins. They become friends with a talking mouse. And they take a trip on the back of a giant ruby-colored bird toward Rainbow Mountain. And it's just like in the book, except *much, much* better.

A Pause

Twisting flames spring high before settling to a gentle burn. A portal no longer, the hearth's radiating warmth soothes and encourages reflection, as does the silence that holds you. Yet even without images unfolding, you sit enthralled by the tongues of fire as you absorb all you've been shown.

"I said before that I found this uncanny," you speak at last, as you find yourself turned toward Zosia again, "and that is even more true now. What a privilege to be offered such an intimate view into the lives of others."

Silence embraces as you seek the words to describe your experience.

"I was not watching from a distance," you continue slowly, "or observing through some sort of window. It was as though I was living *inside* these lives. Their thoughts and feelings, memories and movements were my own. And each experience spoke to me in its own way."

"Yes, I imagine that is so," replies Zosia. "And yet one or two likely called you more sweetly?"

"Yes, that is so," you answer. You say no more, but drink deeply of the calming brew in the mug you hold.

"You are wise to speak little," Zosia says after long moments pass. "These stories abound with layers, as do you. It is best to let their magic sift its way through, sparking as it goes. Perhaps spark*ling* as well."

After many moments elapse, she asks, "Would you like to see more?"

Again you do not rush your reply. "Yes, without question. And yet you tell me this magic needs to move through layers. I want to see more—no, I *yearn* to see more. But may I wait a while before doing so? That would feel best."

"Yes, you certainly may," the Old One answers with a smile and a nod. "These teachings come with no timetable but that which arises from your own sweet soul. Abide in what you have seen and return, my dear, only when you are ready."

With those words, you are facing the hearth once more. The age-worn stones grow dim and dimmer still, though the radiating warmth of its flames remains with you. The room itself becomes hazy now as the swirling and darkening mist returns, glittering once more with flecks of color. Soon all form vanishes, and you are propelled in a gentle but steady backward motion until all movement ceases, and you once again inhabit that vast and silent, dark and utterly safe space that welcomed you at the start. Rest here for a few moments, darling reader. Breathe in all that has been shown you, and on each outbreath feel that magic sifting through your many layers, sparking and sparkling as it goes.

After a time you become aware of the sounds, sights and scents of your own precious life. It calls you to it, and you heed that call. Though as you step again onto your own unique path, you find yourself awaiting the time of return to this other place, a place that is no place, to this dream that is no dream at all.

Leia Marie

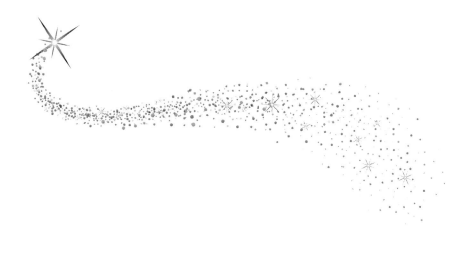

ENCHANTED *A Tale of Remembrance*

The Amble Resumes...

It happens more quickly this time. You enter that immense and inviting darkness, feel yourself swirled forward as you approach a realm quite different from your usual wake-a-day life. As the mists enfold you, I ask again, precious reader, that you bring with you an awakened sense of play, as I once more place words into your mouth and create for you an experience to embody.

The hearth appears before you now, and you are soothed by the warmth of the flames as they dance their friendly frolic within its enclosure. You find yourself sitting in the same chair, though you may or may not notice that the pattern of the material covering its cushions has changed. You are again facing Zosia, who looks much the same as before, though she appears more elegant than ancient to you now. Her dress is a soft rosy hue, and her hair is swept into a bun, with wisps escaping its confines to halo her face and accentuate the sparkle in eyes that gaze into your own.

"It is a delight to welcome you here once again," she says with a smile that crinkles the lines of a face that holds the wisdom of a thousand lifetimes. After an expanse of silence, she adds, "Do you have questions or thoughts you would like to share?"

"I have held this family close during my time away," you begin.

The old woman merely nods and waits as you search for words.

"I'm struck by how easy it is for us to get off track. To forget. To need reminders of what calls us to ourselves. Lana had lost the artist in her, Jessica the athlete. They needed to be reminded, and this enchantment gave them that."

"Yes," she agrees. "And yet, while that is an important facet of this, it is not the whole of it. I would ask that you explore the notion reflected in your choice of the phrase *off track*."

Time passes. You drink of the mug you find in your hand, and the new though still delightful beverage calms as it encourages contemplation.

"I envision that we each have a path through this world," you say at last, "and that events sometimes conspire to knock us from it." You pause again before continuing. "Yet since you ask that I examine that view, I wonder if perhaps my conception of path is inaccurately narrow.

Zosia's nod urges you to continue, which in time you do.

"Perhaps those forays that seem to me apart from the main path are not detours at all. Maybe they, too, are a segment of a course that twists and turns and unfolds as it is walked. Not mistakes or departures from a set direction we are meant to travel, but valuable portions of the path itself, each one bringing us something meaningful. Perhaps experience as a whole is the path, and our task is to walk it fully, no matter where it leads or how circuitous its route may seem."

Zosia beams. "And yet there is wisdom in recognizing what calls at any given point, and in discerning how best to align with it."

"Yes, I can see that," you respond. "And I imagine that is one of the important tasks of being human. Speaking for myself, though I'm guessing that Lana and Jessica might agree, I find it challenging to recognize and to discern."

"It is a challenge, indeed," she concedes, "though you have just said it is an essential aspect of the human endeavor. And here I have a question to ask of you. Do you have plants sitting upon your sill at home?"

Though surprised by this sudden shift of topics, you nod.

"And what have you noticed about their attraction to sunlight?"

"They gravitate toward it," you answer. "Their leaves bend in the direction of the light."

"Indeed," Zosia replies. "And while it is simpler for these GrowingGreens, your kind has the same capacity. It is innate within you, this ability to turn toward what is needed for optimal growth. It is a vital part of the apparatus gifted you at birth."

"And that," you reply," must be why Jack and Ella, still close to their birthing time, seem to have easier access to that inner knowing than do their parents. Yet you say we are all born with this capacity to turn our own leaves, those individual expressions of our lifeforce, toward the Light as well."

"Absolutely," she affirms with a broad smile. "As you have said, honing the ability to choose well is one of the vital tasks of a human life. This is why the sages among you have spoken so often of free will."

You remain quiet for many Earth minutes as you ponder what has transpired. Finally, Zosia speaks again.

"As we have come to contemplate the idea of choice, would you like to see more now, or would you rather have us speak further or sit longer in reflection?"

"I am ready to see more," you reply.

As soon as those words leave your lips, you find yourself facing flames that shoot high in the hearth, gamboling with a tangible glee before settling again. Images spring to life there once more, scenes that draw you from yourself and into the lives of others of your kind.

Ann

She is grappling with the possibilities suggested by the morning's data when her computer dies and the lights in her small office blink out. Through the window she sees the sun dipping toward the horizon and realizes she's again lost track of time. A lot of time. Vaguely registering hunger, Ann grabs a granola bar from her bottom-drawer stash, rips its wrapper with her teeth, bites down, and begins ticking off ways to use her time productively until maintenance fixes the glitch.

Settling on reviewing the research article they'd be sending off next week, Ann retrieves it from the shelf behind her desk. She'd worked in the revisions Jiang had suggested and printed off a hard copy for that final proofing that always seems more effective with paper in hand. Final proofing...who is she kidding? She knows she'll go over it at least half a dozen times in the next few days. Swiveling her chair around to get the most of the waning sunlight, she loses another chunk of time, stopping only when she can no longer make out words on the page.

"What the hell are they doing anyway?" she asks aloud. "They shoulda had this fixed by now."

Grabbing her sweater from the hook, she puts it on and opens the door, intending to storm out kvetching about the facilities management folks, but realizes she doesn't care all that much. Plus, storming is difficult through the gloom of a hallway whose backup lights are as dark as the awful florescent ones. Trailing a hand down the wall to remain oriented, she moves past one closed door after another. Turning the corner, she sees dusky light coming from Rājīv's open doorway, and by the dim light of his own narrow window sees him sitting immobile, staring at a blank screen. When he doesn't respond to her opening gripe, she continues on.

"What an odd afternoon," she thinks as she reaches the exit and steps into the brisk evening air. Color hangs on to the west, but the sky is darkening fast. Definitely time to head home.

She walks toward the parking lot, and on the way passes people frozen in midstride who, like Rājīv, don't respond when she speaks.

"Okay," she chuckles, "*this* is not normal human behavior."

Ann often finds people baffling. She is much more comfortable with numbers than actual humans, though there are notable exceptions. Like Eric. They'd met as undergrads, she tutoring for needed cash and he struggling with organic chemistry. While it could be challenging to tutor in subjects she considers relatively straightforward, people are equations and once she'd found the formula for the way his mind processed information, they'd found a natural rhythm. He'd passed the course with a solid B, something he was happier about than she. They'd worked briefly together the next semester on a calc course he claimed was difficult. However, when she recognized he was rather proficient in the material and told him so, he'd asked her out for coffee. Perplexed though she was, she had agreed, a choice that culminated in marriage a few years later.

They are a Venn diagram, separate spheres with enough overlapping area to have made them viable as a couple for nearly three decades. Mostly they get each other, and what they don't get, they accept, even encourage. Her respect for Eric's yoga is a case in point, as is his tolerance of her need for order and to write when emotions run high. Yet that Venn had to expand with the addition of Eric's father to their household last year. She'd discovered Phil's equation on that first trip back to Eric's hometown the summer before graduate school, and found she could appreciate the workings of his mind. However, Phil and Eric's overlaps seem mostly oriented to conflict, which could be difficult for her. But when the tension between them buzzes across her skin like a swarm of hornets, she's learned to simply leave the room, sometimes the house itself.

Ann reaches the lot, passes cars interrupted in the act of backing out of spaces or moving down the center lane. Though she registers that something is off here as well, she finds it not the least bit disturbing. In fact, all seems vibrant and bright, though she isn't sure what she means by those words when they come to her. She decides to walk home rather than risk her own vehicle stalling out as those around her have done. She'd commuted by foot frequently when she first got the position at the lab. It was only 2.8 miles after all, and she knew the exercise was good for her cardiovascular system. However, as her research ramped up, it seemed a poor use of time, so she'd let it go.

She takes a flashlight from the glove box and, given the rapidly cooling evening air, retrieves a worn blanket from the trunk, wraps it around her shoulders, and starts off. She crosses the lot, follows the road that snakes through the facility grounds, turns onto the boulevard. The streetlights are out, and cars and their drivers are fixed in place. Ann pauses to look closely at an inert pedestrian, and recognizes the signs of normal respiration. When she aims her flashlight toward the man's face, he blinks rapidly a few times but makes no other response.

"Voluntary animation suspended in at least some portion of humans," she comments aloud as she walks on, "but also extending to their technology. How very interesting."

That interest wanes, though, as her focus is drawn to the wide and clear sky where the first stars are now visible. Even though it necessitates slowing her pace considerably, Ann turns off her flashlight to see that sky better. But when she trips over a section of uneven pavement, she decides it best to change tacks. This odd evening is offering an opportunity to give herself to the one thing her ravenous mind craves above all others, and she'd be a fool not to take advantage of it.

Switching the light back on, Ann lets its beam guide her to the wide field that begins 1.2 miles from the parking space she's claimed as her own back at the lab. She steps from sidewalk to grass, makes her way to the field's approximate midpoint, wraps the blanket snugly around herself, and lays down.

And there it is, the cosmos spread out above her. Or more precisely, an infinitesimally small segment of it given current estimates of well over two trillion galaxies, ranging from a mere thousand stars in the dwarf spheroidal Segue 2 to over 100 trillion in the supergiant elliptical IC 1101. It really is beyond astounding, particularly as the grandeur of the visible universe comprises only 5% of the whole.

With artificial lights apparently extinguished for many miles around and the waning crescent moon not due to rise until just before dawn, Ann knows she is looking at more stars than she has seen on the clearest of nights, at least since she was a young child first discovering this passion in a small town near Winnipeg. And she knows that the multitude of stars that will appear as this night deepens would still be but a tiny portion of the Milky Way, a mid-range galaxy of 100 to 400 billion stars, depending on the model used for calculation.

Well, that's enough to stop a human mind in its tracks and bring it to its knees. Almost. Ann's thoughts continue to spin a while longer, from current knowledge concerning the age of the universe, to the untold number of variables that interacted perfectly to lead to those first microscopic life forms on Earth. When she begins moving into the helpless sorrow that often overwhelms her at what humankind's anthropocentric and myopic view of life is doing to the exquisite biosphere of the planet, she finds she just can't go there. Interesting, in that she can *always* go there.

"It seems that this night," she whispers, eyes reflecting starlight, "is for other pursuits."

Ann has found no validity in the concept of a personal God, certainly not the God of her Lutheran parents or the petty and angry god of those who refuse science and choose to believe the planet and its amazing ecosystem was created in seven days a mere 6,000 years ago. She also feels no affinity for Eric's belief in a benevolent and accessible Presence, or the possibility that something called a soul could live on in a purposeful way following the demise of a human body.

Yet in this moment, Ann recognizes this very field as her temple, with grass greening from last week's rain and her human body stretched out upon it, a body containing a multitude of microscopic mysteries of its own. Her sacred book is the evolving science that seeks to understand in its own imperfect way the processes that govern the Cosmos and the only known life-supporting planet within that vastness. And her personal rite is to honor that elegant and ultimately incomprehensible design in whatever way she can.

Tonight, Ann chooses to enact that rite wholeheartedly. Looking up into unfathomable space, she knows herself to be utterly inconsequential, and that fact brings with it an exquisite joy. Her mind quiets at last and Ann dissolves, losing herself to the deep and boundless sky.

Eric

He can hear the television before he even reaches the front door. Sure enough, Fox News assaults him as he steps into the foyer...as does the shrill cry of the smoke alarm.

"What's burning, Dad?!!" Eric hollers as he tosses his jacket on the couch and rushes to the kitchen.

There he finds the burner on full blast under the remains of a can of chicken noodle soup, broth boiled away, noodles melded to the blackened bottom of the pan. Turning off the flame, Eric flips the switch of the exhaust fan, which is right next to an index card taped to the rangehood with the words, "PLEASE USE MICROWAVE, NOT STOVE."

Eric opens the window, and drags over a chair to unhook the battery from the smoke detector, which only makes the blare of Fox more grating. As he retraces his steps to the foyer to open the front door and kick off his shoes, Eric reminds himself to keep it together, that he'd gotten there in time, that all is well...or at least well enough.

"Hey, Dad," he begins as he walks back to the living room, where his father reclines in his Lazy Boy, muttering at the politician on the screen.

"Dad!" he raises his voice louder. No response. "DAD!!!"

"Oh, I didn't know you were home, son. Those bleeding heart bastards are trying to raise our taxes again, just like I told ya they would!"

"Dad, there's something a bit more important at the moment," Eric says, aiming for calmness while continuing to pitch his voice loud enough to be heard.

When he gets no response, he shouts again. "DAD!!!"

"I can hear you just fine. No need to yell."

When he replayed it later, Eric realized that in addition to the continued effects of the adrenaline rush, it was his father's dismissive tone that got him, a replay of an old dynamic between them.

"Yes, I DO need to yell! Cuz you can't hear me unless I yell, cuz you won't wear your goddamn hearing aids and you keep the TV so friggin' loud no one can hear themselves think around here!"

As his father continues to stare at the screen, Eric reaches for patience by taking a few breaths, but as that brings with it the stench of burnt white flour, the effort isn't particularly effective. Grabbing the remote from the end table where it lives amid bags of pretzels, M&Ms, and cheap hard candy, he turns off the TV.

"Hey, I was watchin' that!"

"I'm sorry, Dad, but we need to talk." Eric says in measured tones. "I've asked you not to use the stove. I even put up a sign to remind you. But you did it anyway and then forgot you put your soup on."

"I didn't forget," Phil argues, as he pulls the lever on the side of the chair to lower the leg rest. "I was just waiting 'til this story was over. I'm going in there right now."

"Well, don't bother, Dad. It's burnt." Eric replies. "We'll probably have to throw out the pan."

Never one to listen to his son, Phil reaches for his walker, hauls himself upright, and walk-clumps his way to the kitchen. When he reaches the still-smoking pan, he looks down at what remains of his lunch. Though Eric can't see it from his place in the doorway, shock registers briefly on his father's face before the mask of belligerence returns.

"Well, something must be wrong with your stove then, cuz I just put the soup on two damn minutes ago!"

"There's nothing wrong with the stove, Dad!" Eric bellows. "You turned the burner on high and you went back in to watch TV and you forgot about the soup! Why can't you just admit it?!"

"Cuz I don't admit to what's not true, that's why! I can still heat up a goddamn can of soup!"

Grabbing a sleeve of saltines from the counter, Phil leaves the kitchen and trudges down the hallway to his bedroom.

"Don't walk away, Dad!" Eric calls after him. "You coulda burned the house down!"

"Well, I didn't, did I? You always did worry too much, son. Just relax." And he closes his bedroom door. Quietly, as though to point out that *he* isn't the one with a foul temper.

Well, *that* went well, Eric thinks. In less than three minutes, he'd escalated from relative calm to raging lunatic, ignoring in the process everything he knew about effective interaction. Hell, he'd even co-taught classes in non-violent communication. Wasn't *that* a joke. He supposes it only lent support to the adage, "If you think you're enlightened, spend time with your family." Well, he knows he isn't enlightened. In fact, he's been feeling a lot like a fraud lately.

Eric runs a hand through his hair, switches off the TV, and goes into the kitchen to survey the damage. How on earth could one old man make such a mess in just a few hours?!! In addition to the ruined pan on the stove and the empty Campbell's soup can beside it, the countertop is strewn with jars of Jif and grape jelly, cannisters of Maxwell House and Coffee Mate, a box of crackers, three dirty mugs, an assortment of knives and spoons, an open bag of white bread, a scattering of staling crumbs, and a plate with one cold and soggy piece of toast on it.

Beginning the cleanup process, Eric berates himself for blowing up at a man who's lost everything: job, wife, house, every one of his fishing buddies, the city he'd live in his entire adult life, independence and memory. But *good God*, the man was maddening!

The transition had been hard on everyone, though Ann had never once complained. After the calls from the social worker at the senior housing place had become a near-weekly occurrence, Ann had arrived home from work one day and, without even taking her jacket off, stated in that matter-of-fact way of hers, "Your father needs to come live with us. Lisa has too many kids. We have the spare room." She'd then walked down the hallway to begin her coming-home routine, just as though she hadn't dropped a bomb into their nicely ordered life.

Eric had resisted the idea for a while. He and his father had never had an easy time of it. They got along alright when they saw each other a couple times a year and talked on the phone every week or two, but he knew things would heat up again once they were living under the same roof. Unfortunately, he'd been right. He knows the tension is hard on Ann, but she simply puts on her headphones and goes into the other room, or leaves the house for a walk or a drive. No, Eric is the one who struggles.

With the kitchen put to rights, he walks to his home office, turns on white noise to soften the drone of the TV coming from his father's room, and gets to work on the books for the Studio. Another part of his life that likely wouldn't have come about without Ann's pragmatic nature carrying the day.

When the stress of teaching chemistry to mostly disinterested teens began to aggravate more than excite, she'd pointed out that since her salary was adequate for their needs, he should resign and get credentialed to teach yoga as he'd wanted to do since walking into his first class just out of college. Of course he'd loved Ann before that, but that love was deepened by her encouragement to give himself to a calling she didn't understand. He'd chosen not to renew his teaching contract and had begun the process of earning his RYT-500 cert. In addition to keeping the house running smoothly, he'd then picked up as many classes as he could at the studios around the Twin Cities, relishing the type of teaching he'd always known was possible. Sure, it wasn't in the sciences the west revered, but yoga was simply a different path for exploring what lay beneath the conditions of the visible world. And Eric now knows it is the only path for him.

Ann had done it again when they'd moved here for her job at the lab. After he'd shared his disappointment at the dearth of studios where he could teach, she'd walked in from work one day to announce that he needed to open his own place, quietly laid out how the finances would work, and went in to take a shower.

And here he was seven years later: yoga instructor, manager of a thriving holistic business founded on the pledge to promote harmony in the community, and raving maniac. Yep, fraud.

And with that thought, the world stops. Eric's computer dies as silence blankets the house. At first he, too, thinks it's a power outage of the usual kind, though he immediately recognizes a different *feel* to this one. It is as if everything seems more alive somehow, even joyous.

He walks down the hall, taps on his father's door and, when he gets no answer, opens it a crack. His dad lies on the bed facing the wall, back to the now-silent TV.

"Awww, you weren't even watching it, Dad," Eric whispers as he walks over and sits on the edge of the bed. He places a hand over his father's heart and feels its steady beat, chest rising and falling with each breath.

"So you're okay," Eric says. "Someday, I'll walk in here and find you gone. Can't imagine what that'll be like."

With sorrow weaving strangely through the quiet elation of these last few moments, Eric returns to his office. As he steps inside, his eye is drawn to the floor-to-ceiling shelves that hold anatomy books, manuals covering safe and effective techniques for teaching asana, years of various yoga journals, and texts on spiritual philosophy. His fingers wrap around his favorite exploration of Patanjali's Yoga Sutras, the book falling open to the second pada, in which the Ashtanga, the eight limbs of the yogic tradition, are discussed. Of these, it is the five Yamas that Eric feels calling him.

He knows them, of course. He mentions them occasionally in class, and used them as the basis for a full day's course he taught a few years back. It's humbling, in a delightfully invigorating way, to accept that he has lost sight of these simple teachings in his personal life and needs to revisit them now, not as teacher this time, but as student once again. This afternoon's student, though, is about to take these principles in a new direction.

The first Yama is *Ahimsa*, directly translating from Sanskrit as "without violence". It's concerned with non-harming on all levels...such as the bitter thoughts that often plague him about his father, and the irate tone and words of the last hour's sorry vignette. As Eric turns to face his reactions and look deeply into what fuels them, scene after scene from his early life play across the screen of his mind. Eric has always focused before on the few occasions of overt violence, or the more plentiful emotional lacerations caused by his father's relentless criticism. Now as he looks more deeply, he recognizes the anguish of his father's disinterest, of never having once felt fully seen and loved by a man he adored.

The tears stinging Eric's eyes bring him to the second Yama. *Satya* translates as "truthfulness", and today he knows that means letting go of his many layers of self-protection. He'd accepted long ago that even the best father-son relationship is woven through with at least a modicum of tension, precisely because it is so complex. He'd also recognized that his father's harshness had been learned at the hands of his own father, and therefore had never been about Eric at all. But in this moment, Eric sees that he's used that intellectual understanding to gain emotional distance from his pain, as he has also done through a ready disparagement of anything that reeks of pop psychology or simplistic cause and effect. *Satya* instructs that, until he lets himself fully feel his emotions, he will continue to act them out unconsciously, in ways harmful to both his father and himself.

Which brings him to *Asetya*, which translates as non-stealing. Eric hasn't stolen anything tangible since those few shoplifting forays as a teenager, but isn't it stealing of a subtle sort to deny the full impact of his experience?

To rob the boychild who obviously still lives inside him of the right to feel his pain, and to withhold the love that should rightly be given now to that younger self?

The fourth Yama is *Brahmacharya*, which refers to the proper use of energy. Eric knows that allowing his feelings to rise up safely is what is asked of him now. And letting the tight fist in his chest unclench, well, couldn't that be a subtle enactment of the fifth Yama, *Aparigraha*, which translates as non-grasping? On this odd day, Eric knows it is time to let go.

He returns the book to the shelf, takes his yoga mat from its place in the corner, unrolls it down the center of the room. As he removes his socks, he wonders how long it has been since he did yoga for himself. Since just after his father moved in and turned life upside down? Maybe. Of course, he regularly moves through poses with his advanced classes, but that's public, and always with attention to his students' questions and needed adjustments. But the vinyasa he flows through now is all his own.

With his state of calm deepened, he moves to his meditation cushion. After several minutes of the most soothing of the pranayama breathing techniques, Eric drops into meditation. While he's still managed most mornings to do at least a half hour before his father wakes, today's meditation is quite different. Setting aside the part of his mind that says this is ridiculous—an inner voice he now realizes carries a tone very much like his father's—Eric enters one of the scenes that came to him earlier, from when he was 8, maybe 9 years old.

He feels again the pliers being ripped from his hand, hears his father voice saying, "What are you, stupid? I swear it's easier to just do it myself!" Eric sees again his father turning away, angling to push his son back and make clear he is reclaiming the workbench as private territory. And the back of his father's blue flannel workshirt fills his world.

Eric now puts words to the emotions his small self experienced in that long-ago moment. Standing again in the garage of that Saturday afternoon, Eric feels rejection, shame, banishment, and the certainty that he is utterly alone, the few inches between him and his father a chasm that cannot be bridged.

And from his cushion now, Eric reaches back in time, slipping his arms around the young boy he had been and still is, picks him up and carries him out into the afternoon sunlight. And after the hoarded tears have been set free, they sit and they talk. And Eric knows he no longer needs to withhold as his father withheld, no longer needs to berate as his father berated, no longer needs to judge as his father judged.

Eric knows something else, too. He is not victim, but pupil of a man who has much to teach him about the cost of unhealed wounds. This rigid and harsh man was never meant to be Eric's adversary. In all his convoluted complexity, his father has always been his mentor, urging Eric forward in his quest to be the man he could become.

And with that recognition, one that feels almost like remembrance, tears rise again. These tears stream not for himself, though, but for his father, a man he is surprised to discover he adores still and always.

Phil

He shuts the door and blares the TV to drown out his son's disapproval. As he sits on the bed, places the damn walker to the side and stretches out, Phil thinks for the thousandth time what a fool he'd been to let the kids talk him into moving out here.

He doesn't have one goddamn thing of his own. Well, the few things from his apartment they had room for, but damn if those could replace a life. And isn't *that* the truth. The life he'd built over 86 years is gone now. Just gone.

It hadn't happened all at once. No, it'd been a series of jagged amputations over the span of a couple of decades. First, his knees started giving him trouble, and it got harder and harder to get in and out of the truck so many times in a day. And he swore the stairs he climbed got steeper by the week. Then the arthritis in his hands worsened, so while changing out locksets was still easy enough, gripping the smaller tools—the picks and tensioners needed for the detail work he loved—became more difficult. So he'd taken on an apprentice, had enjoyed setting up challenge locks for him to puzzle his way through, teaching the things that could only be learned from someone who'd been doing it a while. After a couple of years, Jim was nearly as good as he was and so he'd sold him the business. And about drove Jeanne crazy, walking around the house ill-tempered and with nothing to do. Drove himself nuts, too.

Oh, he'd adjusted after a while. Put an addition on the garage, finally made himself a real workshop. After he'd finished the house projects there'd never been time enough for when he'd worked those long hours, Phil got more creative. Bought a lathe, some woodworking tools, and had just finished a decent set of salad bowls when Jeanne got sick. Well, that put an end to those ridiculous notions of selling his stuff at craft fairs. Not that he minded. He needed to be with her as she went through the treatments, needed to take her on some of those trips she wanted in between. And when the cancer came back for what everyone knew would be the last time, there wasn't any place he'd rather be, nothing he'd rather do than take care of his girl.

His son thought he was an S.O.B. and Lord knows he'd given him plenty of reason to think that. But Jeanne knew different. Knew he loved her, maybe not so perfectly at first when he was young and stupid, but his Jeannie was a good teacher, and he'd gradually gotten the hang of love. Good thing, because the end came sooner than either of them could have guessed.

By God, he loved that woman! It was love that washed her down when the diarrhea came on without warning and she was too weak to do it herself. Love that changed the sheets. Love that had him doing his best to make food she could keep down. Love that carried him through that godawful afternoon when she'd insisted on picking out her own casket, standing by her side sure his chest was gonna rip right down the middle. It was love that curled him around her that last night, with Eric, Lisa and the grandkids standing by the bed, seeing him cry like a goddamn baby in the silence that came after her last ragged breath. He certainly didn't expect a damn medal for what he did, because he couldn't have done it any other way. And knowing he'd done his best by his Jeannie had given him a sort of wretched comfort when he'd watched her being lowered into that gaping hole. And as he began figuring out how to live without her after 54 years.

He'd kept the house a while longer, but truth was, he couldn't stand it on his own. He'd moved a daybed into his shop in those first weeks when the house was too damn quiet. Or maybe it was screaming too damn loud that she wasn't there anymore as, truth be told, he'd done more than once himself. There was already a toilet, sink and one of those little fridges out there, but Phil picked up an old Coleman stove from a garage sale and made a little kitchen for himself. Strung a rod in the corner to hang a few clothes, moved the TV out from the bedroom. It got so he only went in the house to shower, which to hear Lisa talk he didn't do as often as he should have. He'd thought it'd all be temporary, but eventually he had to admit he was never moving back in. But when he surprised himself with the thought of setting fire to the house that had been theirs but could never be his, he knew it was time to let it go.

Not that leaving had been a walk in the goddamn park either, but he'd gotten through it with Eric and Lisa's help. Help nothin'. They'd done just about everything, even found him an apartment in a place that served meals and did other things that kept old people living longer than they had any right to. He'd gotten friendly with a few of the fellas, took part in some activities, and was just getting used to his new life when the shit hit the fan again. Truth was, he didn't remember a lot of the details. Too many damn doctors, someone again accusing him of leaving the burner on, obnoxious visits from that nosy social worker he'd never asked to come in the first place, the one who was probably younger than his granddaughter.

And so here he sits in yet another life, still trying to figure out what the hell to do with it. He gets along just fine with Ann. She doesn't talk things to death. Well, unless you got her on one of her favorite subjects, but even then he gets a kick out of her. That girl is one smart cookie, and she doesn't have a problem letting a man be who he is. Not like his son. Always trying to change him, razzin' him about what he eats, wanting him to do yoga, for Christ's sake. He knows he should be proud of his boy for running a successful business. And he is, because he knows what that takes. But yoga? What the hell kind of business is *that* for a man?

He knows they mean well. But you can't sit down and have a beer with either one of them, and he doesn't know a goddamn soul here otherwise. But even if he did, he can't get around much anymore. Wouldn't be able to go fishing or to see a game, so what the hell does it matter. Not a goddamn thing matters, and nothing makes a bit of sense. Like the fact that it's suddenly dead quiet.

Phil turns over, sees the TV has gone kaput. Stays stretched out for a while longer. Calls out to Eric, doesn't get an answer. Good. Means he's gone out somewhere, which gives Phil time to clean up the mess he made in the kitchen. He scoots to the edge of the bed, wrestles the walker into place, stands up, and makes his way into the hall. When he passes Eric's room, he sees him staring at his computer and somehow knows that Eric's lack of reply doesn't mean he's still pissed. Doesn't think much about what it does mean, though. He continues down the hallway, turns the corner and sees the clean kitchen.

"Yeah, you just had to make me look bad, didn't ya?" he hollers over his shoulder. "Couldn't give me a goddamn chance to scrub that pan clean, could ya?"

Maybe it's the anger that has Phil turning the walker too quickly or leaning his weight on it wrong. All he knows is he's now lying on the floor, the wind knocked clean out of him.

"Okay, okay. Let me just lay here a minute and catch my breath."

When he feels steadier, Phil turns his head to take stock of the situation. His walker's tipped on its side near his feet, and he's too far from the counter or table to pull himself up. He gets no answer when he calls out to Eric again.

"So, Phil, we gotta get up on our own," he says out loud.

He reaches his leg out, intending to hook the walker with his foot to drag it closer, but a jolt of pain shoots from his knee straight up to his ass.

"*Christ Jesus*, could this day get any fucking worse?!!" he shouts. "We're on our own and helpless as a goddamn baby!"

He tries to sit up, but that brings the pain back full force. It also makes him register that he's wet in the groin.

"Aw, so ya went and pissed yourself too, did ya?" he grumbles, though his heart isn't really in it. "A goddamn baby lying in your own goddamn piss!"

For some reason that makes him laugh, which lets loose another spurt or two of urine. And now the whole thing strikes him as hilarious, and his initial almost tentative laughter quickly turns into a full-out roar, tears streaming down his face as his bladder unloads fully into his drawers.

When the laughter quiets and Phil wipes his eyes, he wonders how long it's been since he's laughed that hard. Months? Naw, had to be years. And God it felt good, even though it ramped up the pain. Well, a little pain isn't gonna kill him. Which of course brings him to wondering what exactly will finally do him in, since one thing he knows for certain is that's where he's headed, and it won't be long now.

Sure, the kids do what they can, but don't they see that doing for just brings home the fact that you can't do for yourself anymore? And Eric might be able to clean up a mess in the kitchen, but he can't clean up old age, now can he? Can't get old *with* him. Can't *die* with him, for Christ's sake. Phil's on his own with all that. So he better get on with it. Ready himself for it. Figure out how to get between here and there in a good way, a decent way, a way he doesn't have to feel bad about. And he's been feeling bad about most everything lately.

He knows he can be a bear, knows he isn't easy to live with, particularly now in yet another place that isn't home. But as he lies on the cold tiles and plays back all the things he's lost, there seems some sort of twisted truth in it. Isn't dying about getting everything stripped away until, in the end, your body's taken too?

He has no idea what happens after that. Jeanne had been convinced that a part of her, some Jeannie essence, would live on. Phil doesn't know anything about it, doesn't really care one way or the other. He accepted long ago that he just isn't wired to focus on such things. But now he understands that the string of losses in these last few years was just the way it's supposed to be. They hadn't happened because he'd done anything wrong. They weren't his fault. This ripping away of everything that wasn't nailed down is just a natural process...and one he can't avoid.

In his woodworking days, he'd loved that final sanding process, the gradual smoothing that came from using finer and finer grit paper. Maybe what he'd seen as the dismembering of these last years was really just the first steps in some kind of sanding process. At least that might be a good way to look at it, one that wouldn't make him so goddamn furious all the time.

"Yeah, Phil," he chuckles, "all ya gotta do is accept you're nothin' but a chunka wood, and then decide to let life have its way with you. Nothin' to it."

He calls out to Eric again, and still gets no answer. And the sure knowledge that his boy would come in a heartbeat if he could becomes a smoothly turning key that frees something in Phil that has long been bound up. He'd been focusing on the obligation involved in Eric's offering his home. Of course that's part of it, but Phil can see now the love that's there too. His son loves him and is just trying to do the right thing by him, just as Phil tried to do the right thing for his kids over the years. He knows he failed miserably much of the time. Sure, he'd been good with the practical things—keeping a roof over their heads, food in their bellies, clothes on their backs. But the emotional stuff, well, that was Jeanne's area. It came natural to her. But the point is, Phil did what he could then. So maybe he oughta let Eric do what *he* can now. "Even if there aren't two things you agree on," Phil says aloud, "maybe you could cut the boy some slack, and not be such a cranky old bastard."

So if he pulls that off, if he lets life sand him smooth so he can accept Eric's doing what he can, where does that leave him? Still indebted, and doesn't he just hate that. And suddenly another key he hadn't been able to grab before fits itself right in and turns the lock. The point of lying helpless on his kid's floor is to get, really get, that the time for pride is over. Chances are, he'd be in a nursing home if the kids hadn't taken him in, and there wasn't a whit of pride in *that*. Things are slipping away, and soon it'll *all* be going away, every damn thing. And he has no choice but to accept it. No, that isn't quite right either, because he knows he just isn't any good at accepting something being yanked away like that. It just pisses him off and makes him wanna grab on all the tighter. Ahhhh...the point is to figure out how to *give* it away. By choice. To willingly let himself be stripped bare so that when his time comes, he can walk into that whatever-it-is as naked as the day he was born.

"Well, ya got your work cut out for ya, Phil, my boy!" he says with a sigh. "Cuz you never were much good at lettin' shit go. You're a fighter, but even you can see that this isn't a fight you're gonna win."

And truth tell, he doesn't even want to. Ever since he lost Jeannie, life has been just too damn difficult. So why does he fight so hard? Ha, even a fool like him can see it just makes things ten times worse. After all, he's lying on this hard floor with his ass-end killing him and his crotch gone clammy because he'd been fightin' mad. So he'll just have to learn to do it different. Starting right now.

Phil repositions himself so his arm cushions his head, wincing as pain bullets from his hip. When it settles down to a dull ache again, he opens his eyes and sees the late afternoon sunlight streaming through the open window onto the tiled floor. Phil feels the breeze on his face, and it feels good. *He* feels good, despite the pain and the embarrassment of getting himself into such a mess through sheer cussedness.

But maybe that too is how it needed to be. Sure got his attention. Death's coming for him, is gonna grab him and haul him through to whatever, if anything, is on the other side. And he'll have to not only let it, but walk forward to meet it. Yeah, that's it. He has to wave hello, and at some point reach out to shake Death's hand. Turning away sure as hell isn't working, and wanting things to be like they used to be isn't either. Just keeps him pissed off, since he knows damn well they never will be.

"You've been pissed off a long time, Phil. Do you think you could lay that one down? Naw, I didn't think so," he chuckles, "but you can try. Let's try then, okay?"

And lying on the hard tile with pants wet, hip broken, and the late spring afternoon flowing in through the kitchen window, Phil tries. And Phil succeeds.

Pausing Again

The flames stretch high and cavort about in a dance that is both lively and joyful. When they quiet once again, the ping of sleet against pane soothes as you sit for many moments collecting yourself.

"I find it so disorienting," you say at last. "To feel for a time that I *am* these people, and then to return to being simply myself again...well, it is bewildering."

"And why do you think it is," Zosia asks, "that you can feel such kinship with those you have never met, and feel it to such a degree that you nearly lose all sense of an individual self?"

"Well, I want to say it comes from you and whatever magic lives within your ensorcelled hearth," you answer with a smile, as you look now into the depths of her eyes.

"But you are not certain," she states.

"No, I am not. Well, obviously there is magic here," you say, pausing as you await that which is rising up. After a passage of time in which you feel the delight of the unhurried, you continue. "It seems to me that magic can only ever allow a truth to rise into awareness that is already present within."

Zosia nods. "And?"

"And so, I think that what each of these dear souls feels and what their lives have brought them is not so very different from what I feel and have experienced within my own life. Certainly the details are unique. I am not a scientist, nor is my relationship with my father the same as Eric's. And yet beneath those surface differences, there is a commonality that allows me to *recognize* the similarities that do exist beneath the particular details."

You fall silent again as you seek what is emerging.

"So perhaps what I find disorienting is actually a truth," you continue. "Perhaps the usual separation I experience between my life and the life of another is illusion, and this experience here with you, and with them," you say, gesturing toward the hearth, "is clearing me of that. It may be that what I am experiencing is not *dis*orientation at all, but a *re*orientation, an orientation to a deeper reality that I am often blind to. We are not such separate entities, clearly divided one from another in some absolute or permanent way, as I so often think."

"And what does that recognition bring you?" she asks with a nod. "How can it assist you as you continue your EarthWalk?"

As you consider the question, time stretches out in this place that is without time. Finally an answer arrives. "It would be a worthy endeavor to practice this awareness often in my daily life. To not only know with my mind that we are linked in a place deeper than our differences, but to strengthen my ability to actively engage as such, heart and soul."

Zosia nods again. And she waits. Embers glow and wind howls.

"It is time for me to reenter the life that awaits me," you say at last, "the one I think of as my own. Am I free to return again?"

"Absolutely, as surely you know you are," she replies with a sweet smile. "Though the form may change over time, you are ever and always welcome here."

With that, the sights and sounds of this place of magic waver and fade. You feel yourself sliding backward, until you are held again within that vast and benevolent darkness. Rest here for a time, dear one. And when the particulars of your own world call, gather them sweetly about you and step fully into the life that has waited patiently while you journeyed elsewhere.

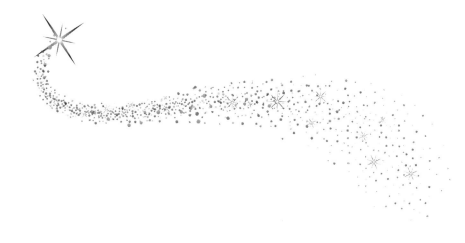

Ambling On...

Welcome back, beloved reader. Allow yourself to again be embraced by that enveloping and soothing darkness as you traverse the terrain from what we like to call the real world into another realm, one in which Guardians devise magical interludes, archetypal beings come to life, and hearths act as gateways into other worlds.

And sure enough, you soon find yourself before the soothing fire of this place you've come to love. But though it is hard to identify, you realize immediately that something is different. You first think it is only the quieting of the storm that you notice. Rain continues to fall steadily upon the roof, but the wind no longer lashes ice against windowpane or howls madly about the walls. The hearth looks the same, though you notice for the first time herbs hanging from the rafters, a glowing hurricane lamp on a wooden counter against the far wall, and a bed in the corner covered with a brightly patterned quilt. You wonder if these are new additions, or if you have just now become aware of them. You turn to ask this question but stop. For it is not Zosia sitting in the chair, but another.

"Ooooh, child," she says kindly, with a broad smile and a chuckle, "if you could only see your face! Remember that all is ever well here. Please take whatever time you need to absorb that which appears new."

Her words merely reinforce the leisurely delight you always feel in this place, the sense that there is time enough for whatever is needed or desired. The woman sitting before you is dressed in a flowing caftan, a vivid swirl of yellows, oranges and reds. Her skin is a deep brown burnished with coppery tones that glow in the firelight. Raven-black hair liberally streaked with gray is intricately fashioned, a topknot streaming into long braids strung with bright beads and adorned with cowrie shells and the feathers of a brightly colored bird. Where you had thought Zosia elegant, this woman is as solid and robust as the Earth itself. And though you did not speak that thought, she throws back her head and laughs, a deep and resonant sound that fills the room.

"Well, that is one way to describe this form that I wear," she says, the pleasing cadence of the West African coast alive in her words. "Solid and robust as the Earth herself. That be quite a compliment, indeed!" When her mirth quiets, she adds, "While some may call the appearances we have chosen stereotypical, as you and Zosia discussed, it is archetypal that we have aimed for. I am known as Nyah, and I will be with you for a time."

"I am pleased to meet you," you say, smiling as you realize you are comfortable in her presence in only these few minutes. "May I ask where Zosia is?"

"You may ever ask what you would in this place, dear one" Nyah assures. "Zosia has not gone far, and it is likely that you could feel her if you but open your mind to the possibility, just as you could have sensed my presence earlier had you thought to seek it. Zosia shall join us again, but I be here with you now. We couldn't have you be gettin' bored, now could we?" And here she slaps her thigh and hoots again.

"As if boredom would ever be possible in this place," you say, laughing yourself.

"You speak truth," she replies. "Yet I think boredom in *any* place demonstrates a distinct lack of imagination. Wouldn't you agree?"

You nod, and silence descends for a time. You again find a mug in your hand, and though this beverage is as curious to you as the previous ones, it is equally as soothing. The smile spreading across Nyah's wide face encourages you to pick up the threads you had been weaving with Zosia, and you are delighted at how easy it is to do so.

"In the time I have been away, I practiced remembering my deep connection with others and acting from that awareness. I found it easy at times, tremendously difficult at others."

"Yes," she affirms, nodding. "And what do you think might cause that variation?"

"Well, it is often affected by my mood, by whether I am rested or not, rushed or at ease, and whether I am able or willing to interact openheartedly with what is. And yet, I find it particularly challenging to feel rapport with those who are outwardly quite different from myself, those who hold contrasting beliefs or behave in ways I find harmful or offensive, even deplorable."

"So," she replies, "you offer two possibilities for the variation you have discovered: your own internal state, or the behavior or inner state of the other, at least as you perceive it to be. I wonder what you might find were you to look more deeply into that dichotomy."

As you consider this, the fire snaps and a gust of wind spins in the night. Finally, your response arrives.

"My original perspective has just expanded. I had one interaction since last we met in which I hardened myself to someone who made what seems now to have been a relatively minor, though insensitive, remark. And yet on another occasion, I was able to maintain a felt sense of connection to someone who objectively had behaved far worse. That suggests that in *both* situations, my reactions stem primarily from my own internal state, and only peripherally have anything at all to do with the other."

"And?" she asks. And with that simple question, this wise woman initiates a call and response exchange between you. Punctuated by long pauses, this back and forth, this to and this fro, brings you into the deeper layers of your own knowing.

"Perhaps," you say, "it would be best to see the conduct of others as raw material offering an opportunity for my own growth and enhanced awareness. Through my reactions, my inner state is brought to the fore, projected onto the screen of our exchange. Hidden no longer, my response allows me to directly perceive what is occurring within my psyche and my spirit. Thus I am provided an opening to become more conscious, more aware, more alive."

"And..." she prompts.

After several sips from your mug, you reply. "I can, just as Eric realized with his father, recognize the other as teacher, someone arriving in my life bearing a gift, no matter how unpleasant the packaging might be."

"And..."

"It seems to me that conflict can be beneficial in growing the soul, a boon camouflaged as nemesis. All might be seen as grist for the mill of my awakening, if I can but recognize it as such and work creatively with it."

Nyah's expectant smile urges you to explore further, and a new facet of your answer appears.

"From there, I have the freedom to craft my own response. Zosia and I spoke of free will. Well, each interaction offers an opportunity to choose who I will be in that moment, and who I will become through the way in which I greet and engage with what is."

"And..."

Again you pause, and again an answer rises up to be known. "Perceiving a deeper connection with another doesn't negate my ability to take a stand, for example, against what I perceive as injustice. And I can only assume that any intervention I make will have a better chance of being effective if begun from a place of warmth and affinity, even camaraderie.

Nyah beams, and she waits.

After several breaths, you speak further. "Reflecting on a particular interaction at a later time will provide useful information, offering a snapshot-in-time of my current place in my journey toward wholeness. Each interaction is an experiential learning opportunity." Surprised into a laugh, you conclude, "Just another pop quiz in the School Of Life."

Your companion also laughs, its resonance seeming to spring from the innate joy she carries within her. Silence returns then, but for the sounds of fire and the rain of this night's softer storm. Insights nestle into the rich soil of your being. Seeds root and buds unfurl, though no further words come to you.

"Are you ready to see more?" Nyah asks after a time. "Before you answer, I must warn you that the lives you are about to enter will challenge you more than those you have seen up to this point. And perhaps one or two may test your ability to find kinship.

After a brief pause, you respond, "I am ready."

And with that assent, you are once again facing the hearth, its leaping flames settling as you enter new lives.

Emma

She can always tell. He doesn't slam the car door, doesn't yell or stomp up the three steps that bring him from the garage into the main house. But she knows.

She and Mommy are waiting by the door the way he likes, but tonight Daddy walks by them without speaking, and the knot in her stomach twists tighter. He turns toward the living room as he always does, walks around the bar to get his first drink just like every night. She hears the familiar clink of ice, the liquor being poured over it. But it's Daddy's silence that's loudest. It's going to be a bad night.

Mommy whispers for her to go up to her room, but they both know Emma won't leave her alone unless he makes her. She waits in the hallway where she can watch as her mother goes to him and, reaching up, helps take off his suit jacket. She undoes his tie and carefully pulls it from under his collar. Mommy drapes both over the back of one of the leather chairs that stretch around the curve of the bar.

"Did you have a rough day, Richard?" she asks in the voice she uses on nights like this. When Daddy's silence is the answer, Emma watches Mommy put her arm through his and walk him to the couch. Silently, he sits and leans his head against the deep cushions. Mommy kneels then and takes off his shoes. She hands Daddy the remote so he can choose music or television, and encourages him to relax while she finishes preparing dinner. She then gathers shoes, jacket and tie, and walks calmly and unhurriedly back toward Emma.

"Please take these upstairs, so I can get dinner on the table, okay, sweetie?" she whispers, with a smile that doesn't match the worry in her eyes. Emma reaches out to take her father's things, and then stands there, looking up into her mother's face. "Don't worry, honey, it's going to be okay." They both know that's a lie.

Emma walks quickly to the stairs, but has to climb them slowly so her shoes won't clatter on the shiny steps and give Daddy a headache. Turning to the master bedroom, she walks into her father's closet, which is nearly as big as her old room in their last house. She places the shoes in the empty spot on the shelf, toes pointing out like all the others. She puts his jacket over the hanger that waits on its stand, making sure the shoulders fit exactly right. She pulls out the drawer that conceals a series of rods, each draped with ties of similar shades. Ordinarily, Emma likes to look at the colors marching down the rows like a box of crayons, but not tonight. She carefully hangs today's dark blue tie with its thin, light blue stripes, but since the tie is slippery and she's trying to hurry, it slides to the floor. When it stays in place on her second try, Emma walks quickly to the top of the stairs and stops to listen before going down. She hears nothing but her Daddy's jazz.

She walks slowly down the stairs, listening hard with each step. She finds Mommy in the kitchen arranging a plate of hors d'oeuvres. Emma stands next to her while she finishes, walks into the hallway with her, and waits as Mommy walks to Daddy.

"Here you go, darling," Mommy says in the voice Emma hates, putting the platter on the coffee table and sitting next to Daddy, long legs curling under her. "I was thinking," she says, stroking the back of his neck, "that maybe I could make Emma a plate and she could eat in the den. That way you and I could have a nice quiet dinner, just the two of us."

Her father doesn't answer right away, but when he does, his voice is icy cold. "This family eats together, Meghan."

"Yes, of course, Richard. Yes, that would be better," Mommy says quietly. "Dinner won't be long now."

Mommy gets up from the couch, walks slowly down the hall, strokes Emma's hair as she passes. In the kitchen, though, she moves quickly, checking the roast and potatoes, making dressing for the salad.

"Honey, please set the table," she says. "Use the white plates with the gold trim and the rounder wine glasses. And make sure everything looks just right, okay? I'll come check in a few minutes."

Emma fills the water pitcher, carries it into the dining room, and is relieved that Mommy has already stretched out the tablecloth, since Emma can never get it to hang evenly all the way around. She puts the pitcher on the table, takes plates, silver, glasses and napkins from the credenza, and lays Daddy's setting first, a voice in her head talking her through each step: "Big plate in the center, salad plate on top, bread plate above and to the left. Knife to the right, spoon next to it, big fork nearest the plate on the other side, little fork next to that. Water glass right above the knife, wine glass to the right." Curling the napkin into its ring, Emma places it atop the salad plate. She then sets Mommy's place on Daddy's left and her own place on Daddy's other side. She puts the butter crock in the middle between the candlesticks, adds the salt and pepper shakers, fills the water glasses, and she's done. Emma usually likes setting the table, loves how pretty everything looks. But it's not fun tonight. As she reaches out to straighten a salad fork, she wishes for morning. But she's learned that wishes don't come true.

Mommy brings in the salad, reaches out to move Daddy's wine glass a little to the right, straightens an already straight knife. "You did a nice job, Emma. I'll go get Daddy."

"Richard, dinner's ready," she says from the living room. "The salad's on the table and the Cabernet has been decanted."

Daddy just sits there...and Emma hates him. No, she doesn't. She loves her Daddy, but not when he's like this. Not when he wants to make everybody scared.

Mommy comes back to the dining room, and they wait together. After several minutes, Daddy gets up and pours himself another drink. After more minutes go by, he comes in, puts his glass on the table, takes the decanter from atop the wine cabinet, and pours some into his glass. Emma watches as he does that swirly thing, tastes it and, still silent, pours more wine into his glass, some into Mommy's, and puts the decanter on the table. After he sits, she and Mommy do too.

Everyone is silent as her mother passes the salad, silent as they eat, silent as Emma gathers up the salad plates and goes to the kitchen with Mommy. The roast is resting on the counter, and Emma watches as her mother cuts several slices, takes potatoes and carrots from the oven and arranges them around the edge of the platter. She asks Emma to get the bread, so while Mommy spoons brussels sprouts into a serving dish, Emma gets the rolls from the warming drawer, puts them into the waiting basket, and wraps the cloth snugly around them. Then she and Mommy carry everything to the table.

Daddy serves himself, takes a bite of roast beef, tastes a potato wedge and a carrot, eats a brussels sprout. "Everything tastes good, Meghan," he says, and Emma's stomach begins to relax. Maybe things will be okay.

But as her father butters his roll, he glances over at her. "So, Emma, have the grades been posted yet? I haven't had time to check."

And Emma's heart begins to pound. She finishes chewing her potato, swallows, and says, "Yes, Daddy."

"Well, what were your grades?" he says as he finishes buttering, lays down his knife.

"I got almost all As, Daddy," she answers, trying to make her voice sound happy, bright.

Daddy stops with the roll halfway to his mouth, puts it back on his plate, turns to look at her, eyes hard, face like stone. He pauses, in that way that makes her feel stupid before saying, "Almost." It is not a question, but she answers anyway.

"Yes, I got As in English, Social Studies, Technology, Spanish, and Health Sciences," Emma says, her voice shaky now.

"And so let's see, what's missing from that extensive list of immensely challenging courses? Oh, I think it might be *math*."

"Daddy, math got really hard all of a sudden," she says quickly. "I've never been very good at it, and I'm *really* bad with fractions. Everybody hates them."

"And what grade did you get, Emma?"

"I got a C+, Daddy," she answers softly.

"And you do know, Emma, that C means average?" Daddy asks, his voice now dangerously quiet. "Are we average in this family, Emma?"

"No, Daddy."

"And do I pay $15,000 a year for that fancy school so you can be average, Emma?

"No, Daddy. I'm sorry, Daddy."

"Yes, you certainly are. And you'll be sorrier if you don't pull that grade up. In fact, I want you to leave the table right now, go to your room, and study your math."

"Oh, Richard, surely she can finish her dinner first," Mommy says.

"Don't contradict me, Meghan!" Daddy shouts, banging his fist on the table hard enough to make Mommy and Emma jump and the dishes rattle. Then he picks up his plate and hurls it against the wall, where it cracks and falls to the floor, leaving the wallpaper streaked with food.

"Emma, go to your room this instant," he says, each word razor sharp. "I want that door closed, and I want it to stay that way until I give you permission to open it again. You don't come out for any reason. Do you understand?"

Emma nods.

"Do you understand, Emma?" Daddy repeats.

"Yes, Daddy."

Emma stands up, pushes her chair in and looks over at Mommy who sits frozen in place, eyes on her plate. As Emma climbs the stairs, she hears Daddy say quietly, "Clean up this mess, Meghan. When you're done, come to the living room. I'll be waiting."

At the top of the stairs, Emma turns into her bedroom, closes the door quietly, and lets the tears come. Why did she have to be so stupid?! It's true, fractions *are* awful, but if she'd worked harder, maybe she could have done better. And then Daddy wouldn't be mad and Mommy wouldn't be scared. It's all her fault.

Emma angrily brushes away the tears that won't stop coming and sits at her desk. She picks up her pink Princess backpack, removes the worksheets Mrs. Rogers gave for extra credit, and places them in the center of her desk. She slowly opens the desk drawer. Pencils and pens run in a perfectly straight row across the front, just the way she likes them. Lined paper is stacked behind them on the right, while her construction paper with its rainbow colors is on the left. Between them are a collection of shimmery stickers she's been saving for years. It all looks so neat, but tonight that doesn't help at all.

Holding her breath, Emma inches her hand into the drawer to get a pencil. And wham! She slams the drawer hard, crushing her fingers. It hurts bad, but she doesn't make any noise. She slams the drawer twice more, because it always takes three times for her baby tears to stop, and for her head to get that fuzzy feeling that's kind of like dreaming. She looks down at her red fingers and knows they will soon turn that ugly purply-blue color. Good. Then they'll be as ugly as she is.

Emma takes a pencil from the drawer, holds it in a hand that throbs with the beat of her heart, and looks at the first problem on the sheet. $\frac{2}{3} + \frac{5}{8}$. She tries to remember how to make the denominators match, but it's hard to think when she's listening for sounds from downstairs. She only hears Daddy's music now, but she knows more's coming.

Emma stares at the numbers for a long time, her mind hopping around like a scared bird. Then Mrs. Rogers' voice comes into her head, and Emma whispers the directions out loud, while she writes the numbers on the paper.

"First, you multiply 3 and 8 together, which is 24. Then you divide 3 into 24 to get 8, and multiply 8 by the numerator to turn $2/3$ into $16/24$. And you do the same thing with the other fraction and then add them together."

Emma lines the numbers up on the worksheet, and is trying to remember how to reduce $31/24$ when Daddy's loud voice makes her forget all about fractions. As the minutes stretch on, Daddy's voice gets louder and louder. She can't hear Mommy, not until she gets near the stairs. Even then, Emma can't hear words, just Mommy's crying. Emma walks to her bedroom door, slowly turns the knob to inch it open a crack. She can't see down the stairs, but she's watched enough fights to know Daddy's face isn't stone anymore, but bright red, with veins popping out and eyes hot as fire. Mommy's face would be streaked with tears, eyes terrified.

"Please, Richard, let's not do this," Mommy pleads.

"Don't tell me what to do, bitch!" he shouts. "I'll do whatever the hell I damn well please!"

Then the rushing click-clack of Mommy's heels on the stairs. But Daddy is faster.

"Don't you run away from me, you fucking cunt!"

And Emma knows he's now grabbing Mommy's pretty hair in his fist, hears her body thump-thump down the steps, imagines him dragging her into the living room. Something shatters against the wall. And then the music is turned up, which doesn't stop the horrible noises, only muffles them some.

Emma closes her door, and stands in the center of her bedroom for a long time. Then she gets Sunshine from his turtle house, and runs her fingers over the golden orange starbursts on his shell. Daddy's allergic to cats, and he says dogs are too noisy and messy, but she's happy with Sunshine. She knows box turtles are smart, faster than white rats in figuring out mazes. But she's sure Sunshine is smarter than other turtles. He can always find the veggies she hides around her room, no matter how carefully she tucks them away. Plus, he's taught her something about hiding when things get scary.

Emma takes a lettuce leaf from the pail, jumps as something crashes downstairs, and takes Sunshine into her closet.

"Now you have *two* shells, Sunshine," she whispers, as she closes the door, "yours and my closet. We'll just stay in here a while, okay? And don't worry, he's probably not going to kill her. He never has before. It'll all be over in a little while. Well, maybe it'll be a long while, but it'll stop. You'll see."

Emma kneels down and crawls to the far back corner where the clothes hang almost to the floor. She wriggles under them and curls up on her side. She puts Sunshine in the curve of her body, and strokes his hard, rough shell. As he munches the lettuce, Emma crumples up a sweater that fell from its hanger, and puts it next to her stomach. And she laughs when the turtle crawls under it, just like she knew he would. "Now you have *three* shells, Sunshine!"

Girl and turtle stay that way for a very long time...until the music suddenly stops. Emma sits up quickly, listening hard. When the silence continues, she sweeps the clothes aside and crawls out. Ears straining for sound, she opens the closet door. She puts Sunshine back in his house, listens a while at her bedroom door. No sounds come up the stairs, no hollering or crying or banging or crashing. When she peeks into the hallway, she sees her parents' door is open, which means they're still downstairs.

Emma tiptoes into the hallway, stands on the landing, hears nothing. And even though she creeps down the stairs as quiet as a little mouse, Emma somehow knows it is safe.

There's no one in the dining room or kitchen. The living room either, but one of the bar chairs is knocked over and another lays on the floor across the room. The coffee table's upside down near the fireplace, and there's broken glass on the floor. One of the paintings is broken over the back of the sofa.

Emma turns into the back hall, walks past the bathroom, and stops at the door to the den. Mommy's lying on the floor with Daddy standing over her. Both of them are as still as statues. She knows Daddy can't move and won't even know she's there, so she kneels next to Mommy. Emma sees her breathing, sees the mark on her mother's arm that will turn the same purply-blue as Emma's fingers. She stands up, turns and looks at Daddy's ugly mad face...and kicks him right in the leg. Hard. But that makes her feel bad, because she knows kicking is wrong. And because she loves her Daddy, most of the time.

Emma isn't scared anymore. She's confused now, jumbled up inside. Kind of like when she and Daddy went on that crazy spinning ride on top of the tall spiky building in Las Vegas. She doesn't know what to do with herself, but she does know that she can't stand to see Daddy's angry face or Mommy on the floor, so she leaves the den. But she doesn't want to be in the wrecked living room either or in the dining room where the fight began. The kitchen is better, but then a memory pops up of Daddy shoving Mommy hard against the counter, so she leaves that room too.

Awful memories meet her no matter where she goes, but they no longer make her feel sick inside. The quiet that fills the house has woven its way through Emma as well. Confusion has turned into curiosity now. The memories feel like pieces of a ginormous puzzle, and she has to figure out how to fit them all together.

In the hallway, she remembers seeing Mommy on the floor last winter. As she walks down to the lower level, she remembers her lying in a heap at the bottom of the stairs after he pushed her down. In the game room, she again watches Daddy throw the remote at the TV. She didn't see Daddy smash one of the big mirrors in the workout room when she was in the second grade, but Mommy wouldn't have done it, so it must have been him.

Emma walks back up both sets of stairs. Outside her parents' bedroom, she remembers hearing Mommy's crying through the closed door. And as she stands in the opening to the master bath, Emma again sees bruises as Mommy gets out of the tub.

A jolt of understanding causes an "Ohhh!" to burst from Emma's lips. She suddenly knows that tonight wasn't about her math grade at all. Daddy was mad when he walked in the house. She and Mommy tried to make everything perfect so he wouldn't explode, but he would have found a reason anyway. He *always* found a reason. But his reasons aren't really reasons, just excuses to get his mad out and dump it all over Mommy and her.

There are more puzzle pieces she can't fit in yet, like why Daddy is always so angry and why she and Mommy don't leave. But for tonight, it's enough to know that it isn't her fault. It makes Emma laugh out loud.

She dances her way back into her own room, scoops her turtle from his house in the corner, sits down, and puts him on the floor in front of her. "You have to help me remember, Sunshine," she says. Though she feels herself becoming serious again, she also feels giggles bouncing around inside her. "I know things are probably gonna stay bad for a while, but I gotta remember that it's not my fault, no matter what he says or does or thinks."

And Sunshine *does* help, because right then he turns away from her, showing his most beautiful scute. While most of his sunbursts looked about the same, the one in the middle and a little above his tail is larger and brighter than the others. Emma knows exactly what he's telling her.

"Yes, Sunshine," she says excitedly. "I need to remember that I have a sunburst, too. That I *am* a sunburst. And I can't let anyone—not my mad Daddy, not my scared Mommy, and certainly not that mean Isabella girl—convince me I'm not, or that I'm not perfect just the way I am."

And with that, Emma closes her eyes and imagines a glowing sun in her stomach where the scared feeling usually lives. That sun makes her feel warm and glittery and strong. Soon, though, she notices something even better. The sunburst grows brighter when she breathes in, and its rays stretch up into her chest and down her legs when she breathes out. And it grows bigger with every breath. Now it's shining past her skin and reaching down into the floor and up to the ceiling. Emma knows that someone with magic glasses, like Violet in that book she read last year, wouldn't only see a little girl when they looked at her. No, they'd see a huge, shining sun.

Emma opens her eyes again, and gives Sunshine a big smile. "But I still need you to remind me, okay? Cuz I'm smart enough to know that my sun won't make Daddy be different or make Mommy less scared. And since I don't have Violet's magic glasses, I won't even know when my sun stops shining."

Sunshine slowly stretches out his wrinkly neck and twists it to look back over his shell at her. And she laughs out loud. "I get it! My sun *can't* go out, just like your scutes don't disappear just cuz you can't see them. And you know what else I figured out, Sunshine? Every time I look at *your* sunbursts, I'll remember I'm a sun, too, and I'll practice shining out in all directions. My sun will remind me that Daddy's mad is not my fault, and that I'm not stupid. And that I don't have to be perfect on the outside, cuz I'm already perfect on the inside, whether anyone sees it or not."

Just like with stupid fractions, Emma knows it'll be important to practice. So as she breathes her sun brighter and bigger, bigger and brighter, she says, "I am a sun, a beautiful and powerful sun. And," she adds, with a giggle bursting free at last, "I'm also a girl who absolutely, completely and totally *hates* fractions!"

Richard

At first, he thinks she's faking it, that the blank look is just possum playing dead. But when he gets no response from a swift kick to her stomach, he wonders if he could have killed her. And boy, doesn't that sober him up pretty damn quick. He knows he hadn't been as careful as he could have been. True, he hadn't hit her in the face, hadn't in years. That was just asking for trouble. And it could be a damn nuisance, too, leading to cancellations of plans already set in place. But she'd really pissed him off tonight, interfering when he was only setting needed limits with their daughter. Coddling was not going to help Emma succeed in the world, and damn if he was going to stand by and allow a child of his to skate through, doing less than she was capable of. Meghan might be out of touch, but he knew exactly what the world required.

So he might have gotten a little carried away, but he hadn't pushed her *that* hard, had he? He steadies himself, takes a good look. And the breath he hadn't known he'd been holding escapes in a rush when he sees the rise and fall of her chest. Best to just let her be for a while.

Richard walks into the living room, vaguely registering the damage as he goes behind the bar to pour himself another drink. He's too far gone to waste the good stuff, so he pours himself another Glenlivet 12 year, neat this time. Doesn't want to fuck with ice. Since he also doesn't want to sit surrounded by mess, particularly that Barceló he'd just bought a couple of years back, he goes down to the Game Room, racks the balls on this year's purchase, the Teckell 9 foot, and runs through a game each of 9 ball, fifteen in a row, and 3 ball. Then he brushes up on his air hockey skills, before settling on the couch.

A part of him registers it odd that he had light enough to play, since it's full dark now and the power outage that silenced his music continues, but mostly he doesn't think much about it. He just lets jazz play in his head, a skill he has that sets him above the rest. Once something's in his brain, he doesn't forget it. Comes in handy in business, but he knows it can make him broody otherwise. And Christ Jesus, isn't this the perfect night to brood. So as Kamasi Washington's latest streams on his internal drive, he thinks back over the day…the Wisterson account he isn't making headway on, the slight from that scrawny little asshole Peterson, the godawful traffic. And then to be disrespected in his own fucking house, well, there's no wonder he lost it.

And that makes him think of Emma. He knows she'll still be in her room working on math. Sure, she slacks off occasionally, but she's a good girl and when he makes the rules clear, she follows them. He'll go up now and see just what the fuck she finds so difficult about fractions.

Richard considers getting himself another drink, but knows he'll pay for it in the morning. He climbs the stairs to the main floor, cuts through the kitchen to avoid the living room, climbs the stairs to the second story, sees with satisfaction that Emma's door is shut just like he specified. He knocks, something Meghan is probably right about since their daughter isn't getting any younger, but announcing his intention to enter and waiting a second or two is one thing. He'll be goddamn if he'll ask permission to enter any room in this house. He turns the knob, sees the math worksheets on her desk, but no Emma. Must be hiding in the goddamn closet again.

Richard yanks the door open, and sure enough, a pink sneaker peeks out from under the clothes hanging in the corner. He feels the usual fury that comes whenever he sees someone cowering, but something about that sneaker stops him from reaching in and hauling his daughter out. His body goes rigid and his breath catches in his chest. Slowly he stretches out his arm and pushes the clothes to the side until he's looking down on a tightly curled little body dressed in purple leggings and a blue princess top with a scattering of silver sparkles.

Rage continues pressing its way up only to be stopped by something stronger, a thing writhing in his chest. He lets the clothes fall back into place, leaves Emma hidden in her spot on the floor, staggers from the closet and into the hallway. His breath is coming now in wrenching gasps. Bloody hell, he needs a drink! He takes the stairs two at a time, swings into the hallway and through to the bar, grabs the bottle of Glenlivet, and races down to the Game Room. He drinks straight from the bottle, not for enjoyment or even relaxation, but to banish that image of Emma on the floor. Something about that pink shoe kicks him right in the gut.

The enchantment of this time lasts days for Richard, stretching into a week and more of drunken stupor. On occasion, he roams the house, always avoiding the den, always ending up at Emma's closet staring at that pink sneaker. Twice he pulls the clothes back to see her little body tightly coiled. Then he stumbles away and resumes his drunken prowl.

One morning, though, Richard knows he's had enough. He'd come to in a chair, feeling like shit and stinking to high heaven. Christ, if he kept this up he'd be like his old man, that sorry-ass excuse for a human being. Richard climbs the stairs, strips off his clothes, walks into the shower, turns the water on hot and sharp, and stands for a long time as it sluices over his skin, the wall jets easing some of the knots along his spine. He dries off, takes a few Tylenol, puts on a pair of sweats, and goes down to the kitchen. Even though the power outage hangs on, the fridge seems to be working and flames shoot up the second he turns the knob on the gas range. Only then does he realize how lucky he'd been to have hot water upstairs, because Lord knows he needed that shower.

Richard scrambles some eggs while the coffee maker hums, vaguely wondering when he'd eaten last. The toaster isn't working, but almond butter on a couple slices of bread tastes damn good with the eggs. He takes his third cup of strong black coffee downstairs, and starts on the NordicTrack, which luckily is getting some juice, though not enough to light up the display. A good long run and the Tylenol dull the headache, but he still feels sluggish as he goes through his lifting routine. Well, what does he expect anyway, after that bender he'd been on?

And that just gets him thinking again about his no-good father. Drunk all weekend, every weekend, losing job after job when he got so he couldn't keep it together during the week either. Finally, his mother'd had enough and kicked him out on his sorry ass. Didn't see much of him after that, and good riddance.

Richard racks his last set of weights, grabs two bottles of water from the gym fridge, guzzles one down and takes the second with him out to the lower deck. The sun has cleared the trees to the east of the property, and its rays shine down on the lush expanse of bluegrass leading to the river. Richard follows it down, turning back for a view of the house on its rise. Damn, he'd done well for himself. He knows this isn't the last house he'll buy, but it's a fine one, landscaped to perfection and filled with most of the things he'd always told himself he'd get one day. He's nothing like his shitbag of a father.

Sure, he enjoys a drink after a long day, but it isn't a problem. And he doesn't drink that rotgut crap that was all his father could afford. Richard only drinks the good stuff, Glenlivet for every day, but Johnny Walker Blue 25 year or Macallan for special occasions. And he works hard to earn the right to it. Pulls in 6 figures, has that much again in stocks, while his father had settled for unemployment any time he could get it. No, he's nothing like his goddamn father, that's for sure.

Richard goes upstairs for a second shower. As he towels off, he catches a glimpse of himself in one of the full-length mirrors. He knows he looks good—tall, muscled and tan. Nothing like his flabby ass father, who couldn't have cared less about staying in shape. Richard pulls on a pair of Ralph Lauren's and a polo shirt and feels like himself again.

And with that thought, the lure to Emma's bedroom returns. He ignores it for a few hours, goes into his office to sketch out plans for a new dock, thinking maybe he'll put an addition on the boathouse this year for extra storage. But he just can't get that pink sneaker out of his head. It exerts some sort of weird gravitational pull that makes his chest ache.

Finally he gives in and stands again in the doorway of the closet, staring at the pink sneaker, noticing how tiny it is. But when he pulls back the clothes and looks down, it's not his daughter he sees in the corner. It's his sister. And though the grown Richard stands anchored in place, he sees himself as he was then, thin and scrawny-legged, crawling in next to Becky, both of them trying to escape the battle raging in the other room, though each word and slap cut like a knife through the cheap walls. How many nights had they huddled together in the closet of one apartment after another before he was big enough to brave the storm, protecting their mother by taking the beating himself? And how many years has he tried to block out the later realization that, while his mother was tending to him after the violence ended, his father was dragging his sister from her hiding place to do to her what no man should do to a child?

Richard's stomach spasms, vomit rising to his throat. He barely makes it to the toilet before it spews out in great wracking spasms that leave him curled on the bathroom tile, empty and weak. And in that moment, as time stands still and all's quiet, Richard knows that while his relationship with his mother had been complicated, his love for Becky had been as pure as any emotion he'd ever felt. And the fact that he not only hadn't protected her, but had opened her to harm by his absence...well, it's unforgivable.

Fuck, but he needs a drink. Richard races down the stairs, but his legs betray him, carrying him through the back hallway to the door of the den. Meghan lies twisted up against the wall, his fingerprints visible in the bruise on her upper arm. And superimposed on the image of Meghan is his mother's body as he'd seen it many times, eyes blackened and nose bloody.

Richard tears from the house and down to the river. He strips down to his boxers and heaves himself into the water like a man pursued, swimming until he hasn't the strength for another stroke. Then he turns onto his back and lets the current carry him. Finally, he makes his way to shore and treks back upstream to his own property. Richard stands then in the warmth of the late afternoon sun and looks up at his house on the hill. But he sees it now for what it is, some strange and twisted shrine to his father, a facade he's created to show their differences, while hidden at its core lies the truth of how alike they truly are.

Yes, he has a prestigious job, makes far more money than necessary. He drinks expensive booze, and lives in a large and impressive house. But that little pink sneaker and the woman lying on the floor scream a truth he hears at last. This home, built in opposition to everything he hates about his father, is filled with as much fear as any he'd lived in growing up. As is he. Because Richard sees as clear as day that it's not rage he feels when he sees someone cower. The feeling that twists his gut, that compels him to do something, anything, to make it go away, is not anger at all, but some noxious mix of terror, helplessness, wrenching guilt and self-hatred that he carries with him always. Fury and an excessive need for control are just his desperate attempts to outrun them. And in the process, he's meted out to Meghan and sweet little Emma the very emotions his father heaped upon his own family.

"Well, Richard," he says aloud now, "you've spent a lifetime telling yourself how different you are from Dad. It's time now to take a hard look at the similarities, and to figure out just what the hell you're going to do about them."

And with that statement, Richard becomes aware of a tingling sensation traveling across his skin. The air seems somehow alive, vibrant and glowing. The guilt in his gut is as strong as ever, as he knows it should be, but a tightness deep inside has begun to loosen. Richard knows he isn't going to run any longer, that he doesn't need to, that he doesn't even want to.

And for now, that's enough.

Meghan

Suddenly, he stops. Meghan waits, eyes averted, not giving him anything to latch onto. She's learned his ways over the 15 years they'd been together, and knows that when he's in a rage like this, or gearing up for one, it's safest not to assert herself in any way, best to let him make the next move and hope to God she can respond in a way that calms, rather than incites him further.

She'd been stupid to disagree with him tonight. She should have known it would only make things worse...just as she knows now that she can't afford any more mistakes. So she lies crumpled against the wall, his current silence as terrifying as his red-faced shouting had been. More so, actually, because it's unexpected and makes her fear what might come next. His shoes are inches from her face. In her peripheral vision, she sees his hands clenched into fists at his thighs. But he's just standing there. Is he playing with her, waiting for her to make a move so he can strike again?

Yet as the seconds stretch into minutes, her heartrate begins to stabilize and her breathing gradually slows. It's as though her body registers the diminished threat, even as her mind seeks frantically for what might come next.

"Richard?" she says at last, quietly, tentatively.

When she receives no response, she slowly turns her head, alert for the slightest indication of danger. Finding none, she looks fully into his face, sees how fury has twisted it into a thing grotesque, teeth bared, lips contorted. His eyes, though, are distant now, no longer spitting fire. They still look down on her, but she knows he sees her no more.

Meghan sits up, haltingly stands and waits a few moments for the mild dizziness to pass. She takes stock of her injuries. Her right hip hurts where it slammed into the wall, and the wrenching of her arm has left her shoulder tender. Her scalp throbs, her fingers filling with loose strands as she combs them through her hair. She'll have bruises for certain, but she's grateful nothing is broken and that she has full range of motion everywhere, but for the flareup of that old shoulder injury.

She edges around Richard and walks into the disaster that is the living room. She stifles a swift spike of anger by reminding herself that this is what happens when she provokes him. She knows how hard he works to provide them with a beautiful home, a far cry from the squalor of his youth. He hasn't talked about it since the early days when, filled with remorse after an angry outburst or those first violent eruptions, he'd let her know just how terrible it had been. Childhoods like that leave scars, scars others can't see and wouldn't understand if they did.

Despite the years that have passed, a mix of shame and anger rises now as she remembers Lauren walking into the boutique's changing room despite the drawn curtain, and seeing a string of bruises stretching down one side of her back from shoulder to waist. In the mirror, she'd seen the shock on her friend's face, heard the sudden intake of breath.

"Yeah, I know," Meghan said, as quick on her feet as ever, "it hurts like hell, too. Heels are just no match for those basement stairs of ours. Slid right out from under me. Lucky I didn't break my neck!"

But Lauren hadn't been fooled. She'd never liked Richard anyway, and was always looking for evidence that her opinion was justified.

"C'mon, honey," Lauren said, her voice pleading. "You can tell me. We're friends, right? Let me help. We can figure this out together."

"There's nothing to figure out and I don't need any help," Meghan insisted, her voice sharper than she'd intended. "Everything's fine."

Lauren turned away then, hanging the slacks on the hook and leaving the dressing room, but not before Meghan saw her eyes fill with tears. Things had cooled between them after that. They'd been growing apart anyway, but she couldn't stand to see the concern in her friend's eyes. It felt like pity, and Meghan couldn't abide being pitied, in large part because it was completely unwarranted. She wasn't some victim, an abused woman who couldn't think straight. Just the opposite. She was strong, strong enough to help a wounded man heal. Richard's pain was so deep that, of course, it would sometimes erupt. But he wasn't evil. He was damaged, and she loved him enough to help him mend.

That perspective, though, had begun to waver in the past few years. Richard rarely shows his sweet side these days, and his apologies exist only in the memories she carries. As Meghan begins the cleanup now—righting chairs, sweeping up pieces of the shattered vase, blotting the water that pooled on the floor, and moving the Barceló to the garage to be taken to Wilson's for repair on Monday—she realizes his increasing harshness with Emma is shifting something inside her. He's always been strict and with high standards, but he no longer seems to delight in their daughter as he once had.

Thinking of Emma has her on the stairs in no time, albeit after a quick look into the den to find Richard's immobility holding fast. She gives the bedroom door a few light taps before entering, calling out so Emma will know it's her. School supplies are spread out on the desk, but Emma is missing.

Meghan crosses over to the closet, opens the door, sees the pink sneaker peeking out from under the hanging clothes. She stands transfixed, heart pounding, lungs unable to draw breath, eyes incapable of turning away. Her arm trembles as she reaches out to push the clothes aside, and a strangled cry rises from deep inside when she sees her sweet girl curled into a ball. And in that moment, all that Meghan has held in abeyance comes bursting through. She falls to her knees, hand covering her mouth, body convulsing as long-held sobs rip free from the cage that has contained them for so long.

Meghan remains on that closet floor for an interval that is neither too long nor too short. When she stands, though, obstructions that had distorted her vision have been swept away. Pacing back and forth across Emma's room, she begins to plan her next move.

She'll call Rachel. Though she and her sister have never been close, particularly since her marriage to Richard, Meghan has not the slightest doubt that she'll help. And who better than an attorney to make certain Richard's threats won't pan out—threats to kill her if she tries to leave, to sue for full custody, to disparage her among mutual friends and her remaining professional contacts. Rachel's also in a financial position to help Meghan get on her feet as she makes her way, step by step, back into the career she'd left when she became pregnant.

Richard won't make it easy for her. She knows he'll put roadblocks in her path at every turn. But she can see now that he's been making her life impossible for years anyway. How could she have been so blind?!! And why did it take seeing the harm done to Emma to wake her to the truth of her life?

Of course, she knows the reason. She'd come to question her own worth, while still knowing in every fiber of her being that her daughter is precious beyond measure. She will ensure that Emma is treated that way from now on. And she'll learn to insist that she herself be treated the same as well, faking it until she can come to believe it is true.

Meghan goes back into the closet, stretches out on the floor facing her daughter, and reaches out to stroke her hair. Soon, Sunshine creeps out from under the sweater in his slow turtle fashion. As he cocks his leathery head toward Meghan, his red-orange eyes take on an inquisitive look that elicits a giggle from her.

"I know, Sunshine," Meghan answers. "I can't imagine how it's all going to work either. We'll just have to find out, though, won't we?"

Pausing Anew

Though images no longer play in the flames, you continue to peer into the depths of the hearth, soothed by the fire's crack and sizzle. And though the wind no longer keens outside, you recognize a howl wanting to burst forth from within as you reel from all you have seen.

You speak at last, looking again into the inky depths of Nyah's eyes. "I am stunned and deeply moved by what has been shown me. And yet I believe it best to let these three individuals live within me for a while, rather than do them a possible disservice by speaking too soon."

"Yes," she agrees softly, the tenderness of her gaze washing over you. "And it is also good soul-care to allow time to settle into what you have just experienced. It is our sense that your kind often attempt to rush past heartache in an effort to outrun it, as though it might dissolve into nothingness if not fully felt."

The fire soothes as time again expands. At last you find words. "And you suggest that approach is in error, and I must agree with you. Heartache not fully experienced seems merely to await an opportunity to rise up again. In the meantime, though, it can exert a pull outside our awareness, causing a dampening of spirit that closes us off to life, while making us vulnerable to all sorts of other confused expressions.

"And if avoidance is your main coping strategy," Nyah adds, "you then require ways to keep your feeling nature submerged, yes?"

"Yes," you nod. "Enter any number of addictive and otherwise harmful behaviors. Or as Richard has just demonstrated, we might unconsciously dole out our unfelt pain to others. You used the term 'feeling nature' just now. We are a species that feels, aren't we?"

Registering her smile, you continue. "Our task, then, must be to choose how best to feel what we feel, as fully and as safely as we can, trusting that doing so will lead us forward." You pause before adding, "So how do I fully and safely feel my emotions about all that has just now come to me through your fiery portal?"

Silence, a gentle smile, and an unending well of compassion are her only answers. You receive them, and as you hold her gaze for many long breaths, you find yourself gradually guided forward.

"I realize you are not allowed to give firm answers, but I am grateful for the soft incursion of these last moments, for they have taught me something. From your silence, I am reminded first to be still and to wait. To not run from my reactions, whatever they might be, nor to act upon them too quickly.

"And from your quiet smile, which tells me I am welcomed here without conditions or expectations, I realize that I need to not only be still with my emotions, but to *welcome* them and receive them into my awareness, just as they are. As I offer them refuge, they will then reveal themselves, letting me know them and teaching me both about myself and life as a whole.

"And as your gaze settles on me," you continue, "I feel bathed in love, cherished and held in the light of compassion. If I can greet my emotions with that same love, if I can receive them into my heart without rushing to make them other than they are or use my mind to quickly explain them away, they will feel fully received. Heard. Known. Isn't that all they ever wanted?"

Nyah beams, broad and deep. "Yes, dear one. Your kind has been gifted a strong feeling nature. Yet there is no doubt that this gift may often be experienced as burden. Challenges, though, never come without compensation, without other gifts to lighten the load. One of these is that emotions fully felt transform into something else. Have not the sages spoken of impermanence?"

"Yes," you answer. "The Buddha particularly. So it comes to me now that when we try to avoid emotions, we inadvertently lock them down, turning them into concrete, but a concrete that is apt to fracture under the right conditions. Yet when we allow our emotions to remain fluid and alive, they more easily move through us, like a swiftly flowing stream. They can then shift and morph into something new."

"Indeed," she agrees with a nod. "And another gift lies in your ability to share your burdens with others. While I know this can be hard, particularly when the lacerations are deep and the pain prolonged, your kind is not meant to soldier on, independent units disengaged from the rest. Lives—and heartaches—are meant to be shared, though the form of that sharing can vary greatly."

Silence returns. You close your eyes to enact what you have learned. You seek an inner stillness and finding it, you turn toward your feelings for Emma, Meghan and Richard. You consciously welcome these emotions into awareness, breathing them into your heart and breathing them out, listening with an inner ear to what they have to tell you. As logs shift in the grate, your feelings respond to this welcome and roll through you in rapid succession, their intensity increasing and softening, with much doubling back as each reaction bumps against and rolls with the others. Dread. Shock. Helplessness. Fear. Outrage. Compassion. Horror. Sorrow. Disgust. Fierce protectiveness. Hate. Admiration. Impulse to harm. Recognition. Desire to avenge. Affection. Kinship. Wonder.

As Nyah has modeled for you, you simply receive, bathing each in acceptance, washing each in love. And when the tumult at last subsides, you brush tears from your cheeks and open your eyes, noting the moistness in the eyes of your companion as her gaze again holds yours.

"Well?" she asks with a gentle smile.

"That was quite a ride!" you respond with a laugh. "Intense, but not awful. I certainly understand my urge to avoid such emotion, for it is indeed painful. And yet, it felt almost good to simply feel it. It certainly felt real. True. It was definitely survivable. And the very *liveliness* of the process suggests that when I close down to the intensity of affect and don't let myself feel, I must die a bit. Yes, closing down feels a little like death. Dying at the very least to a full experience of living. Of course, emotions can feel like they're killing me, too," you laugh, "but *feeling* like and *being* like are not the same thing."

Silence returns. You drink from the mug in your hand and find you have no need of speech. You rest until, at the most opportune time, the hearth begins to dim. You feel yourself pulled back into that safe and enveloping darkness. You rest there as well, until the particulars of your own life begin to materialize around you. Welcomed back into your own world, you carry with you the memories of this last sojourn and let them simmer as you await the time of your next return.

ENCHANTED *A Tale of Remembrance*

Ambling Again...

Yes, the time has come once more, sweet reader. With a quick and rousing call to your powers of make-believe, you are again pulled forward. The passageway is well-known to you now, and you travel its length quickly. Welcoming darkness swirls about you and gradually resolves into the details of your wise companions' mythic abode. With a sense of anticipation, even elation, you greet Nyah, as she smiles a greeting in return. She looks much the same as before, though her dress swirls now with vivid greens and blues, and her braids wrap 'round the top of her head and are circled by a knotted scarf reflecting the pattern of her dress. Patiently you both await the arrival of words.

"Meghan, Richard, and particularly sweet Emma have remained with me while I've been away. I have thought of them often and have reflected on my reaction to each."

"I am not surprised," Nyah replies. "Will you say more?"

"Yes, of course," you answer. "You had warned me that I might be challenged to feel kinship with all members of this family. You were prescient indeed...though I suspect that comes with that whole archetypal thing ya got goin' on," you say with a grin.

She winks before erupting into laughter that elicits your own and fills you with delight. You find it odd, though, that you can feel such pleasure while also holding awareness of pain so recently witnessed. When your laughter is spent, a lightness remains that makes it easier to revisit your reactions.

"Richard was the hardest to like or to recognize as kin. I was repulsed by the terror he created for Emma and Meghan, and still find it angering to remember. But while simply detesting him would be easy, I soon recognized that it would be *too* easy. Richard's choice to look at the ways he was like his father compelled me to look at the ways I am like Richard. I too have been insensitive to the pain of others. I too have been selfish. I too have let my unhealed wounds from the past wreak havoc in the present, for both myself and those around me. I recognized that my challenges are not so very different from Richard's, varying mostly in terms of magnitude. And the compassion I began to feel for him—and importantly, *with* him, as I *was* him—in response to the pink sneaker, led also to a greater self-compassion. We are all learning here. And we all make mistakes, even if some of those are more disastrous than others."

Time passes, hearth glows, rain falls beyond the walls and upon the roof. Finally, more words arrive.

"My reaction to Meghan was mixed as well. I felt her pain and her fear, but also found myself angered that she didn't do more to protect herself and her daughter. And then I again realized judgment has no place here. When humans have been beaten down, sometimes quite literally, they become so wrapped up in trying to survive that their vision shrinks and perspective is lost. The enchantment provided an opportunity for Meghan to see more clearly, and to expand her vision to a larger perspective...and she did. While my heart goes out to women who don't have wealthy attorneys for siblings, I am overjoyed that Meghan can see at least her very next steps.

"And I also recognized that my own vision often shrinks as well, and I lose perspective myself. I am like Meghan, as well as her husband. In this moment, it seems to me that the similarities we humans share are so much greater than our differences."

Your companion smiles and nods before asking in a gentle voice, "And what of Emma? Are you ready to share your response to her?"

"My heart broke," you whisper. "How was Emma to make sense of such intense emotion, such turmoil going on around her and directed *at* her? She tried, though, and her conclusion—certainly helped along by her father—was to think that *she* was to blame and to work hard to make up for it. Yet in entering her experience, I felt how this belief had burrowed even deeper inside her, leading to the conclusion that she was not only to blame for what she *did*, but for who she *was*. In her young mind, a striving for perfection was the only way she could hope to make up for what she believed was a failing at her core.

"Each time the hearth took me into her room, I was struck by how orderly it was. It was not the room of a child actively engaged with life. Books and dolls lined the shelves with an unusual degree of precision. Her bedcovers had not a single wrinkle in them, and her stuffed animals were arranged against the headboard and across the windowsills like little soldiers standing for inspection."

You pause for a time before continuing.

"As I've said before, your hearth allows me not only to see *into* these lives, but to feel as though it is I who am living them. So I experienced Richard's rage from the inside, its intensity as addictive as it was frightening, and felt Meghan's fear viscerally. I felt, too, Emma's self-loathing. But to be with her as she intentionally harmed herself—as punishment, but also as a way to share her mother's pain and to manage her own—was devastating. Just devastating.

"But then," you say, with a broad smile blooming, "to walk with her through the house, to experience with her the growing realization that the shame was not hers, that she was not responsible at all...well, *that* felt miraculous. Like those moments of Grace when clouds part and the sun shines through once again, everything inside me brightened. I knew Emma's clarity and felt such delight as she sought ways to remember. I am in awe of her wisdom. What am amazing child!"

Sounds from the hearth's fire fill the silence until words rise again.

"But perhaps Emma is not so unique. Maybe all living beings have this aptitude. It could, indeed, be our birthright, this ability to listen deeply and respond in a life-affirming way. Like plants turning toward the sun, as Zosia and I spoke of earlier. I know you can't give me firm answers, but can you tell me if I'm on the right track?"

Nyah's smile and dancing eyes are her confirmation.

"But I sense there is more," you continue. "As I joined with Emma particularly, though I also sensed this a bit with her parents, it did seem that her insights were not altogether new. She was aware of feeling hate toward her father at times, which shows me that on some level she knew it was *his* behavior, *his* state of being that was the problem. Perhaps this enchantment simply gave her a chance to deeply know what she'd already sensed but couldn't quite grasp, and to release herself from the responsibility that on some level she already knew was not hers."

You sip from your mug as the rain continues to sound in the night.

"And though I know you cannot tell me," you begin, "I want to know if Emma will remember. Though I just realized," you say with a quick laugh, "that I don't need your endorsement. Emma's recognition of her own worth was real. I *felt* it! That recognition is now a part of her, anchored in some deep place inside. I trust she will find her way."

"Oh, my dear, " Nyah says, softly "do you have any idea what a precious gift your trust is?"

Surprised by the joyful dampness in the old woman's eyes, your awareness leaps to a new level. "Ahhhh, our trust is blessing. When we have faith in another's awakening, we fund their ability to awaken. Our believing in them encourages them to believe in themselves. And our remembrance sparks their own." After a pause, you add, "And seeing this now, I choose to also keep faith that Emma's parents will remember as well. I trust that they cannot *un*know the truths they have perceived, can not *un*see what clarity has shown them. This enchantment has given each person the opportunity to come to stillness in order to access the truth hidden away in the raw material of their lives. Whether they will act on those truths—and in what way—is theirs to decide. They may, indeed, forget and be lulled back into unconsciousness again. And yet, even so, I believe they will remember again."

After much time passes, you continue. "This dance of forgetfulness and remembrance, of somnolence and awakening, is so pervasive within the human experience that it cannot be an aberration. In fact, as I've sat in this place of magic with you and Zosia, that dance seems to have a meant-to-be flavor to it. I wonder if one of the purposes of the human experience—if indeed there is any purpose to it—is to develop the ability to recognize when we have fallen into unconsciousness and to rouse ourselves into awareness once again. It's as though it is the *mechanism* of transit that we need to learn, both the things that numb or harden us to the richness we live within, and those that bring us back into direct experience of it. To see how we close off to Grace and to know how to open to it again. And each time we do return, the path is better known to us, the *process* is better known to us.

Your eyes are suddenly wet as you look at this old woman who, along with Zosia, has become so dear to you. "Just like my travels to this place, the pathway becomes more familiar with each passage. To stray and to return," you muse, "to drop into sleep and to awaken. Could that, broadly speaking, be the point of it all?"

"It just might be, my dear," Nyah replies with another wink before a long pause holds you both. Finally she speaks again. "Are you ready to see more?"

"Yes, I am," you reply. "I am *thirsty* to see more."

"Then we shall step now into the lives of another family," she says. And with those words, you find you are facing the hearth where golden tongues of flame leap and sway.

Kayla

Well, *The Overstory* certainly isn't the light read she had in mind when she decided to go for the extra credit option listed on the syllabus. True, she'd had second thoughts when she saw just how BIG the dang thing was—over 500 pages, and in a tiny font, too!—but she thought fiction would be a nice escape from a demanding semester. And since she only had to write a short personal essay to prove to the Botany prof that she'd actually read the thing, she'd carried it to the register along with a cute tank top she couldn't resist and a couple of crazy expensive textbooks she'd decided to buy rather than rent online. She'd swiped her card, shoved it all into her pack, and walked out of the building, not knowing her life was about to change. Again.

Now she's holed up in her room unable to put it down, mesmerized by dendrologist Patricia Westerford's research. Kayla'd already been online a gazillion times determining that the information shared through this fictional character was not fictional at all, but well-documented science, albeit couched in somewhat lyrical language: the detailed wonders of photosynthesis, the wisdom of growing things, the hidden magic of the forest performed at a pace too slow for humans to perceive. And now Dr. Westerford speaks these words:

> My whole life, I've been an outsider. But many others have been out there with me. We found that trees could communicate, over the air and through their roots. Common sense hooted us down. We found that trees take care of each other. Collective science dismissed the idea. Outsiders discovered how seeds remember the seasons of their childhood

and set buds accordingly. Outsiders discovered that trees sense the presence of other nearby life. That a tree learns to save water. That trees feed their young and synchronize their masts and bank resources and warn kin and send out signals to wasps to come and save them from attacks.

Here's a little outsider information, and you can wait for it to be confirmed. A forest knows things. They wire themselves up underground. There are brains down there, ones our own brains aren't shaped to see. Root plasticity, solving problems and making decisions. Fungal synapses. What else do you want to call it? Link enough trees together, and a forest grows aware.

As she reads those last words, the lights go out and the background mix of musical genres streaming across the dorm falls silent. The timing of the power outage feels to Kayla somehow *intended*. It not only punches up the power of those last few printed words, but creates the conditions to absorb them...perhaps even a plea to do so. A request Kayla gladly grants.

Her eyes travel of their own accord from the book in her hand to her own small forest, its various hues lit by late afternoon sunlight. Of course she knows the difference between an old growth forest and her own meager collection of green, but she really likes her own meager collection of green. Needs it, in fact. Pots range across the windowsill, circle the edges of her desk, hang from hooks anchored (explicitly against dorm policy) above the window, drape from atop the two cheap wardrobes on either side of the door, and fan out across the floor. With the addition of the ailing ivy she rescued just last week from a room down the hall, she now has 25 pots housing a forest of 14 species, including pothos, hosta, peperomia, spiderwort, aloe, snake plant, calathea, peace lily, spider plant, schefflera, Christmas cactus, three types of geraniums, two ivies, and two begonias. Not bad for a 12 by 18 foot room intended for two humans, though Abby now spends most of her time at Tyler's place, which pretty much gives Kayla a room to herself. Sweet!

As she drinks in the silence of the green, Kayla wonders if a collection of houseplants, confined each to its own pot, can communicate with one another. While she's learned that much of such communication in a forest occurs deep within the ground, she's also learned that trees send signals through the air as well, chemical messengers carrying important information. Maybe her plants do the same. She hopes so. They certainly are thriving in their tiny forest. While much of that has to do with regular watering, feeding, and grow lights for the sun-hungry, she also likes to think that they sense each other's presence...and her own. She wants them to register, in their own green way, her gaze falling on them throughout the day, wants them to feel her love, wants there to be some sort of communication loop linking her lifeform to theirs.

As the silence stretches on, she becomes sure that's the case. If the compounds emitted by the needles of sequoias can bring peace to stressed humans, then she and her plants can surely have an effect on each other. With this thought, a tingling runs along Kayla's arms and her mood buoys with each inhalation. Though the budding scientist in her is aware that she's probably totally making shit up, still she gives herself to the sensation, choosing to believe that such communication is not only possible, but is occurring with each breath.

Relishing whatever weird thing is going on here amid the silence and through the quivering dance across her skin, Kayla's eyes come to rest on the spider plant hanging in front of the window, sprouting babies. And that's when she knows. It is time. Time to approach a door she closed over 2 years ago, one she's been barricading ever since with anything handy: working two jobs to stash money away, finishing her last year of high school crammed with honor courses for college credit, applying at universities around the country, and settling on one half a continent from home. And while that wild outer storm raged, she'd kept her sweet baby swaddled deep inside, almost as though the birth itself had never happened.

Dear little Sophia.

Kayla'd gotten pregnant toward the end of her junior year in high school, a result of a few fumbling sexual encounters with bad-boy Ethan. After a third pregnancy test confirmed the truth of the other two, she'd told her two closest friends, then her parents and siblings, and eventually was successful in tracking down Ethan to let him know. Not surprisingly, everyone thought abortion was the way to go. Kayla knew that was a viable option, since she totally believed in a woman's right to choose what to do with her body. And in that vein, she decided she would choose what to do with hers.

Family lore was replete with stories of Kayla's determination: brow creased in concentration as she learned to walk, to read, to skip; doggedly seeking out intermediate footholds when her little legs couldn't reach the ones her older siblings used to climb the backyard trees; getting back on her bike after crashing, knees streaming blood, and furiously pumping to catch up with the others.

Kayla had channeled that same trait into exploring each option available to her, in order to find a choice she could live with. During those first few weeks, with a hand resting on her still-flat belly, she let herself swing back and forth from one option to another, playing out possible scenarios to see how each felt. She imagined conversations with her fetus-becoming-baby. She scheduled the first gynecological appointment of her life, and got answers to her long list of questions about both pregnancy and abortion. Kayla'd even met with Sister Constance-Marie, an ancient nun in a convent in the northern part of the state, who listened attentively as Kayla talked and talked and talked, and whose only advice was to be still and trust that an answer would come.

And gradually it did. After making herself a little crazy going this way and that, Kayla landed in the certainty that she would give—that she *wanted* to give—this collection of cells an opportunity to become human, to burst into the world as its unique self and live a full life. She also knew just as certainly that she would not be the one to raise this child. Her gift would be to offer her bodily resources to grow a baby who could live in the world and, once there, be guided by others. Not a popular decision, not for her friends, not for Ethan, and not at first for her parents.

She remembers the moment her mom and dad finally accepted her decision. It was a Saturday evening and the three of them were at the table, the dishwasher humming away across the room. Her mother had just offered their help should she choose to keep the child, even offering to raise him or her themselves if that's what Kayla wanted.

"We're worried," her father added, "that, down the road, you'll regret having your child adopted and..." His voice broke then and her mother reached out to take his hand. After a few breaths, he finished, "We just don't want that for you."

Though her parents had never said a thing about this being their grandchild, Kayla knew she was choosing not just for her baby and herself, but for her parents as well. And it broke her heart in two.

With tears streaming down her cheeks, Kayla said, "You two are the very best parents a child could hope for, but I can't ask you to do that. You've already raised three kids, and when I'm on my own you'll be able to do something *completely* different. You've talked for years about going off in the RV to live like gypsies, maybe settling down in the mountains somewhere. It wouldn't be fair to ask you to let that dream go. But I know having your grandchild adopted isn't fair either.

"I'm soooo sorry I'm hurting you, but whether I have the right to ask this or not, I'm gonna ask it anyway. I ask you to trust me and trust my decision.

I know it's the right one."

After a few moments of silence, her father rose from his chair and said, "Mom and I need to talk. In a little while, we'll come up and tuck you in, okay, sweetie?"

As goofy as it was, she still loved those nights when they tucked her in. "Okay," she answered, standing to wrap her arms around her dad. And then her mom joined in for a three-way hug, what a much younger and more carefree Kayla used to call a Kayla sandwich. All of them were crying as though their world was breaking, which it was. But she knew her parents had accepted her decision, knew they'd accepted there was no choice but to let their world break apart and find a way to put it back together again.

From that point on, their support was strong and sure, the steady ground under her feet. As the months moved forward, as her belly rounded and her breasts grew heavy, they helped Kayla research agencies and options. They read home studies together and narrowed those down to a select few, welcoming each set of prospective parents into their home for an initial interview. They hired an adoption attorney to handle the legalities, including Ethan's refusal to be involved in any way. And they encouraged Kayla to take the year off from high school, understanding that she had more important concerns now and didn't need the flack that had started coming from some of her peers...or the support of those who gave her the creeps, assuming she was a right-to-lifer.

Her parents liked the Marinos as much as she did. They even drove her to Michigan where Kayla spent a few weeks with Mia and Antonio, getting to know them better and trying to picture what life would be like for her daughter there. It was toward the end of that visit that indecision gave way to a quiet certainty.

On a gorgeous fall day, she'd set off for one of her long walks, but came back about twenty minutes later when she had to pee yet again and the thought of balancing her 7-month pregnant self for a squat in the woods seemed more trouble than it was worth. As she turned into the drive, she heard raised voices coming from the back deck. Feeling only a little guilty, Kayla walked quietly down the side of the house, stopping near the back corner so she could hear without being seen.

"Don't tell me what to do, Antonio! You can be so goddamn controlling, you know that?!!"

"I'm not being controlling! If you go at it that way, you're gonna ruin the fitting. You want me to just stand by and let you fuck up the grill?"

"I'm not going to fuck up your precious grill! I'm just getting in there to clean the gunk you didn't get off last time."

"That *I* didn't get last time? Why is it *my* job to clean the grill?"

"Because every time I touch the thing, we get into a stupid argument like this!"

"Keep your voice down, okay? Kayla'll be getting back soon and we don't want her to think we're a couple of crazy people."

"Oh, Tonio, the girl's smart." Mia said, her voice losing some of its sting. "She wasn't raised in some lab, ya know? She's heard arguments before. Do you think she expects us to be perfect? Do you think she expects us never to get annoyed with each other, to never fight?"

"You're right, Mimi. Of course you're right. This has just been so bloody stressful, it's a wonder we haven't gone batshit crazy."

"I know. What if she says no, Tonio? What if she decides to keep the baby? Or what if she decides to go through with the adoption, just not with *us*? What if she decides she doesn't *like* us?"

Kayla heard Antonio's footsteps crossing the deck, coming closer to Mia, closer to where she herself was standing. The soft rustle of fabric against fabric let her see their arms wrapping around each other.

"God, I don't even want to think about that. But the truth is, she might. I have a good feeling about this, but yeah, she might say no. And if she does, she does. We know how much we want this, know when we're not busy being scared—or batshit crazy—that we'll make great parents."

"So if she says no," Mia said softly a minute later, "she says no. And I'll again pick up the pieces of your broken heart, and you'll pick up the pieces of mine, and we'll start over. We'll start over again-again, okay?"

"Yeah, we'll start over again-again," Antonio replied. After a couple minutes of silence, he added, "I'm sorry, Mia. I love you...even though you don't know how to clean a grill."

"Hey, don't push your luck, Mister Gotta Do It My Way," Mia answered.

And they both laughed.

Yep, that's when Kayla knew for sure. When she told them after dinner that she'd eavesdropped on their argument, she didn't apologize but explained she needed to see who they were when they weren't on their best behavior. And though it confirmed what she'd been feeling all along, it was the final piece falling into place.

After that, things moved quickly. Antonio and Mia arranged to work from home, though home was an apartment they'd rented near Kayla for those last few weeks, in case the baby came early. They chose the baby's name together, and attended doctor appointments with her and at least one of her parents. All of them met in various combinations with her therapist, Jenna, to talk through the confused emotions and strengthen the already deep trust that had grown so quickly. They met with the attorney to sign the initial documents and approve the ones that awaited signatures down the road.

And they not only attended the birth, but assisted in it. Kayla's parents were her coaches, but Mia caught Sophia and Antonio cut the cord. And when they then laid the beautiful red-faced and squalling baby on her chest, there wasn't a dry eye in the room, not for the family members, not for the medical folks. Thinking back on it later, Kayla suspected Sophia's birth must have been even more special than most, in a room overflowing with a fierce love born of fear and struggle, of heartbreak and hard-won trust.

And a few days later, Mia and Antonio took her little girl, took *their* little girl, away into her new life. And Kayla shut down. Oh, she cried when it was expected, often when it was not. But it felt like it was her *body* doing the crying, while she herself was wrapped in gauze someplace far away. She continued to see Jenna, though less and less frequently. The next fall she participated in planting the aspen tree in the backyard, placing Sophia's placenta deep in the hole before they wrestled the tree into place. But it all felt so *unreal*.

And now that sweep of memories finds her in a tiny dorm room 27 months later, tears streaming from eyes locked on a spider plant glowing in the late-day sun. It had been her very first plant, bought at the same time as the aspen. While her parents were out in the nursery getting information for a successful transplant, Kayla had wandered through the greenhouse and stopped at a hanging mass of slender, two-toned leaves. It was pretty, but that wasn't the draw. What captured Kayla's attention was the one little baby reaching out from the tip of an arching stalk. Though Kayla was not aware of any emotion, tears had again risen unbidden, and she knew she needed that plant. The aspen would remain at home growing in the yard as a sort of public remembrance of Sophia, while she'd take this smaller piece of living beauty wherever she went, a private honoring of her own.

That plant was the mother not only of a succession of its own babies, but indirectly of the rest of Kayla's personal menagerie. And possibly, she realizes now, a career focused in one way or another on nurturing the growth of green life in the world.

Kayla laughs out loud that she'd not seen the connection before. After Sophia's birth, she'd needed to take an active part in growing things, needed to be surrounded by the abundance of life, ached for tangible proof that such vitality was never-ending and that it could take many forms. And yet, there was more. Kayla had never kept even one of her spider babies. She'd bought pretty pots, rooted the spiderettes in the loamy soil they preferred, and had given each and every one of them to others.

Jenna liked to remind her that making peace with Sophia's absence was a process that began when she first knew she was pregnant and would continue into the future as feelings welled and thoughts about Sophia arose. And Kayla knows now that it's true. Without ever realizing it, through this spider plant she had enacted again and again the process of relinquishing Sophia.

And something else comes to her now. Just as she formed little Sophia from the stuff of her own body, she realizes that Sophia has formed her in return. Her baby's very existence forced Kayla to dig deep to find her way forward, gave her the gift of discovering at an early age that she could trust herself to find her own answers. And perhaps Sophia was helping Kayla even now to understand her own purpose in the world: to nurture life for life's sake, to create to the best of her ability the conditions for it to thrive in the world, and to release it to do just that. Yes, Jenna was right. Each step on her path was simply what making peace looked like in that moment.

Kayla knows she is ready to take another step now. She reaches into her nightstand drawer and removes the small wooden box her oldest brother had made for her in shop class years ago. Opening the lid, she takes out the photos Antonio and Mia sent for Sophia's two birthdays and both Christmases, photos Kayla had looked at with a dulled heart before tucking them away. Now, though, she lets herself see, really *see*, her baby girl. And her heart breaks all over again, though not in a bad way. Well, it does hurt like hell, but there is something else woven through the pain. Something that feels like a quiet sort of joy. Something that feels like a heart coming alive again.

Brushing tears from her cheeks, Kayla picks up her laptop, raises its lid, and clicks on the birthday video she has yet to watch. And there's her girl: climbing playground equipment while Mia guides her feet; working a puzzle and looking so much like Kayla herself, forehead creased in determination; shaking a tambourine as large as her head while wiggling her butt and singing; dissolving now into helpless giggles.

Kayla never regretted her choice to have Sophia adopted. Well, not for more than a little while anyway. But seeing her baby, really *seeing* her baby, thriving and so full of life is a gift, one that reassures her that she made the right choice. And Kayla welcomes the permission this gift brings, permission to thrive herself and to bloom in her own way. Her baby is happy, and she can be happy too.

As the video comes to an end, Kayla takes three framed photos from the suitcase stashed beneath her bed. She places one on her nightstand, one on her desk and, taking a poster from the hook on the wall, hangs the other so it will be the first thing she sees when she walks through the door. She may not keep them up for forever, but it feels right for now.

As she sits back on her bed, Kayla recognizes that something tight and hard inside her has loosened and is beginning to unfurl, a bud opening and relaxing into the petals of a flower. And she promises herself that she won't close down again. In fact, she will reach instead, and does so now.

The tingling fills her whole body as she takes the photo from her nightstand and gazes at her daughter through the eyes of an opened heart. Gaze, though, is such a tiny word to hold the enormous outpouring of love she now beams toward Sophia. Kayla knows, in that moment and without any doubt whatsoever, that love is always welcomed and never wasted, and that communication—that *communion*—can occur across distances regardless of humankind's current inability to fully measure it. And Dr. Westerford's teachings come back to her now, but with a new depth and a new application.

"You and I, sweet Sophia, are wired up underground, too," Kayla says aloud. "Our connection exists within our DNA, and it exists beyond it as well. It can travel miles. And today, this is the wish I send you: Live well, my Sophia girl. Know that I will never forget you and will hold you near always. And know that our love goes on and on, on and on. Forever and forever."

Mia

She and Antonio stretch out on the bed, enjoying the peace that arrives with their energetic daughter's afternoon naps. They'd considered making love, but are again using this uninterrupted time to talk, something there never seems to be enough time for these days.

"She wanted to read Brown Bear again," Antonio says, "and I swear she knew *all* the words."

"But I bet she insisted you read them out loud with her anyway, right?"

"Of course! But after I closed the door I heard her singing, "Brown Bear, Brown Bear, What do you see? I see a red bird looking at me,' " he sings, making Mia laugh with his near-perfect imitation of their girl's high-pitched singsongy rendition. "And in the Children, Children section, she got through almost the entire menagerie before her voice got drifty. White dog was the last one I heard."

"That's nearly the whole book! And that was from memory?"

"Yep. I took the book with me. She was totally wiped from the park, and we know what would've happened at the restaurant tonight if she'd spent naptime reading," and here, Antonio uses air quotes, "rather than sleeping." He then puts on his Sophia-beginning-to-lose-it face, followed by a pitch-perfect impersonation of her test cry rising rapidly to a bona fide shriek, though thankfully many decibels lower than the reality would be.

And that's when the world stops. Eyes glazing, Antonio silences mid-cry, and the soft background hum of the baby monitor disappears.

Heart racing, Mia jumps up, rushes down the hallway to Sophia's room, and finds her child on her back, limbs akimbo, chest rising and falling evenly. Mia drops into the rocker, thinking, "I've gotta stop this. She's okay. She's safe."

But Mia knows that won't always be the case. Life will do what life does: dish up trouble in the form of falls from bikes, mean kids making her cry, and a variety of disappointments, both minor and spirit-crushing. But Mia has no idea how to *live* with that fact.

She remembers she hasn't always been a nutjob. In fact, she'd been pretty adventurous, loved ziplining and rock climbing, anything with a bit of risk. But some switch in her brain had toggled on when Sophia arrived, and she couldn't figure out how to toggle the damn thing back off again. She could worry about anything, it seemed. Even dumb stuff, like a power outage that turned off the baby monitor, but set off internal alarms that convinced her disaster had finally struck.

She stands, leaves Sophia's door open as she returns to the bedroom, stretches out next to her husband. What the heck *is* this? She thought it would go away once the danger of SIDS passed, but it hadn't. She thought it would end when the final adoption papers arrived, but it didn't. If anything, it had grown stronger in the last few months. And she knows at least partially why. Her child is increasingly and inexorably moving out into the world and into her own life, where parents aren't always there to protect. She trusts the in-home daycare provider completely—a grandmotherly sort who'd taken care of the children of two of her friends—but it always throws her when Sophia comes home babbling about a kid Mia doesn't know or shares a new word or some piece of recently acquired knowledge that hadn't come from her or Tonio.

She knows that adoptive parents are often hit harder by this excessive feeling of responsibility. After all, a child didn't just happen for them. They had to choose it, had to jump through all sorts of hoops, had to compete against others for the chance to parent. With all that preparation, you better not fuck up the main event.

But Mia knows it's more than that, too. Sure, it's normal to feel anxiety about your children, to feel uneasy when they're away from you for extended periods of time, to know you can never meet your own or anyone else's standards perfectly. But she knows this is not mere anxiety or simple worry. This feeling that electrifies her limbs, that sends her blood careening through her body, that leaves her awash with cortisol, exhausted yet unable to sleep, this feels more like panic. No, not panic. Terror. She feels terror. Not all the time, of course, but it seems always in the wings, waiting for an opportunity to barrel onto the stage to steal the show.

And in the stillness of this late afternoon, it comes to her. The memory of large hands rough between her legs, ugly words whispered in her ear. Memory only in technical terms, she feels those hands now, hears again those vulgar words along with the threat of what would happen if she told anyone.

Fear floods her body again, confirming that what fuels her current anxiety is, in large measure, the nightmare of those 3 years her family lived in the apartment building across town, the one with the disgusting neighbor who seemed always to catch her alone in the stairwell. She recognizes, though, that there is something else here in addition to the onslaught of fear, something noxious and soul-crushing. Shame. She feels the shame of a 7-year-old who had no one to explain the shame was not hers.

Though emotions still rush through her as she lies beside her dear and immobile Tonio, the simple act of naming has caused them to diminish a bit. No, that's not quite right. The feelings are still strong, but there's clarity now. At least she know what's happening. She's not crazy. And this clarity helps her see that, in addition to the flashback terror of her own experience, she feels a gut-clenching rage and horror that there are people in the world who would harm her precious Sophia in that same way...or worse.

All of this comes to Mia now. Though she knows it will take time to sort it out, she recognizes she's taken the first step in righting something that has been skewed, and that awareness brings with it a little buzz of interest, even some rising excitement mingling with the dread. True, this is not the ziplining sort of eager enthusiasm, but now that she knows what she's dealing with, she also knows what her next step will be. She'll reach out to Andréa, the therapist she saw to deal with infertility, and she will heal this thing. Yes, that feels exactly right.

The mother she has become, though, knows something else is needed right now. It is something she has practiced every time Sophia has awakened from a bad dream, and each time her daughter has shied away from an unfamiliar person or animal. In those times, Mia soothes Sophia. She holds her child's fear while offering the context and reassurance that Sophia hasn't had the life experience to offer herself. In short, when Sophia is upset, Mia loves her. She engages her, actively. And Mia knows it is time to turn that love toward herself, to be both the giver and the one who receives.

"It's okay," she whispers aloud, placing a hand on her heart as she imagines talking to her young self. "You're safe now. You made it. That bad man can't hurt you anymore, and you'll never be alone with him again. And you'll never be alone again at all, because you've got me with you now. We're going to meet with someone who can help us both, but one thing I want you to know is that it was never your fault. You are not to blame."

The tears she hadn't realized she was shedding become more intense. After a time, though, they lighten as her system calms and her heartrate settles back to normal. Mia rises from the bed then and walks into her child's room. She looks down at Sophia, and lets love flow through a channel grown larger—if that's even possible—as some of the debris lining the pathway has been washed clean.

When Kayla first placed Mia's hand on her rounded belly, Mia had known that Sophia was her daughter. During those pre-adoption days, she'd waited for a rush of guilt about the pregnancy she'd terminated in her early twenties, but it never came. Abortion had been the right choice then, just as welcoming Sophia into her heart was the right choice eight years later. Just as healing the remaining vestiges of abuse is now, so that she can delight in Sophia's moving out into the world and claiming the life that is hers.

"My precious girl," Mia murmurs as she gently strokes her daughter's hair. "I may not always be able to keep danger at bay, but I will do my absolute best. And I'll give you the skills you need to deal with this crazy world, and that includes making sure you keep the confidence you were born with, so that no one will ever be able to take it from you. And so you'll always know you're special, my bright, sweet and wonderfully bold little girl."

Antonio

Mia's laughter stops abruptly during his impression of their usually good-natured child's capacity for exhaustion-induced, though truly prodigious, meltdowns.

"What, after all this time you've become inured to my adroit impersonation skills?" he asks turning to face his wife directly. Though her lips still form the crooked grin he adores, she looks at him without seeing. The air shimmers with strangeness, though he senses all is well. Getting up to check on Sophia, he finds her sleeping soundly. After gently sweeping a hand over her curls, he walks to the kitchen for a snack to tide him over until they meet Mia's parents at the kid-friendly restaurant for an early dinner. He brings chips and salsa back on a tray in case Mia wants some when she rouses, leans back against the headboard and finishes off the bag—there weren't *that* many left—puts the tray on the floor, and curls on his side to face his wife.

God, he loves this woman! It wasn't exactly love at first sight, but damn close. Her profile on OkCupid was the perfect mix of hilarious and deep, but he was a goner after their first date. He knew she liked him too, and by the time she fell hard, he'd gained an equilibrium that allowed him to steady her. Neither had been looking for long-term commitment, but both knew it was foolish to quibble about details when love presented itself. So they'd done the long-distance thing for a while—and wasn't that a bitch!—until he could arrange a transfer to her city.

Marriage had never been important to either of them until they started talking about kids. At first, they'd been happy just to let nature take its course, abandoning various birth control methods and making good use of an extra reason to have sex. When they still weren't pregnant a year later, Mia speculated they were "giving the Universe a mixed message" by saying they were committed to raising a family but not making themselves legally into one. So they got married, and the stress of that experience led to another solemn vow: to never get divorced no matter what, because they didn't want to go through *that* again.

But still no baby. They then got serious, first by working with Mia's cycle length and fucking like rabbits between days 8 and 19. When that didn't work, they added in early morning temperature readings to pinpoint ovulation more precisely. Then it was the CycleBeads app before trying a couple different ovulation predictor kits. Nada.

Antonio had been supportive, reassuring Mia it would happen when it happened. They'd always enjoyed sex and never had any problems in that area. And while sex on demand certainly took the spontaneity and a good bit of the fun out of the sex act, he'd always been, ahem, up for the experience.

Then they started the doctor routine. They weren't surprised to find that Mia's endometriosis might be a factor, though the gynecologist didn't think her condition was severe enough to be the sole cause. She'd suggested Antonio see a colleague of hers, explaining that difficulty conceiving often involved both partners. He had no problem getting checked out, mostly because he doubted there was anything wrong with his plumbing.

So he made the appointment, got the blood draw, and jerked off into a very uninspiring container after choosing a little encouragement from the truly monumental collection of porn helpfully provided. And was stunned when the doctor gave them the news that his sperm were deficient on every measure: number, motility and morphology. And that lovely test was repeated twice more, since "specimens" can vary greatly. Those repeats confirmed that he had Oligoasthenoteratozoospermia. The only good part of the whole thing was getting a diagnosis with such a ridiculously laughable name. After a series of tests gave him an otherwise clean bill of health, the doctor laid out the next level of infertility treatments as their only hope if making a baby was their goal.

"So *is* making a baby really our goal?" Mia asked on their drive home from the clinic that day. "Isn't our goal to become parents of a little being and to love that child into becoming the adult human he or she is meant to be? Do we really need that child to be *biologically* ours, particularly given the fact that the planet is overrun with humans as it is?"

After talking it every which way, they accepted that what they wanted was a child, maybe two or three, to love and to raise. They wanted a family. So while having a little Antonio or Mia running around held a certain appeal, that was vanity, not necessity. It was ironic, though, that after all those years of worrying they might get pregnant before they were ready, there they were, ready but unable to make a baby. Go figure. The whole thing was more a surprise than anything else.

Well, shock was the better term to describe Antonio's reaction. He was fine with adoption and leapt right over the goddamn moon the first time he held Sophia...and every day since. But in a completely separate part of his brain, having weird sperm did a number on him and, truth be told, he'd yet to come out the other side on that one. Who knew it would matter so much to him that his little lads were so scrawny? He'd always been comfortable with his masculinity, with absolutely no need to do the macho thing. But yeah, lame as it was, there's a part of him that feels less a man. And when you add to that the many months when sexual interest and pleasure took a back seat to getting pregnant, the nature of sex itself changed for him. For them.

He knows the inventiveness and frequency of sex often plummets for exhausted new parents. But while that is a factor—how the heck could it *not* be?—he also knows just as strongly that it is more than that for him. Oh, they still do the deed at regular though significantly less frequent intervals, but the passion seems to have been leeched out, for him at least. And he knows Mia misses it, is even a little hurt by the change in him. Of course he's tried to explain it to her, and he guesses she understands as much as she can. But it wasn't *her* fault they couldn't conceive.

He'd been on edge during most of the adoption process. It was just so damn unnatural...providing written answers to a slew of personal questions, taking part in interviews, doing the formal evaluation to make sure they were stable, or at least as stable as other parents-to-be. And it had been godawful when things fell through that first time. And it was all his fault. If his sperm weren't defective, he wouldn't have had to be polite when the father of some teenage girl called to tell them his daughter had decided to keep her baby.

"Honey," Mia pleaded, when he got stuck in the gloom, "you've got to stop this. I'm crushed too, but our child is out there somewhere, and we need to be patient so she can find her way to us." Sounded reasonable, of course, but his struggles had nothing to do with reason. No matter what Mia said, he felt it was all on him. His failing.

But then they'd found Kayla, and that had been another kind of love at first sight. He knew she was the one. Of course, he didn't let himself fully believe, once burned and all, but it certainly *felt* different. And *he* felt different about it. Kayla blew him away with her courage and wisdom. She was so much like Mia, and that had to be a good thing. He certainly hoped he didn't have anything in common with that little panty waste of a man-child Ethan, but having a birth mom who was so much like his wife just had to bode well.

And it did. The whole process had been intense, of course, but better than they'd dared hoped. As recipients of Kayla's generosity in welcoming them to her doctor's appointments and the birth itself, they were bonded to Sophia before they'd ever held her, and were already a family when they brought her home. He almost couldn't remember how things had been before she'd turned their lives upside down and blew his heart wide-open. Who knew he could love so deeply, so fiercely?

Mia had been right, of course. Sophia *was* their child and this was simply the route required to find her. If his sperm had been more plentiful, faster, and had aced the Kruger morphology assessment, they might have had another child, but they wouldn't have Sophia. Even the thought of that makes his chest ache. They call her their little meant-to-be, and that's what she is. And he wouldn't have it any other way.

So why is he still hung up on sperm? Maybe it was all part of that adjustment to adoption thing that Kayla's therapist had mentioned. Their story was their story, with its own unique components and innate timetable. Making peace, Jenna had said, was usually an ongoing process and she'd encouraged them to be alert every step of the way for what was offering itself for transformation.

Maybe he's ready for a bit more of that now. He reaches out to Mia, runs a hand over the lush brown hair he loves, loops an unruly curl behind her ear.

"Hey there, my brown-eyed girl," he whispers, "woman of my heart. I've been yours from the very beginning, and I'm so lucky you're mine. You're bright and funny and sexy and courageous, even though you have been wigging out a bit lately."

And then he stops cold, as a new possibility plows into him. They don't know what's causing Mia's anxiety, but always thought it was something about becoming a mom, since neither of them noticed it until they brought Sophia home. But he's learned enough from being part of a couple for over a decade now to know there's seldom a firm line between partners, that it's hard to always know where one stops and the other starts. He doesn't want to make Mia's struggles all about him, but wouldn't it make sense that an increased distance between them could be a factor? True, they're totally connected on the parenting thing, and they work well together on all the business aspects of family life. But their time together is focused either on their 27-pound whirlwind of near-boundless energy, or on just doing what needs to get done. Their marital relationship has taken a backseat to all of that.

Not unusual, he knows. But being stuck on his defective sperm has further complicated some of the unavoidable realities in a young family's life. Certainly, it's made it harder to recover from the make-a-baby-now pressure and allowed their sex life to be less than it could be. And in the process, it might also have conveyed to Mia on some unconscious, primal level that he wasn't fully there for her.

"Oh, sweetie," he continues now, eyes swimming with tears, "you and I are gonna have to talk about this more. I miss that part of us and I want to get it back. And I want you to feel connected and that I'm here for you, Mimi. *Really* here, cuz I am. I know you know that, but I want you to *really* know that, okay? All the way down to those lovely toes of yours...and every place in between."

Antonio walks around to Mia's side of the bed and climbs in behind her, spooning his body against hers, an arm wrapped around her. And content with the knowledge that a shift is occurring, he falls asleep, just like he used to when he held her like this after lovemaking. Just like he knows he will again.

Sister Constance-Marie

Pausing on the landing to catch her breath, she gazes through the window at the lengthening shadows and feels a comparable shadowing within her own spirit, the darkening of mood that so often comes with the gloaming. It is true, her bones ache, but it is this other ache that plagues her, a companion she has grown accustomed to, though she misses it not a whit when it lifts completely and flies elsewhere for a time.

Sister Constance-Marie has just left Chapel after gathering with her Sisters for Nones, one of the canonical hours the convent observes daily through readings, prayer, meditation, and song. She has not held a formal job in nearly two decades, which allows her the freedom to attend each observance. Even when her heart is heavy, *especially* when her heart is heavy, she finds the rhythm of the Divine Office soothing, the psalter, canticles and hymns a balm that settles what is so often unsettled. After a lifetime of practice, she recognizes each portion of the day as sacred and deserving of honor, just as she knows the greening of the land outside this window is holy, a gift from the Lord whose existence she often questions.

She can't remember precisely when doubts first arose. She wonders if they have always been present in some form, a trait visible to others even when she herself had been blind. Perhaps it was that which led Reverend Mother Adrian Thérèse, three decades dead now, to choose Constance-Marie for her religious name. Untried as she had been and with her share of youthful hubris, she'd initially hoped that, in the name Constance, the steadfast quality of her devotion had been recognized. Thankfully, she did not share that notion with a soul, speaking only of how she sought to emulate Saint Constance who chose a life of service after being healed of leprosy at a sacred well.

Soon, though, Sister Constance-Marie learned the deeper significance of her name. It was not evidence of an unwavering faith, but an exhortation to grow that quality. The name was not given her because she *was* constant, but was offered as an aid in *becoming* constant. As constant as the star of the sea, the French meaning for Marie. Or perhaps constant in her search *for* that shining star.

She became aware of doubts, painfully so, about a decade after taking her solemn vows. Being bilingual, she'd been assigned to the migrant community, and the depth of poverty and nobility she found there soon grew that work into a vocation. It felt as though she'd been born to care for the young and the aged, to assist in simple medical procedures, to receive with an open heart the stories that needed so desperately to be shared.

It was people's questions about the teachings of the Church that disturbed her. At first, she'd given the standard answers she herself had been taught. When in confusion, despair or anger they pressed her further, her responses sounded to her own ears like platitudes: It is part of God's plan. All shall be revealed. We must trust in Him and pray for the strength to follow the example of his Son, Jesus Christ.

Soon, all such answers felt wrong. Well, it was not the answers that prickled like wool against winter-dry skin. It was that so many believed those answers were *hers*, when all she was doing was parroting the doctrine placed upon her tongue by others. She never doubted that Love was a powerful force, or that practicing it was her calling and her salvation. But the rest of it…who knew? Certainly not her.

"Enough of this falderal" she says aloud now and without the slightest embarrassment. "Yes, I talk to myself. A refusal to rein oneself in is a benefit of age I gladly claim," she continues as, one hand holding tightly to the banister and the other negotiating the cane on the carpeted steps, she completes her slow journey to the first floor, turns down the hall and into her cell. "An hour of study, and then to the kitchen to help ready the evening meal."

Sister Constance-Marie likes to be of use. As the Church's support of nunneries declined over the years, her vocation found various outlets in the world, and she looks back on them all with profound gratitude. Though she no longer brings in regular income, she helps now with meals, laundry and light housecleaning, and is available for those who knock upon the convent door, unannounced or by appointment as is their wont. True, she no longer advises. Instead, she listens with an open heart, welcoming into expression and holding tenderly the suffering that is so often hidden. *That* she can do, and that she does. The bereaved and the sick, those confronted with a crisis they feel incapable of managing, pregnant women and girls, frightened and confused. She sits with them all, sharing their pain and their turmoil, their grievances and their misgivings. And their doubts.

No matter the burden that led them to journey along backcountry roads, they are lighter when they leave the convent walls than when they arrived. A cross, after all, is less crushing when another bears a bit of its weight. And yet time and again, these dear souls find more than simple solace. Through being *received*, just as they are and with no attempt to educate or correct, they find their own path forward. It is a wonder and a delight to witness. So yes, she is content to leave the larger theological issues to those with the brilliance to explore them. And she is grateful for being gifted her own much simpler calling.

The afternoon passes as others have before. She reads and she prays, weaving sacred words through her gloom. Her melancholia accompanies her as she makes her way to the kitchen, and it assists in the chopping and the simmering. It goes with her as she returns to Chapel for Vespers, eases some when the nuns who work in the world return and the full community sits for evening meal. Her malaise returns, speaking to her in the silence as she makes her way to Chapel for Compline, the final office of the day. And there, it is cradled by the familiar cadence of prayers recited across decades, hymns sung through the ages.

"Guide us waking, Oh Lord," her voice, reedy with age, joins with her Sisters for the *Song of Simeon*, the final antiphon," and guard us sleeping; that awake, we may watch with Christ, and asleep we may rest in peace."

And she realizes hers is the only voice chanting that last line.

She considers being embarrassed that she missed some cue or, after all these years, confused this service with another. But she feels only a deep peace as she stands gazing at the image of Christ above the plain altar favored by the Sisters.

Time passes. When pain in her left leg finally rouses her, she looks at the other nuns and finds them each entranced, standing immobile and silent. Sending a prayer that this uncanny quietude soothes them as it does her, she makes her way to the door. Discovering that the hallway lights are off, she walks back to the altar, bows, and asks to remove one of the lit candles to guide her safely to her room. Sensing permission granted, she takes a taper in its holder and makes her slow way from Chapel. At the stairs, she hooks her cane over her candle arm and, gripping the bannister tightly with her other hand, slowly climbs the stairs and turns into her cell. She readies herself for bed and says a prayer of gratitude for the many gifts of the day. She then wets her fingers, snuffs the candleflame, and drops into a deep and dreamless sleep.

Sister Constance-Marie needs no external clock to wake her for 2 a.m. Vigil. The rhythms of the day live within her, and she awakens naturally and unusually well-rested. When a pull of the lamp chain does not illuminate, she combs through the one drawer in her bedside table and, finding the matches there, relights the candle.

"Lord," she recites before donning the habit, "prepare my soul interiorly while I prepare my body to go to Choir. Clothe me, O my God, with the fervor of Thy Divine Spirit and with the precious gifts of Thy Grace."

Although she no longer wears the full habit that was traditional in her youth, every article of clothing still has its corresponding prayer. She recites them each as she dresses, making sacred even this simple act. Placing the matches in the pocket of her tunic, she takes the candle in one hand, cane in the other, and reverses the path trod through the darkness a few hours before.

Upon arrival at Chapel, she finds her Sisters still enraptured and the candles on the altar burned to nubs, wax pooled in their holders. She places her own candle on the side table and enters the supply closet. There she chooses three votives in glass containers, and walks them one at a time to the altar. When all three are present, she recites *The Prayer To The Holy Trinity*.

"Glory be to the Father," she softly intones, lighting the first candle, "who by His almighty power and love created me, making me in the image and likeness of God."

Lighting the second, she prays, "Glory be the Son, who by His Precious Blood delivered me from hell, and opened for me the gates of heaven."

"Glory be to the Holy Spirit," she continues as she lights the last votive, "who has sanctified me in the sacrament of Baptism, and continues to sanctify me by the graces I receive daily from His bounty.

"Glory be to the Three adorable Persons of the Holy Trinity," she bows, "now and forever. Amen."

Sister Constance-Marie sits then. And she turns to face her gloom and doubts head-on. She has had a number of Confessors and Spiritual Directors during her 67 years in the order, and has learned to discern quite quickly those with whom an open sharing would be beneficial. Her current mentor, Sister Mary Clare, is a bouncy little fireball of a nun filled with wisdom, verve and the ability to listen from the heart. With her, she has shared all, and the words spoken between them just last week return to her now amid the silence of this sacred night and place.

She gives little thought to the suggestion that she consider medication for her melancholia. Who would she be, after all, without her longtime companion, the intractable friend who has gifted her with a heightened sensibility to the suffering of others? It is true that it has created challenges to living in awe, but it has also helped her grow a practice of seeing the Light within the murk. She has learned to surrender to this cross, to let it teach her its lessons, and oftentimes to carry it with a quiet joy. However, she realizes now a certain freedom in remembering that medication is an option. Yes, the cross rests more gently knowing it is a choice. And her choice for now is to remain as she is.

On the subject of her theological doubts as to the nature of God and the teachings of the Church, Sister Mary Clare shared words she'd heard spoken long ago by someone named Joseph Campbell in a discussion with journalist, Bill Moyers. "I don't have to have faith," he'd said. "I have experience."

Those words set a bell to tolling in some deep inner place and it has been ringing ever since. Amid the silence of this early morning hour, gathered once again with her Sisters before the altar, that bell ceases to ring and comes to stillness itself.

It is true, she has not been constant in accepting without question the doctrine of the Church. The mind she was born with apparently will not allow it, and she knows that is unlikely to change at this late stage. And yet she suspects this is not solely a matter of temperament, for how could anyone, no matter the brilliance of their mind, grasp anything true and substantial about God?

The gift of those words, though, was the light they shone upon her felt experience. Theology might hang her up, but in the wealth of the many years she has been granted, she's never doubted the dynamism of Love.

"Love is God in action," she says aloud now. "Love is God as a verb. Love is God expressed through a human life in the world."

She knows these are not novel ideas, just as she knows that antidepressants did not arrive in the world yesterday. But in this early morning hour, these are no longer intellectual constructs or realizations held in the upper regions of her mind. They have moved deep inside her and have found a home there. Or more accurately, they have landed in such a way as to awaken what has always been present.

As she sits in Chapel beside her entranced Sisters, awe blossoms as scenes and faces from across the sweep of her long life play in rapid succession upon the screen of her mind. A multitude of infants clamoring their red-faced way into the world. Those of all ages who are given final release from their earthly bodies, often after much pain and struggle. The weeping, shouting or quiet acceptance of the aggrieved, frightened or shamed. Affection and profound commitment expanding, flourishing even, amid seemingly unbearable hardship. And through all of it, she recognized—sometimes clearly, often only dimly—the One Love. And she knows herself blessed to not just have discerned it with her mind, but to have felt, in bone and sinew, this One Love shining through a multitude of guises.

It is all so very clear to her now, and she is surprised again. What a marvel it is! After a lifetime of prayer and study, Grace descends once more, alighting upon a soul ever hungry for it. And she prays for remembrance of the gifts of this silent night, this holy night. And she wonders if perhaps this is all faith is, the ability to remember and to trust the awe that filled us on another day, when shadows return and deepen as they most certainly will.

"Holy Mother-Father God, you are the Star of the Sea and Love is Your Light," she whispers, as tears flow down cheeks deeply lined with age. "Of that, I am certain. I am and have always been just as you made me: Constance-Marie, constant in my devotion to Your Star, Your Love, Your Light. I vow to the very best of my ability and by your continued Grace, to behold your Love in all things, to attune myself to it, and to let it shine through me and out into the world. With my enduring gratitude, Amen."

Pausing Once More

The portal closes and the fire becomes mere flames again, albeit flames that continue to radiate magic as most fires do. You return fully to your body, gradually registering warmth from hearth and mug, the patter of rain against the roof, and the calming smell of woodsmoke. When words begin to press for expression, you find yourself again facing your wise companion.

"As you know, I often wait to speak my thoughts," you begin, "but excitement has found me and wants to be given voice." You laugh and Nyah's smile encourages you to continue. "I have been struck by the expressions of spirituality your hearth has shown me. Sister Constance-Marie has committed her entire life to a path she chose as a young woman, despite the doubts that assailed her at times. And the wisdom of the yogic tradition had such a deep impact on Eric that he created a successful business to share it with others. For both, this enchantment has revivified the magic they'd already found.

"And yet there seems to be something of a spiritual nature unfolding in *all* these lives," you continue. "Obviously, the wonder overtaking Ann as she looks up into the cosmos feels similar, though she would never use the word spiritual to describe it. But the hard truths both Richard and Phil have come to see, and Jessica's reclaiming what had been abandoned along the way... well, those all feel quite profound. And the children embody something that, while not overtly spiritual, certainly has the potential to point their lives in a heartfelt direction. So this is my question: How do religious or spiritual orientations fit into our path of becoming?"

"And what are your thoughts, my child?" is her only reply, but for a smile and a wink.

"You just aren't going to give me any direct answers, are you?" you say with a grin.

"Soft incursions only, remember?" the Old One answers with a chuckle.

"Yes, I remember." As you consider your own question, a log shifts in the hearth. "Sitting with you in this place of magic, a few things come to me. First, I'm not sure our spiritual beliefs matter all that much. Long ago, I heard an interview with the Dalai Lama in which he shared his view that no one religion was objectively better than another. His words return to me now, though this may be a paraphrase: "If it gives good heart, is good religion. If it does not give good heart, is not good religion." That felt true to me then, and it feels true to me now. In each life you have shown me, the individual has found her or his way back to that which grows good heart.

"I also think," you continue after many heartbeats, "that by responding to what calls us, we honor ourselves and take another step on the path that is uniquely ours, no matter the label we or others might place upon it. And when we find our own particular way—whether it's Lana's painting, Kayla's love of the natural world, or the soul searching Meghan and Richard have begun—we are brought into a rich experience of being alive."

Nyah nods, but remains silent sensing new words bubbling up inside you.

"To live as the fullest versions of ourselves," you continue, "we must dip down into that which runs like an underground stream beneath the particulars of our existence. And because that channel is always there, its water ever available to us, there simply *must* be an untold number of ways to tap into it. What's most important seems not the avenue we choose, but the life-giving nourishment it brings. While some may find a specific spiritual tradition or community immensely helpful in their journey, others will likely find a different way."

"So," Nyah says with a smile when you fall silent, "it seems you had an answer of your own after all."

"I suppose I did," you reply, smiling in return. "It is through discovering our own path, the true one that calls us ever to it, that we grow good heart. And it is by honoring the mystery within our own souls that we touch the much larger Mystery that holds us all."

Nyah nods and adds, "I believe one of your sages urged you to "Let the beauty we love be what we do. There are a thousand ways to kneel and kiss the ground.'"

"Rumi, yes," you respond, though you suspect she knows his name full well. "I have also read that the quote continues with, "...there are a thousand ways to go home again." The important point seems to be to find our own unique ground-kissing endeavors, those that most easily and continually bring us home to ourselves and to life itself."

Nyah nods and adds, "Another sage, the one you call Buddha, said that spiritual teachings and practices are fingers pointing to the Moon. They may provide direction, but should never be confused with the Moon itself."

After several sips from your mug, you speak again. "I believe it might be wise to avoid attempts to hem in the Mystery of All That Is. The workings of the Cosmos simply *must* be far grander than our conceptualizations could ever hold, whether we're speaking of the Universe itself or the human lives unfolding within it. How could we ever fathom the unfathomable? And yet my mind often tries to do exactly that, even wanting to run the show by imposing its ideas on what is. It is difficult to let my mind act as the helpmeet it was intended to be."

"Indeed," Nyah agrees. "Another of the challenges of being human, blessed with a mind that wants to know and yearns to make sense of things, yes?"

"Yes," you nod. "Perhaps the task is to discern which matters rightly belong within the purview of the mind and which require another faculty altogether."

Long moments pass as all that has transpired here, all these Moon-pointing fingers, find a resting place in your soul. At last, you are ready to return to your own world with its many opportunities to kiss the ground. The magical room begins to fade as sweet darkness envelopes you yet again. Precious moments pass for you here, offering respite as you await the return of your own life.

The Amble Continues...

It is time to journey once more from the world that is yours to the other one that now and evermore welcomes you to it. And so, imaginative and playful one, you enter that lively darkness, feel its swirl as it envelopes and soothes. Gradually you perceive the particulars of the space that was fashioned just for you, though you immediately recognize it has been altered again. The storm has passed now and air, fresh and smelling of the lushness of the natural world, spills through the open doorway to your right, whispers across your skin. Crickets trill in the night.

You are standing before the hearth, which is as it ever has been. Yet as your eyes drop to the ground, you see that your feet are bare and stand not on wooden floorboards, but upon rugs brightly woven, you somehow know, from vicuña wool. And with that recognition, you hear the distant sound of a pan flute streaming through the open doorway, its haunting melody bringing with it images of the high Andes, boundless sky stretching forever.

You sense the presence of an unknown someone nearby. Your curiosity grows until you find yourself turned and seated on the floor in front of a man of abundant years. He sits cross-legged as well and is dressed in the Peruvian style, a poncho of brightly dyed wool draping his compact frame, and a woven hat covering his head, its earflaps tied off with red tassels. His round face is dusky and deeply lined, with full lips that curl into a smile as the onyx pools of his eyes meet yours, and draw you deeply in. He speaks then, and though his words are in the Quechuan language foreign to you, you understand them effortlessly, as you know he will understand your own words in return.

"Welcome. I am called Icaro. Be at rest and know that you are safe with me here, as you have been with my sisters."

"Yes, I sense that," you say after several breaths. A warmth radiates from him, as does an ancient wisdom. Neither surprises you. However, you are surprised that you feel comfortable enough, carefree even, to joke with him after being in his presence mere minutes. "I just want you and your sisters to know that you have again succeeded in keeping boredom at bay."

"We are quite pleased to hear that," he replies, his smile broadening.

You sit together in silence, as you again feel the love in which this space has always steeped you, a love that brings to mind the phrase "Love is patient, love is kind." Though you have always felt both kindness and patience here, you suspect these thoughts also stem from the reflections that have claimed you during your time away. You sense Icaro's invitation to share those thoughts now.

"I assume you are familiar with those I've met in the flames as I sat with Zosia and Nyah." Receiving his nod, you continue. "I have been thinking of the people I met on my last visit. I was deeply affected by the love they entered into more fully. Kayla's willingness to both part with her infant girl and find such a unique way back to her was so very beautiful. And I was also quite moved by Antonio and Mia's choice to face that which had, at least to some extent, been blocking or confusing love's expression. And what can I say of Sister Constance-Marie's lifetime devotion to Love and the further step she took into it? I found each inspirational."

You pause for several breaths before continuing, panpipes playing on in the distance.

"I spoke with Nyah about good heart, and that good religion is whatever helps us grow it. It is clear to me, though, that this enchantment is not just *bringing* good heart, but returning each to it, perhaps also amplifying it for a time. The goodness is already there, and I suspect that might be the case for us all."

After some time, you speak again. "I have heard of the phrase Original Grace and find it a *much* more wholesome and life-affirming view than the Original Sin some hold to be true."

"Yes," Icaro nods, when you fall silent again, "I am familiar with these concepts as they have been used within your culture. I wonder, though…do you find no merit in the notion of Original Sin?"

"Well," you reply, "humankind certainly has shown a propensity for behaving badly. We certainly do not claim Love and Light in our every moment, and it would be foolish to pretend otherwise. There is a thorn within us, a fly in the ointment for sure which, I suppose, could be called Original Sin. But it seems that most, if not all harmful actions arise from pain or from ignorance. Even when we harm consciously and of our own free will, a little searching can usually uncover many layers, as it did with Richard. Our bad behavior is seldom, if ever, a simple thing.

"I sense we are learning as we go," you continue, "and learning requires us to make mistakes. Our paths loop about and include many of those seeming detours Zosia and I spoke of earlier. And the terrain they carry us through is often rough, with rocks and brambles and other obstructions that trip us up. So it is a given that we will stumble along the way. Much practice is needed to develop the skill to lead with Original Grace within the nitty-gritty of a human life, particularly in the modern age when we have been cut off from the weave that would sustain us."

You pause now, listening to the duet of crickets and flute. At last, words rise again.

"As I sit with you, one who appears to be connected with at least one stream of indigenous culture, I'm reminded of the various branches of modern science that are discovering what some societies have long known: mutual cooperation and support have been and continue to be far more essential for the survival of all communal life forms than competition. So that would mean that we would have been *designed* for such cooperation, which would seem to entail a well of goodness at our core, what I am calling Original Grace. And yet, our learning curve necessitates that we err often, sometimes with a magnitude that is alarming, if not downright calamitous. This is our thorn."

After a pause of many breaths, you proceed. "I have heard that the word sin means *missing the mark* or *going astray*."

"Yes," Icaro nods, "your English word is thought to have its roots in the Greek hamartia or the Hebrew hata, both of which carry those meanings."

Surprised not in the least that this wise man, skilled in conveying meaning through words foreign to you, is also proficient in a variety of ancient languages, you continue. "So though goodness is central to who we are, missing the mark repeatedly is how we improve our aim and build the skill to hit that mark with greater regularity. And this must be the case both individually and collectively."

After several breaths, you find your way forward. "So if by sin we mean this process of missing the mark as we learn a truer aim, then yes, Original Sin is wired into us. And yet Original Grace exists there as well, exerting its influence even when we are unaware of it. And free will, which has also been spoken of before this hearth, is what allows us to ultimately choose Grace over Sin, allows us to learn from our errors as we hone our skill, as we purify our intention, as we perfect our aim. It is also what allows us to learn the mechanism of return, and choose to employ it when we have become estranged from Grace. So Original Sin may be woven into us, but I see it as being in the service of a fuller expression of the Original Grace at our core."

Long moments pass now as you reflect on the words you have heard yourself speak, and as you consider other thoughts that came to you while you were in your own world.

"I have mentioned before," you start anew, "that I am not merely witness to the lives that unfold in this hearth. While I *can* see them from the outside, I also share their experience in a way I cannot understand. This was certainly so with Sister Constance-Marie at Compline and her revelation of the One Love she has seen shining through a multitude of forms. That knowing was so strong and heartfelt that I will never forget it. I carried it with me during my time away, and practiced recognizing the One Love shining through its many masks." You laugh suddenly. "I just remembered Ram Dass encouraging us to see everyone we meet as "God in drag". I think Sister was there well before him, and I will cherish her teachings always."

After a pause, you speak again. "I have one other thing and then, if there is more to see, I would very much like to see it."

"Young one, there is always more to see," Icaro replies with another smile, "and only when you are ready."

You smile in return and continue. "As I was taken into that last segment, Nyah referred to these individuals as family, even though only two were related by blood and Sister Constance-Marie was not related in any conventional sense of the word. So that has made me consider what she meant by the word family. And since I know better than to ask," you grin, "I am ready to share my hunch."

Registering the old man's assent, you continue. "It seems that we each have our own story, our own ever-evolving path through this world, one that is not merely laid out for us, but one we have a hand in creating through the choices we make and the attitudes we cultivate. And yet that path intersects with the paths of others, some for mere minutes, as was the case with Kayla and Sister Constance-Marie, while we might walk with others for decades. So I suspect the definition of family here is much broader than in our common usage. Family would be those persons whose paths converge in meaningful ways.

"But then," you continue," I dug more deeply into my definition of meaningful. As I remembered the parade of people of all ages whom Sister had touched and those who had touched her, I realized that every relationship *could* be meaningful if we approach it as such. And *that* blew my concept of family sky-high. We could see everyone we interact with as family, if we but develop a clearer vision."

After another pause you add, "I just now dug deeper still, and realized there need be no limits to this sense of family. All who share the planet with us are family if we open our minds to the possibility. Certainly we come biologically from one ancestral root seeded back in the annals of history. Every one of us, family to one another. I like that, and it rings true," you say, smiling. "Each of our individual stories is part of a larger Story that holds them all and links us one to another. Some we have more intimate knowledge of, more affinity for, but all are kin."

You fall into silence until at the right moment you are facing the hearth again, its flames leaping in excited greeting before they quiet once more and draw you into the lives of kin, far-flung but nevertheless known to you.

Aingeal

Her makeup is done, her hair styled, and what she thinks of as her costume for the evening is laid out on the bed: a short and swirly emerald-green dress, a crotchless teddy with a plunging neckline in delicate white lace, garters and nylons, and a pair of black stilettos. Yes, he'll love this mix of naughty and innocent, will enjoy ripping off the dress and fucking her hard and fast in the foyer before dinner. In addition to a range of sex toys, her bag is packed with a blood-red dress in the same style, in case he damages this one as he often does. It's a hot look and will ensure that sex stays in the forefront of his mind as they go down to dinner. A more leisurely seduction will happen later over drinks in the room. Then he'll get sad, and she'll hold him as he shares it all. A room-service dessert and one more cum for the road, and she'll be off. Yes, she knows him well.

There are three men she meets with regularly for sex play, juggling them between the two nights a month she sets aside for such interactions. She keeps the frequency down, in part to remain fresh and in the right frame of mind, but also to leave them aching for more…and willing to meet her price. She certainly couldn't afford her two weeks away on the salary the accountant couple pays her for managing their office. Sure, she gets the going rate, but with the cost of living sky-high these days, it doesn't allow for extras. Which is why she lives in this one bedroom walk-up, and supplements her income with something she's particularly skilled at. She oughta be, since she's been intuiting—and fulfilling—the needs of men for most of her life. A portion of each payment goes for clothing and the various accessories to keep things spiced. The rest goes into her travel fund.

Still in her robe and with the sweet strains of Sakiya's flute coming through their shared wall, Angie pads barefoot to the kitchenette to nuke some leftovers so she won't starve if Niko veers away from the usual game plan. Bringing her dish to the small table set into the window alcove, she eats while scrolling through travel websites. She does this mostly to satisfy her longing, rather than for the often-questionable trip advice they offer. She's driven all over Ireland already, has hiked her way through its green hills and along its rugged coastline with air fresher than she's ever known filling her lungs. Her flight and rental car are already paid for, and she has a standing reservation for the end of April at Sidheliath in a sweet little inn she loves. They don't even make her pay in advance anymore for her favorite room, the one that overlooks the harbor on the opposite side of the house from the pub two doors down, so she can get to sleep early and be up before dawn.

She lives for these trips. When she was younger, it was always someplace glamorous. Paris. Mykonos. Florence. Ibiza. Zurich. But once she found Ireland, she never went anywhere else. She was a little older by then, and clubbing or baking on a beach had long ago lost their appeal. But she knows she'll never tire of Ireland, even though she doesn't fully understand the hold it has on her. It's beautiful of course, but many places are beautiful. There is just something about it that calls her back again and again. Though lately she's been thinking of changing her plans to go to New Zealand instead, with this afternoon's surfing landing her on a site for Fiordland National Park. Image after image of glacier-carved beauty...and then the power blinks off.

Angie closes her laptop and finishes her rice and veggies while looking down on the small park across the street. She doesn't see it, though. Despite having just been dazzled by photos of New Zealand's stark beauty, Angie finds herself back in Ireland again, at the O'Connors' on that first visit. Cianán had just taken her bags up to her room, and after insisting she call him by his first name and working with her pronunciation, he joked that he was finally living up to the name's meaning, his creaky bones and wheezy lungs the very embodiment of ancient. She'd insisted then that he do away with the Miss Jenson and call her Angie.

"But your given name is Angel," Cianán had said, confused. "And to be sure it is a lovely name. Might I call you that then?"

Usually, when men use her given name she stops them by saying, either with a practiced sort of coquettishness or outright sluttishness as suits the occasion and always gets a laugh, "Honey, believe me, I ain't no angel." This time, though, she said only, "Maybe not. You see, that name never really fit."

She'd turned quickly to look out at the Bay, and hoped Cianán hadn't noticed the tears filling her eyes. He'd walked up behind her—something she never let men do unless it was part of the game—placed a hand on each shoulder, and said, "And how would Aingeal do then? It is how we say it here when we meet one."

The kindness in his voice and hearing her name spoken in the traditional Irish way with an accent she was still learning to decipher...well, it just undid her. She'd nodded quickly, and waited for him to leave. She then hurried into her hiking clothes, grabbed her jacket, and headed out. She found her way to the path Aoife had told her about, the one that stretched high above the village and received the full blast of wind off the Atlantic. It whipped the jet lag from her travel-numbed brain, and by the time she got to the pub for a quick meal, she'd felt brighter than she had in months. She was back at the Inn, tucked into bed and sound asleep before music from the pub spilled onto the street.

The next morning, Aoife put out a full Irish of eggs, black pudding, fried tomato, field mushrooms, potatoes and toast. And though Aoife wouldn't let her help with the cleanup, she did invite Angie to sit with her in the kitchen over mugs of strong tea. That settled it. Though Angie hadn't intended to stay in one place for more than a night or two, those plans changed when she learned the O'Connors could accommodate her for the entire trip.

During those two weeks, and certainly in the subsequent stays over the four years since, her comfort increased and she grew at ease in the O'Connors' company. She'd reminded herself at first that it was just a business relationship for them, but there was just no denying the warmth of their welcome when she arrived, the light in their eyes whenever she returned from a hike or a day trip to another part of the country, or the thrill she felt each time they called her Aingeal. And when Aoife began allowing her to help out during her last two visits, particularly on the weekends when the other three rooms were occupied, even Angie couldn't deny that she'd somehow graduated to the status of family member.

And it delighted her to no end. Whether carrying platters of food to the breakfast table, hanging out freshly-laundered sheets, or helping Cianán tend the plants that bordered the winding pathways of the gardens, she felt a sense of closeness that was unusual for her. She still spent hours each day walking in the bracing air, but she rarely ventured far, her role as tourist all but forgotten.

"Okay, Aingeal," she says to herself now, as she takes her bowl to the dishwasher, "it's time to get on the road." But when she tries to call the Uber, she finds the display dead despite having fully charged her phone an hour or so ago. She only then notices the deep silence that has been pressing at the edge of her awareness. Sakiya's flute is quiet, and the background hum of city traffic has disappeared. Dusk is falling now, but looking outside she notices the streetlights are as dark as the night will soon be. Cars are spaced unmoving down the center of the road. But even odder are the pedestrians paused in midstride and a lone cyclist frozen in place without falling to the pavement.

Though it all seems rather strange, Angie immediately accepts that there's no way she'll be able to get to the hotel, given whatever has shut down the city. She stretches out on the couch and lets the unaccustomed silence fill her. And again, the miles between her apartment and Sidheliath evaporate, as do the months since that last night with Aoife and Cianán.

Aoife had asked if they could have a word with her in the private parlor at the back of the house. Angie often passed the evenings with them there. Sometimes they read, each immersed in their own books, though they often took turns reading aloud from a novel or a book of poetry. On other nights they conversed, the couple infinitely patient as Angie bolstered her growing facility with the Gaeilge language. And sometimes the women joined forces to beat Cianán in chess, something they'd managed to do exactly one time, which he claimed was proof he was coming down with "a quare and grave illness." There was something oddly formal about tonight's invitation, though, and Angie's first thought, one she couldn't shake though she knew it was ridiculous, was that she'd done something wrong and they didn't want her to come back next year.

"We have something to ask ye, Aingeal," Aoife began when they were seated. As the night was a cool one, a fire had been laid and lit, its warmth doing little to soothe Angie's nerves. Silence stretched out, and Angie knew she wasn't imagining the tension filling the room. Finally, Cianán cleared his throat and turned to face her, his pale blue eyes holding none of their usual teasing.

"Neither Aoife nor I are gettin' any younger," he began, "and the truth is it's been right nice you steppin' in to help us out when you're here. We can still do well enough on our own, but we aren't fool enough to think that will always be the case now. Ye know we weren't blessed with weans of our own, and the nieces and nephews are all away to the cities, with young to raise and no interest in livin' in a place such as Sidheliath."

Cianán stopped and looked away, shocking Angie into the realization that he was nervous himself.

"What is it, Cianán, Aoife? Is something wrong?" she asked.

"Nothin' but aging," Aoife answered, "and we all know there's not a thing wrong with that either, it bein' just the way of things. But we won't always be able to keep up with the runnin' of the place...climbin' the stairs, hooverin' the rooms, changin' the beds. Without your help with the outdoor work these past two springs, Cianán woulda had to hire much of it out. And the truth is, we'll be needin' more help as the years roll on. And," she finished in a rush, "we're wonderin' if ye'd consider comin' more often, maybe movin' here if it might suit ye."

Angie felt the breath she'd been holding leave her body. Her heart pounded and she couldn't speak.

Misunderstanding her reaction, Cianán rushed in to reassure. "Now don't get to troublin' yourself with it. We knew ye might not be wantin' this. It can be a whale of a time visitin'—and learnin' a bit of the language while you're at it—but livin' here would be a different thing altogether."

"It'd be that," Aoife agreed. "Ye've a life of your own beyont the water. We know that. But we want ye to know, Aingeal, that you're welcome here whenever ye'd like."

"And we won't be any longer chargin' ye for your stay," Cianán said firmly. "Ye keep sayin' no to that, but now *we're* sayin' it. Your American dollars are no longer any good at the Bank of O'Connor."

"They are not," Aoife said with the same note of finality. "Ye'll be noticin' that I never charged your card for this year's stay. And that's the way it'll be from now on."

"I thought you were angry with me," Angie spoke softly into the silence that followed Aoife's words, tears filling her eyes.

"Ach, go way outta that, lass!" Cianán exclaimed. "Where'd ye get that notion in your head? Ye've done nothing wrong...unless ye've hidden it mighty well!"

They all laughed then, and the tension that had been thick a few minutes earlier flew from the room. They didn't talk about the details that night. Aoife said she would share their thoughts by email—Cianán wouldn't go near the computer himself—and that knowing Angie'd consider their offer was enough for now.

As promised, Aoife wrote with suggestions for equitably sharing the finances and the workload, now and as they aged further, and stating their intention to deed the house over at their death...or earlier, if owning a business would help her get approval for an indefinite stay, citizenship if she wanted. And in the last email, Aoife quoted Cianán as saying, "Now tell the lass we'll be adopting her official if that'll help her come to stay. And be sure to be sayin' that I mean it!"

And it was as though Angie read those correspondences, particularly that last one, from underwater. For just as sound and light waves distort as they pass through liquid, Cianán's words seemed to twist and warp as they moved beneath the surface understanding Angie had of them. Of course, she dutifully answered and said all the expected things, but she wrote those words from the bottom of a sea, her feelings heavy and blurred. Though the word *adopt* kindled her deepest longing, it seemed her heart wasn't fully there once the overture had been made. But she sees now that her heart was *always* there, just waterlogged from a lifetime of yearning.

Angie had always prided herself on her courage. She'd been taken from home young, but had always found ways to survive. When she realized her life was going nowhere fast, she'd moved a thousand miles for a fresh start and, without knowing a soul, had built a life all on her own. And though she downplayed it when others expressed admiration for her daring to travel the world alone, their recognition strengthened the sense of fearlessness she'd always valued in herself.

And Angie knows it's true. She *is* brave...in all things but one. She is not fearless in love. She does not risk there. Two good and simple souls love her, need her, and are offering a home in a country she treasures. Aoife and Cianán want to call her kin. And here she is, thinking of a trip to New Zealand.

"Aingeal, you've been practicing courage for a long time, " she whispers into the silence of this odd night, "and here's your chance to take it to a new level. Talk with them. Trust them with your fears. Let them love you and let yourself love them. It's time to jump now, lass. So jump, dear Aingeal. Jump!"

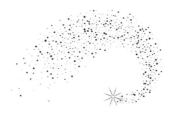

Sakiya

She plays on, the ticking of the metronome loud with the sudden elimination of traffic noise. She'd set the speed to 126 for her scales practice today, and is finishing up arpeggios and inversions before moving to more focused work on BWV 530, the Bach piece arranged for flute and piano that she's preparing for next month's competition. She still isn't pleased with some of the passages in the third movement, so she spends another hour on two of those.

Sakiya plays the first section several times through at various speeds, beginning with lento before moving to adagio, andante and finally allegro, while also varying the dynamics between forte and pianissimo. She then allows her fingers to have some fun, dancing through the passage with the skipping rhythm method, varying the length each note is held from long-short-long-short to short-long-short-long. When her fingers become comfortable with the sequence, she zeroes in on the transition points until the passage is smoothly linked to the notes that precede and the ones that follow. She then repeats the process with the second passage on this afternoon's roster. Finally she plays the entire piece through as Bach intended, and marks the passages she'll work on in the morning.

After noting the particulars of the session in her log book, Sakiya disassembles her flute and, while singing the Bach aloud, uses the rod and swabbing cloth to clean the instrument. She's always found this ritual soothing, particularly after a productive practice like the one this afternoon. Sakiya returns her instrument to its case and places it back on the shelf before running through neck and shoulder rolls, arm stretches, the yoga posture gomukhasana, and a series of finger and wrist exercises, all necessary to keep pain at bay given the asymmetrical positioning the flute requires. Though this is her usual post-practice repertoire, the silence that forms its background accompaniment today is absolute and altogether new. It strikes Sakiya as quite loud, making her smile at the thought of fortissimo silence.

With the kinks worked out, she walks to the window and looks down onto a scene she thinks would make a lovely still-life entitled of *City At Dusk*. Her thoughts don't linger however, soon returning to the competition and how much she needs a strong showing. Progressing to the final round will put her that much closer to Japan's Kobe competition, her dream since she first began playing nearly two decades ago. The Kobe is one of the few international competitions dedicated solely to flute, a reason in its own right for application. However, the city of Kobe is only 1,000 kilometers from the Tōhoku region of Japan, the area in which her paternal grandparents were born and several relatives still reside. She can think of little else these days.

Sakiya has always had one-pointed concentration. She never had to be bribed, cajoled or forced to practice as a child. Playing had always been for her a sort of joyful breathing, even when she struggled to perfect a new skill. To this day, her mother will tell any willing listener how Sakiya's small fingers would move up and down the body of a dream instrument as she slept, air sometimes escaping through lips held in a perfect embouchure. Her father showed his pride by continuing his pet name for her until his death from an ugly bout of cancer nearly two years ago.

"I hear a Little Bird," he'd call out when he came home to an apartment filled with the sound of her flute. "Where might she be?" She'd continue playing, trying not to laugh as he went from room to room, drawing ever closer as he looked in closets, behind the shower curtain, atop bookcases and finally beneath the bed in her room, muttering all the while, "Where *is* my Little Bird? Her singing is so much louder now, so she *must* be right here." Then he'd look directly at her, eyes opening wide in surprised delight, and proclaim her found as she dissolved into giggles.

Playing at Kobe would have made Papa so very proud. And though she needs that one-pointed concentration to get there, she recognizes she has again moved from disciplined effort to obsession, a shift that is not good for her playing or for her overall health—physical or emotional. So it is time now to turn off the flute thoughts, what James calls "muting the fluting". Though he hadn't cracked that joke lately, hadn't joked about or even noticed much of *anything* lately. Ever since the death of that little boy the same month her father died, James hadn't been himself. He seemed to be going through the motions of life, his usual exuberance lost. And it certainly didn't help that he was smoking way too much weed, stoned every evening and the whole weekend long.

Recognizing he should have been home by now, Sakiya moves away from the window to check for texts, but finds her phone dead. It is a testament to the magic of this time that she readily accepts that she has an evening to herself, one she refuses to spend welded to her flute. She dismisses the idea of taking a walk, despite the sunset colors spreading across the sky. Nor does she feel like reading. She wants to DO something, she just doesn't know what.

"Okay, maybe something productive. How about that mess of a closet?"

She walks into the bedroom and opens the closet door. Starting with the floor and working her way up, Sakiya rearranges shoes—James' on the right, hers on the left—restacks sweaters and turtlenecks, sorts the hanging clothes. She then hauls boxes from the upper shelf that stretches the length of the rod. This is the project's real goal, deciding what to keep and what to pitch from her early life.

As the power seems to have gone out, Sakiya gathers candles from around the apartment and lights them. She opens the first box, and arranges its contents on the bed by category: years of journals, a folder of likely embarrassing poetry, a few essays and papers she'd kept from college. And then she sees it, nestled between stacks of recital CDs, recordings of her work with the Shimmering Winds Quartet, and the performance DVDs required for entrance to various competitions.

A tingling dances across her skin as she removes the Tarot deck from the silk cloth she'd wrapped it in years ago. And she wonders now why she'd ever packed it away. She's always *loved* the Tarot, consulting it for questions both major and minor, sometimes simply pulling a card in the morning for the magic it brought to her day. She never put much thought into wondering how it worked—whether by accessing some sort of Divine guidance or simply awakening one's own intuition—but always balked at the cheapening that seemed to come when others used it as a fortunetelling tool or parlor game. What Sakiya loves most is the mystery of it all, and how the Tarot provides a direct link to that aspect of life. Plus, she nearly always found its insights helpful in providing clarity, often moving her forward in a new way.

Closet-straightening and possession-winnowing forgotten, Sakiya tosses a pillow to the floor and sits cross-legged upon it. With the candles arranged in a wide crescent around her, she relishing the familiar feel of the cards sliding between her hands as she shuffles and waits for a question and a layout to arise.

"I ask for guidance about my career as a flutist," she speaks aloud into the evening's silence, seeing a three-card spread appear in her mind's eye. She lays the deck on the oak flooring in front of her, picture-sides down, and sweeps the cards into an arc. She hovers her left hand above them until it feels drawn to a particular card. However, as she extracts it from the others, she finds a second coming with it. Thus she has two cards for this first placement, the one signifying her current position on her career path. Laying them on the floor, she turns them over.

The Ace depicts a hand offering a Wand from the ethers, a symbol of the raw creative power of the Cosmos. The Priestess of Cups shows a woman, sensitive and experienced, surrounded by life-giving waters that are available for her to draw upon as needed.

Sakiya sits back and lets the message settle. Yes, something has been offered her, and from a very early age. And though she is only 29 now, she has a wealth of experience, not only with the flute itself, but with the qualities of focus and sensitivity needed to create music and let it flow into the world.

Her hand moves over the cards a second time, though she decides she will be drawing now for the third position in the layout, the outcome card. She turns over The Magician, a powerful image of mastery and success. As a card from the Major Arcana, it seems to indicate a soul lesson underway, a direction to aim for. Sakiya places this card on the floor near the other two and sits for a few moments, opening to its message. She knows it is confirming that she's on the right path, one perhaps her soul intended for this lifetime. The card encourages a steady progression of skill and confidence toward a greater proficiency.

For the bridge card, the one offering guidance in moving from where she is now to a fuller mastery, she draws the Eight of Discs. Showing a craftsperson at work, its message could not be more clear: Continue as you're doing. Increase your skill through regular practice. Seek opportunities to perform. In addition, as none of the cards depict a group endeavor, it may be encouraging her development as a solo performer, a role that doesn't come easily to Sakiya due to an innate shyness, but one she yearns to inhabit all the same.

The cards amaze her, as always. It's not that they've told her something new tonight. They have, though, offered reassurance and support for what she already knows. "And that," she says aloud, "is *huge*. Thank you."

She returns the cards to the deck and considers continuing her closet project. She finds, though, that after being reunified with this old friend, she's not ready to let it go quite yet. Her mind immediately goes to James. Though she's always felt that she should ask questions for herself only, she feels the need now for clarity about what's happening inside him since he's not sharing much. At first, he said he just needed space, but if anything, he seems further away now than he was in those first few months.

Speaking aloud while again shuffling the deck, she says, "Please help me understand my husband, where he is and what his struggles are. I promise to be respectful and behave honorably with any insights given me." As the cards move back and forth between her hands, a four-card spread appears in her mind. The first and last card have the same place meaning as the reading she did for herself, but in this spread, the middle two cards will offer information about the conscious and unconscious influences at play inside James. When Sakiya feels ready, she again sweeps the cards into an arc in front of her.

The first card, reflecting where James is currently, is The Moon. Its image shows a rather severe-looking Moon above, with two wild animals howling and a crustacean eerily emerging from a pool below. Though other decks may show a friendlier image, all suggest a time when fears and unconscious influences come to the fore for the purpose of integration. And given that it is a Major Arcana card, it speaks to an important soul lesson or opportunity. She nods her agreement. James seems awash in all the emotions his usual buoyancy would tend to hold at bay.

The second card is the Five of Discs and its placement indicates James's unconscious mindset and attitude. The image shows two beggars in the cold of a stormy winter's night, walking beneath the lit window of a church, seemingly with no thought of going in for physical warmth or spiritual sustenance. Tears come to Sakiya's eyes as she recognizes the truth of the image. Her husband feels himself abandoned to the cold, lost in the darkness.

She chooses the third card, the one showing how James consciously perceives his situation. It is the Eight of Swords, depicting a person standing blindfolded, arms tied close to the body, with eight swords impaled in the ground around him. And yet, the individual's feet are unbound, a stream runs across the otherwise barren earth, and a castle can be seen in the distance.

And importantly, there are no swords directly in front of him. He could walk if he chose. This feels accurate to Sakiya as well. Her husband sees himself trapped with no way forward. And yet this is a misperception. Importantly, the number eight often signals a change underway. So this rather bleak card bodes well for James's ability to shift his perspective and find a way out. Sakiya then draws the final card representing the outcome.

It is the Death card. Another from the Major Arcana signaling an important juncture in the soul's journey through the world, it can be easily misunderstood. It does not signal a physical death, though Sakiya does note that two deaths—the child's and her father's—seemed to have initiated James's dark night. Still, the traditional interpretation fits, particularly when put together with the other cards in the reading. It affirms that this situation offers an opportunity for healing and deep transformation. And the rising sun in the background of the Death image promises the dawning of a new day.

Sakiya gets a tissue from the nightstand, wipes her eyes, blows her nose. The reality of her husband's pain washes over her and she gives herself a few moments to simply feel it. Then she sweeps the cards together again, shuffles, and chooses one card for herself, asking "What can I do to help?"

The Priestess of Swords. Just as with the earlier Priestess of Cups, it shows an experienced woman, but without any of the dreaminess or heightened emotionality of the Cups suit. This Priestess is all about intellect and objectivity. She is independent and seeks only a dispassionate clarity, no matter the situation in which she finds herself.

"So I think you're telling me," Sakiya says with a laugh, "that this weepiness won't help James. Of course I will continue to be sensitive to his situation, but I need to recognize that this is *his* work, *his* challenge, not mine. When it's appropriate—and this Priestess will certainly know when that time arrives—I can offer a clear-eyed assessment of what I see going on and encouragement to shift perspective. But I need to respect his ability to find his own way."

Sakiya waits, sensing more. Finally, she adds, "And yet it's also important to be direct about what I need as well, both to myself and directly with James. It feels like I lost my father and my husband at the same time. And I miss them both. A lot. And I realize I'm angry about that. My father is gone now, but my husband is still right here...except that he's not."

Another pause. "No wonder I'm having such a hard time muting my fluting," she says, with tears flowing for herself now. "I have nothing else to draw me out. It's like the flute is all I have. That's crazy, of course, but that's what it's felt like, that's what I've been *acting* like. So no matter what James decides to do, I need to turn things around for me. And I need to be honest with him. I miss him. I miss his sweetness, his attentiveness, his goofy sense of humor. I want him back, and I have a right to say that."

Sakiya retrieves her most recent journal from the stack and is shocked to see it only a third full, with her last entry six weeks after her father's death. And that brings another realization. James isn't the only one who dealt with loss by shutting down. He lost his bright light, and she has taken her love of the flute into dangerous terrain and lost touch with some essential part of herself in the process. Playing continues to be a joyful sort of breathing for her, and the Tarot seems to confirm that it is indeed her calling. Yet she sees even more clearly now—a Priestess of Swords insight, for sure—that she needs a better balance. And now that she has reconnected with the Tarot, she doesn't even need to draw another card, for one spontaneously appears in her mind's eye. Temperance. An Angel, one foot on land and the other in a stream, pours water between two golden chalices. It represents the universal drive toward balance in all things.

"Well, that couldn't be any clearer," Sakiya laughs as she collects the cards and wraps them again in their silk cloth. She does not, though, return them to the box. Instead, she places them on her nightstand, along with two of the candles and an intention to create a space devoted to the Great Mystery from which all life flows. And she knows once again that music is about more than hitting the notes perfectly or finding the pure tone. While these things are crucial, it is the Unnamable Something they convey that matters most. Being true to *that* is her calling, however she expresses it in the world.

Sakiya takes pen to hand, writes the day's date on the next blank page of her journal, and blocks out in bold letters the word BALANCE. Surrounding it in a flowing script, she writes the word MYSTERY. And she knows both of these are vital, each informing the other and weaving through her life moment to moment. Balance between the flute and the rest of her life, between work and play, between the outer world and that which lies within. And yet it is Mystery that holds Balance, and Balance that is needed for the fullest expression of Mystery.

"Playing the flute," Sakiya writes, "is a joyful sort of breathing for me. That will never change. It allows me to express what's in my soul and the Great Mystery as it comes through me. But the flute is NOT my soul, nor is it the Mystery itself, though it is for now my best expression of both. I must nurture my soul in order for my playing to be soulful. Soul-Full, Full of Soul. And I vow, here and now, to do so, to live and to play Soul-Full-Y."

James

He steps onto the path that wends its way through the park...and it is a blessed relief, the workday over, the commute done but for this last segment beneath the trees. The sky has begun to color, but its beauty doesn't penetrate the shadow that has held him these many months. Yet here among the trees, anonymity returns. He can drop the public face he has worn since leaving home this morning and, as painful as it is to admit, the one he's worn since Sakiya greeted him with a cup of coffee when he stepped from the shower just after dawn.

Unzipping the inner pocket of his jacket, he removes the vape pen with its cartridge still attached and takes his first hit. Numbness descends and the image that all day has pressed at the edge of his awareness recedes, shrouded for a little while by smoke. But he is not fooled. He knows that visual will be with him always.

James doesn't go straight home, but instead makes a few laps through the park, taking a hit now and again. It's the fortification he needs before Sakiya wraps him in a hug that will do nothing to connect them. Lately he's begun to wonder if he should set her free, explain he just doesn't have it in him to be with anyone, that she deserves so much more. He doesn't want to see the pain those words will cause her, though he knows he's hurting her in another way by continuing the charade that he remains a man capable of love.

The magic of this day descends soon after James enters the Park, but it doesn't register. Several times he passes Gretchen, the neighbor from Apartment 3C, hand frozen in the act of feeding pigeons. He repeatedly walks by the same late-day joggers and dog walkers, an inline skater, and commuters immobilized in their own journeys home. Closed in on himself, he sees none of them. He lives in uninhabited territory.

After his fourth or fifth orbit through the curving pathways, he knows he's as ready as he'll ever be to go home. He returns the pen to his pocket, crosses the street, registering the stopped cars only long enough to walk between them. He climbs the outer steps of the building, pushes through the door, steps into the lobby. He checks the box to find that Sakiya has already retrieved the mail. He climbs the stairs to the third floor, inhales deeply before placing his key in the lock and stepping into the darkened apartment.

Sakiya does not greet him tonight. He dimly sees her standing motionless, flute to lips, both silent. And James, giving little thought to the oddity of the situation, is shamed to feel only relief. A few more minutes to himself, time to exist without pretense.

He lights a candle and carries it with him as he exchanges chinos for sweats, a button-down for a long-sleeve tee. Since the stove doesn't seem to be working, he can't start the pasta dish they'd planned for tonight's meal and settles for a quick sandwich and a glass of milk. He then returns to the living room and collapses on the sofa.

Cannabis usually dulls memory. As he lies here tonight, though, memory arrives with a vitality not softened by time or smoke. It is a movie unfurling, one that refuses him the safety of spectator. It rips James from the now, and hurls him right smack into the middle of the then.

Again he climbs the stairs to that downtown apartment. Again he sees the door gaping open. Again he knows something is terribly wrong. Abby is once more collapsed against the wall in the corner, and again he knows she's already dead. He doesn't linger on that thought now any more than he did at the time. He's already running back to Noah's room, screaming his name even though he knows. And again he sees the small naked body sprawled on the bed, little buttocks and the sheet beneath stained with blood.

And James begins again that long walk into the land of emptiness, a void that is his very own flavor of grief and guilt. In memory, his body remains frozen in place for several moments, but eventually a stranger rises from within to remove the cell from his pants pocket. It is that James who punches in 911, who gives the dispatcher the pertinent details. It is he who walks across the room when the call is complete, careful not to tamper with any evidence. It is he who looks down on the curling blond hair against the pillowcase and sees the odd tilt of Noah's neck and the imprint of adult-sized fingers in the pattern of bruising there.

Eventually, that James hears footsteps on the stairs. It is that James who the police officer again asks to step aside. Another officer leads that James to the kitchen, where questions are asked and answers given. And it is that James who notifies Noah's grandmother, who attends the mandatory counseling sessions the Agency arranged, who receives condolences and the reassurance of coworkers, who continues to walk like a specter through life, who lies now on this couch on this odd night with a frozen Sakiya in the corner with her silent flute.

Now the movie doubles back on itself. He stands again looking down on Noah, dead from decisions James made as caseworker and advocate. Without any transition at all, the movie suddenly jumps back further now. He's sitting with Noah at an outdoor table, watching the boy try unsuccessfully to keep up with a melting ice cream cone. When Noah is done, James dips a napkin into the plastic cup of water, and begins cleaning the chocolate that covers the now giggling boy, face, hands and shirt.

"You made me *all* clean again!" Noah says when James is finished, small arms stretching above his head, fingers splayed wide.

"Not quite," James answers with a smile, "but it'll have to do for now."

"Yes, it'll have to do for now," Noah parrots in his high-pitched 5-year-old voice. "And when I go back to live with Mommy, you will come with me and stay with me so I'll *always* be clean."

"No, Noah," James says. "I can't do that."

"But I *want* you to," Noah says, his impossibly big eyes filling with tears. His voice is pleading now, holding none of the delight of a few moments ago.

"When you go back to live with your Mommy," James says, his heart breaking a bit as he drops to one knee so his face is level with Noah's, "I'll visit you for a little while to make sure things are okay, but I can't live with you."

Noah quickly looks down, brow creasing in a frown. James has been with Noah long enough now to wait, knowing more will come. He can almost hear the gears spinning in that wise little brain.

"You can't be my daddy because we don't match, right?" Noah says at last, looking up as he puts his small light-colored hand over James's dark one that rests on the arm of the chair.

"No, it's not because we don't match, Noah," James answers, his heart breaking a little more as he looks into Noah's trusting blue eyes. "Skin color has nothing to do with love. You're a great kid and any daddy would be lucky to have a son like you. But I can't be your daddy, because there are lots and lots of kids I have to take care of and keep safe. If I became your daddy and stayed with you all the time, I couldn't do that."

Silence stretches out, and once more James waits.

"I know," Noah says quietly, before nodding his head and adding with a sudden earnestness, emphasizing each word. "It's important to keep kids safe."

"Yes," James says aloud now into the silence of this strange night, "it's important to keep kids safe. And I didn't keep you safe, Noah. I didn't keep you safe."

And then the movie shoots him back to Noah's room, and he again sees that tiny, broken body dead on the bed. Tears come then. These are not the quiet tears that came at the funeral despite the layers of gauze that bound him, or the few shed in front of the counselor. They are not the impotent, enraged tears that came when he finally made it back to his car after the hearing that sent that sick-fuck to prison for 30 years to life. His tears tonight are different, great racking sobs that convulse his body as his heart fully shatters at last.

James lies very still when the final wave has rolled through. At last he sits up, stands and walks to the bathroom. Blows his nose, wipes his face, takes a leak. He returns to the couch, and though he considers taking a toke, he finds he doesn't want to. He lets his mind go back—and finds he wants to let it go back—to little Noah.

Of course, everyone told him it wasn't his fault. Addicts relapse, often without warning. He certainly knew it could happen, no matter Abby's apparent sincerity in working the Steps. He'd just never imagined how bad the consequences could be: Abby dead of an overdose at 28 just 3 weeks after getting her son back, and Noah dead of strangulation, a broken neck and a ravaged body mere exclamation points at the end of his short life.

In those early days, people liked to remind him that the decision to return Noah was not one he made alone. The therapist agreed. The CLR agreed. Noah's grandmother agreed. The judge agreed. It was Noah's first time in care, and Abby had gotten clean and jumped through every hoop they'd set for her. During sleepless nights, James revisited each and every interaction he'd had with her and everything reported to him by the others involved.

He'd shared the conversation at the ice cream parlor with Noah's therapist, leading to several mother-son sessions that seemed to have deepened Noah's level of trust.

There was not one thing James had missed, no concern he'd neglected to follow up on. And that was supposed to make him feel better?!! When something like this could happen without warning, what chance was there of protecting any child? And how could he be anything but a cheat in calling himself a child protection worker? And how could he show up, *really* show up, for another child?

Yet in the silence of this night, a new realization comes to him. He knows that wherever Noah is now, he's not in pain and fear any longer. Noah is safe. And as the truth of that begins to lodge somewhere inside, James feels something he hasn't felt in a very long time. James feels peace. Not a lot of it, but some.

And with that thought, James looks over at Sakiya. He sees for the first time all over again, her long black hair gleaming in the candlelight. He longs, as he hasn't for many months, to hear the magic that comes as her breath flows through the silver of her instrument, yearns to hear the sparkle of her laughter. He looks around the room that holds so many pieces of the life they built together, and he knows he wants that life back. He wants *himself* back, a stranger no more.

And for that to happen, James knows he must drop those layers of numbness that he may have needed at first, but doesn't need any longer. And to do that, he knows he needs to let himself hear again the words spoken in the sweet voice of a generous and wise 5-year-old.

"It's important to keep kids safe."

And James knows he now needs to answer.

"Yes it is, dear Noah. I'm so very sorry that I wasn't able to keep you safe. I tried. I really did. But I just couldn't."

James pauses then, gathering himself to speak the rest of the words he needs to say.

"And I've been pretending to be dead myself, partly as punishment and partly so I wouldn't have to let you go. But being dead myself doesn't make you any more alive. And as awful as it feels to say this, *you* are dead, but *I* am alive. I need to live, even though you can't. It's awful AND it's true."

James waits now, recognizing he is doing what he saw Noah do so many times before: sensing an idea coming and waiting for it to fully form. When it does, James puts the thought into words.

"I realize I've been asking myself the wrong question in these months since you were murdered. I've been stuck on the question of why such evil exists in the world. What I should have been asking myself is what I can do about it."

And here, James takes a deep breath before going on.

"Even though I won't always be able to keep kids safe, I have to try. Just like I tried with you. I know that's what you'd want. And so that's what I'm going to do."

James cries a little then, but the tears are different this time. Softer, but also more loving. It's like he's gotten himself back, and in doing so, he's gotten Noah back as well. He sees the boy doubled over in laughter again, sees Noah's pride when he makes it to the top of the climbing dome at the park, sees his delighted excitement as he unwraps the birthday present James gave him a few months before his death. Image after image flood into him, fill him. And James feels his heart beginning to knit together again.

"I'll never forget you, Noah," James whispers into the silence of this night, putting a hand on his chest. "You'll always be here, right in my heart. Forever and ever."

Pausing Yet Again

Images fade away as the hearth reverts to a functional structure for the lodging of flames. Its radiating warmth soothes the disorientation that always comes from your abrupt return from elsewhere. The mingled aroma of woodsmoke and storm-cleansed air bring ease as well. Long moments pass before you find voice.

"It feels wise now to practice what Nyah earlier called good soul-care. Rather than try to step around or outrun my emotions, I would like to be still to welcome them and bathe each in love. I want to ask if it would be okay to do that now, but I already know it is."

"It most certainly is," Icaro replies, with a quiet smile. "And you need never ask—here or at any time of your life—for permission to do as you deem best. Your next footfalls are only ever for you to determine and ought never be put to a vote by others."

You nod and close your eyes. And you do, indeed, welcome what comes, receiving every emotion as an honored guest come to pay a visit, allowing each to stay as long as it wishes before moving on. Horror. Sorrow. Wonder. Numbness. Kinship. Resistance. Love. Helplessness. Resolve. Delight. Emotions that are a mixture of several and for which a single appellation does not suffice. You sit as each one intensifies and diminishes, though a few return several times before you sense a fuller release. At last you open your eyes, though you remain silent for a time.

"What strikes me in this moment," you begin, "is how challenging it is to love openly and fully. Aingeal was courageous in all things but this, and even though it seemed that Sakiya and James were able to love well, when hurt came—both the expected loss of a parent's passing and the unimaginable anguish of Noah's murder—they both shut down. I certainly understand that response, particularly for James, and I can only assume that it was a similar level of pain that led Aingeal to protect her heart so vigorously."

"Perhaps it was," Icaro agrees. "And yet, is protection possible?"

"No, I don't think it is," you reply, "for the very methods we use to insulate ourselves merely wound us in a different way. We become a bit less alive, a bit less open to the Mystery Sakiya accessed through her cards and her flute. Love brings not merely the potential for heartache, but the certainty of it. We needn't expect a brutal murder, but an open heart *will* be wounded in a variety of ways in any relationship, from simple misunderstandings that occur to a variety of partings, a death in old age at the very least. Love is a prescription for heartache."

"Yes," the old man concurs, "it is so. Love opens the heart, and that is a beautiful thing. And yet, a heart opened will experience pain as well as joy. "

"It seems the ability to love," you suggest after a few breaths, "is central to who we are. It is to our hearts as oxygen is to our lungs. And just as lungs circulate oxygen to every part of the body for the good of the whole, loving actively circulates something essential throughout every part of our being. It seems to be the sustenance that comes to us from the great Mystery, and in some way I can't articulate, I suspect that receiving that sustenance gives something back to the Mystery itself. Certainly it allows us to remain an active part of the flow, to be part of some great, self-perpetuating loop, cycling and recycling forever and ever. To block it is to interfere with that process.

"Though perhaps I am being too narrow with that last thought," you say with a smile, "acting arrogantly as though I could possibly know. If our detours and apparent foibles are part of the path of evolving consciousness, our efforts to block would be an aspect of it as well. All part of the whole, unfathomable Mystery at the core of life. At least that's the way it seems to me," you say with a laugh. "How I do go on!"

You are beginning to suspect that the laughter that bubbled up so easily for Nyah is simply not Icaro's way. His is quieter, softer, and yet the smile that lights his face now conveys a similar delighted joy in your conjectures. Clearly rejecting any charge of arrogance on your part, it is apparent that he appreciates your efforts to feel your way into that which lives beyond word or thought.

    Silence stretches out until you feel ready to return to your own life. And with that awareness, once again the details of this place become less substantial, and you feel yourself pulled backward into the dark's gentle embrace. You reside there until the details of your own world materialize and welcome you home.

Rambling Onward...

Perhaps the living of your own life has held you for mere minutes or many more. However it has played out, you voyage back now to this time out of time, this place that is no place you recognize from your own world. You enter again that sweet darkness and are held there for as long as feels right. You again give me permission to place words upon your tongue and to imagine thoughts for your mind, knowing this is done in the spirit of make-believe. So as I now suggest heat emanating from the hearth, you feel its warmth and soon see its glow, and as I draw your attention to the freshness of the air streaming through the open doorway, you feel it dancing upon your skin and again hear the Andean pipes playing somewhere in the night. And as I remind you of Icaro, you sense his presence. Yet it is only when he speaks that you discover yourself sitting cross-legged on the rug before him, your gaze held by his own.

"It takes such courage to be human, does it not?" he says, the words still in a foreign tongue though their meaning is clear. "Life on the earth plane entails pain. Attempts to avoid and evade are not only fruitless, but harmful to a human heart. Certainly the wisdom gained through your EarthWalk helps you choose more consciously a way forward, avoiding some of the pitfalls that earlier claimed you. But no matter how wisely you choose your steps, pain will often be your companion. There is no escaping that fact."

"Yes, it seems to be so," you nod when Icaro falls silent. "I suppose, in addition to choosing wisely, we must gain skill in relating well to heartache. Allowing it, yes, but also shaping and transforming it into something that shapes and transforms *us* in return, not leaving our hearts shattered, but ultimately strengthening and deepening them, making them more alive and capable of a greater love."

You pause, preparing yourself to speak your next words. "When I walked with James to the door of Noah's bedroom, I was right there, seeing that little body ravaged by hate and feeling James's reaction to it. It was unbearable. And I was also with him as he walked through his life as a shadow. As I thought of it later, I certainly understood why that happened. It would have seemed impossible to do otherwise. And yet, that experience allowed me to know in a deeper way the cost of closing down. And the beauty of opening again."

After many breaths, you continue. "Something remarkable occurs when we quiet ourselves and turn to face, even to welcome, pain as our companion. It's not exactly magic...though maybe it is, a bit. If pain is an inescapable part of life, then maybe pain itself is *filled* with life, with something that is *enlivening*. When we turn to face our woundings, the animating force held within them seems to respond. The pain awakens, yes, but it can also then shift into something new, as the life held within it is freed to become fluid once more, as it was ever meant to be, fluid and ever-changing. And we are brought along for the ride. In allowing that life to flow anew, we are made new ourselves."

You pause to breathe deeply of the fresh air before continuing. "The change that occurred inside James as he turned toward his emotions was palpable, within him and within me as I was there with him. We felt the sharp initial piercing as feelings long pushed away were allowed to return. That is to be expected. And then those feelings intensified, which made sense as well, since they were finally allowed to be expressed. But within a relatively short time, a calming and soothing arrived. The heartache was not erased, but it could now be held within a more expansive field. Maybe in his efforts to avoid, James had shrunk himself down, as did the others I've seen in your hearth, and he was now expanding—*we* were now expanding—back to our true form."

"And yet," Icaro suggests when you become still once again, "you seem to be saying more than that facing pain is an essential route to healing it."

"Maybe I am," you say after a few moments of reflection. "I never before understood how *realigning* it can be. It's as though in honoring what is true, we return ourselves to a larger truth. And while we may need to block for a time, or pace ourselves when confronting a particularly deep wound, if we try to live in that state indefinitely, we pull ourselves out of the flow. We become less alive. We shrivel. We limp along, not fully living. Because fully living requires that we fully feel. That we fully be."

Icaro smiles and he nods.

"I find," you continue, "that I trust James to walk forward as himself again. And I suspect that not only will his interlude as a specter be over, but that he will have grown deeper and more loving than he was before the murder. And wouldn't that be a lovely tribute to dear Noah? To take that sweet boy's death and grow a heart capable of a greater love."

"Yes, it would be," Icaro agrees, his voice soft. After a time, he asks another question. "Do you have thoughts about the others you joined with this time?"

"Oh, yes!" you say with a nod. "Aingeal seemed to make a similar shift when she chose love. While I completely support a woman's right to do as she wishes with her body, the persona Aingeal needed to inhabit when she met with men for sex seemed at odds with who she truly was at her core. There was a sweetness, a vulnerability there that was awakened when she first heard her name spoken in an ancient language, and it continued to grow during her times with the O'Connors. For her, it was fear she needed to face, though likely that fear was also born of significant heartache. But still, an ongoing replenishing and realigning occurred during her stays in Sidheliath. I trust that will continue. Yes, I am sure of it.

"This process is, indeed, magical," you finish with a smile. "And if she and James shrink again, it will only be temporary. Life will call them back. Love will call them back. And they will respond."

Quiet descends again. Fire hisses and cracks. Finally, you share a few last thoughts.

"I gotta tell you, I just fell in love with dear Sakiya. I was right there with her too, able to hear the artistry and elegance of the music streaming through her flute. Her efforts to find balance between such strong dedication and the rest of her life struck me as just one example of a challenge we each have. In this Yin-Yang world of opposites in which we live, it seems that this quest for balance is one we each might share. The particulars are our own, but I bet there are few people who have this balance act figured out.

"And I was also affected by Sakiya's love of the Tarot. I know that a huge part of the benefit folks gain from any type of oracle work comes from the inner stillness required. In fact, this enchantment itself seems based on the belief—or maybe it's fact?—that stillness is almost curative, in that it allows us a chance to listen deeply to our insides. But perhaps there is more to it than that. Perhaps quietude allows us to not only listen to our inner knowing, but to access a wisdom that comes from beyond.

"I'll tell ya one thing," you conclude with a laugh, "after my experiences here with you, I'll be opening to magic in whatever way I can!"

The Old One beams, dark eyes dancing with delight. No further words come to either of you, but when his eyes ask a silent question, you nod and find yourself facing that fiery portal again as images come to life in its flames.

Nikki

Thank God the Happy Hour crowd had been thin. Sure the tips sucked, but she'd been on her feet since before dawn, so when Danny suggested one of them leave early, Nikki'd jumped at the chance. She pulls in front of the triplex now and wants nothing more than to sit here alone for a few minutes. Not true. She wants a hot bath something fierce, maybe with bubbles and a few candles around the edge of the tub. So she turns off the ignition, grabs her bag, and steps onto the walk. Halfway to the stoop, her heel hooks on a broken paving stone, and she nearly goes down.

"Cheap fuckin' bastard," she mutters as she rights herself and continues to the door. Walking in, she sees Hunter immersed in an Xbox battle scene, fingers working the controls like the expert he's becoming. She toes off her shoes, kisses the top of his head and asks if his homework's done. A grunt and a nod seem a decent enough answer. She doesn't mind his obsession with games. He's a good kid, gets As without much effort, and if this is the way he and his friends hang out, she's got no problem with it. She's not one bit worried about her boy.

Her daughter's another story, though. As Nikki starts up the stairs, she yells for Chloë to turn down that godawful hip-hop she's got cranked up way too loud. But of course she's ignored. Again. Shit, the bar was quieter than this.

"For God's sake, Chloë" she says, throwing open the door to her daughter's bedroom, "turn that..."

And she stops, taking in the scene. Chloë in jeans and a purple bra kneeling on the floor, back to the door. A boy she's never seen before leaning against the pillows, pants down at his ankles, fingers pumping her daughter's head up and down against his crotch. Chloë straightens and turns toward the door.

"Mom!" she shouts, grabbing her sweater from the floor and pulling it on. "What are you doing home?" she asks as she reaches over to turn down the music.

But Nikki doesn't answer. She locks eyes with the boy, a boy clearly years older than her daughter. She's pleased to see a bit of fear mixing with his initial shock.

"What the fuck are you doing?" she manages, her voice deadly.

"I...We...Never mind," he stutters, hiking up his jeans, but not before Nikki gets a view of his wilting hard-on. "I was just leaving."

"Not so fast, asshole," Nikki spits out. "Do you know how old my daughter is?"

"*Mom!*" Chloë yells, "Stop it!"

"I asked you a question?" Nikki says, ignoring her daughter.

"Well, ma'am, it really didn't come up," he replies with just enough cockiness for her to get that it's a good thing she doesn't have a gun in her hand.

"Well, she's 13 years old. *Thirteen.* And I'm guessing you're quite a bit older than that, right? So if you come anywhere near my daughter again, you'll be talking it over with the cops. Got it?"

He nods, grabs his shoes and jacket and brushes past her, barrels down the stairs and through the front door. Chloë jumps up and stands glaring at her mother, arms crossed over her chest, chin tilted up at that defiant angle that's become so common. Nikki registers the makeup now, mascara heavy on her lashes, eyes and lips lined with several shades of purple. Silence stretches out until they hear an engine start up and tires squeal away from the curb.

"So, who is he?" Nikki asks then, making an effort to steady her voice.

"No one," Chloë answers with a shrug. "Just a guy I met at the mall."

"What's his name?"

"Josh."

"Josh, what?"

Chloë doesn't answer.

"Josh, what?" Nikki repeats, louder this time. When her daughter remains silent, Nikki takes several steps forward. "Josh, what?!!"

"I don't know, okay?" Chloë shouts. "I just met him. I don't know every single detail about him."

"Every single detail like his goddamn name?" Nikki shouts back. "You brought that boy into this house, put his dick in your *mouth* for god's sake, and you don't even know his last name?!!"

Chloë is silent, though the look on her face is tirade enough.

"Three nights a goddamn week I pull a shift at the bar to make the money needed to keep this house running for you and Hunter, and you can't do your part. Has Hunter even had dinner? No, let me guess, you have no frigging idea, right? I've been up since 5 this morning, did my shift at the café, took time to put dinner together before I went to the bar, and you can't even put a casserole in the goddamn oven?"

When silence is Chloë's only response, Nikki sighs. "Get in the bathroom right now and wash that shit off your face. You're too goddamn young to be walking around looking like a little slut."

"Oh really," Chloë says, dropping her arms to her side and taking a step toward her mother. Her next words are laced with venom. "Just how old do I have to be, *Mom*, to walk around looking like a little slut? Uh, 15 maybe?"

And that's when Nikki slaps her. There's no decision involved. Her arm reaches out of its own volition, palm striking Chloë's cheek. For just a second, Nikki sees the face of her little girl—her little girl's *real* face—shining through the layers of makeup, shock and hurt in eyes that immediately begin to tear. And then time stops and the house falls silent.

"Chloë, I'm sorry," Nikki says quickly, though even as she speaks the words she somehow knows Chloë can't hear them. Slowly, Nikki takes the hand that just hit her daughter and brings it gently to rest on the red splotch already forming on her cheek. "I'm so sorry, honey" she whispers, her own tears flowing now.

Nikki moves closer and wraps her arms around this child of her heart, this child who can now barely tolerate any form of touch from her mother. Nikki doesn't spare a thought as to what's caused the world to pause and her daughter to freeze, but she does see the opportunity it offers to swaddle her child in love. As Chloë is nearly her own size now, they stand chest to chest, and she feels their hearts beating with the same rhythm, feels the beat slowing in unison.

Finally, Nikki steps back. Seeing the imprint of her hand on Chloë's cheek, she again brushes it lightly with her fingers, whispering "I wish I could take it back," but she knows she can't. Nikki turns then, intending to go pee...and sees Hunter standing in the hallway just outside the bedroom door, eyes wide, cheeks wet with tears, right hand frozen in the act of yanking his hair.

"Oh, no, Hunter," she moans, "not again." But of course he'd have heard them arguing through his game haze, particularly after Josh's race down the stairs. Hair-pulling is a new thing, something he does whenever he feels anxious. "My head gets all buzzy, Mom, like it's gonna blow up," he'd explained in his usual, creatively odd fashion, "and my hair's like these handles that help me pull the buzz out."

Nikki holds him close as well, sparing a moment to be grateful that he doesn't reject such overtures. Not yet, anyway. She pours her love into him too, and wonders how things ever got so messed up. She'd never known she was capable of the fierce love she has for her two children. It's the reason she does all she does. And she doesn't resent it, not at all, though she'd understand Chloë believing she did after the things she said. She just needs a little help, that's all. And Chloë had always been so willing to give it before, even when there wasn't enough money for an allowance. Until a switch flipped with puberty and Nikki had suddenly become the enemy.

And that dig just now about Nikki being a slut when she was young was *so* unfair. And cruel. Nikki had never hidden her past, had always openly acknowledged her mistakes. But she hadn't slept around. Kyle and she'd been in love, or at least in what they thought of as love. And when she'd gotten pregnant with Chloë at 15, they'd decided to keep their baby, had gone up together against their parents, the school counselor, even her pediatrician. And they'd won. And even though she'd made a mistake in trusting that Kyle would mature as she had and do what his family needed, she'd never regretted the children he gave her.

Giving Hunter a final squeeze, Nikki drops her arms and continues down the hallway to the bathroom. Pees, blows her nose, and splashes water on her face, marveling at the calm that's settling in now. She turns on the hot water, pours in some lavender-scented bubbles, and leaves the tub to fill as she walks back down the hall. She sends a smile to each child that they give no indication of perceiving, and goes into her bedroom. She undresses and wraps herself in her terry robe, and then goes down to get some sparkling water from the fridge. And finds, sure enough, the casserole sitting right on the top shelf. She fills a tall glass with ice, finding herself soothed by the sound of the fizzing bubbles as she fills the glass. Returning to the bathroom, Nikki places her drink on the edge of the tub, lights the candle on the back of the toilet and another on the window ledge. Sliding off her robe, she steps into the tub and melts into the water's heat. And as she lets the steam carry her away, she's keenly aware that, beneath the current crisis being played out, all is well.

When the water begins to cool, Nikki bathes her body, washes her hair, and shaves her legs in the flickering light. After toweling off, she pulls on her robe to go to the kitchen to put the casserole to warm in the oven. But her feet stop at Chloë's doorway, take a detour into her room. She's about to lie on the bed, but then the image of that slimeball of a young man comes back to her. She grabs the comforter—a present for her daughter's last birthday—bunches it into a ball and throws it down the stairs to put in the wash later. Stopping at the hall closet, she grabs Chloë's old quilt from the top shelf, spreads it over the bed, lays down, and looks at her children.

"How did everything get so screwed up?" she asks aloud, but this time a bit of curiosity is laced with the guilt. "My daughter giving head to a guy she doesn't know, my son so anxious he's game-obsessed or tearing out his hair, me working too many hours and still needing credit cards just to make it all work."

But as the silence stretches out, Nikki lands on the most upsetting thing of all. Somewhere along the way, maybe in the last couple of years, they'd ceased being a family and had become three individuals sharing one lousy rental unit. And Lord knows her kids are too young to be on their own.

Nikki sees she's been ignoring what's right in front of her eyes, and that needs to change. She needs to have another sex talk with Chloë, despite the eye roll she knows she'll get. But there's something more here, something about Chloë kneeling on the floor while that piece of shit scumbag of an excuse for a human being lays back against the pillows taking what he seems to think of as his due. This time the talk needs to be about more than simple mechanics. Nikki needs to let her daughter know she should never kneel before a man unless he's proven himself worthy time and again, and unless he's willing to kneel back and honor her in every way.

She also needs to set limits on Hunter's game time and make sure he has some real-life interactions to take its place—with her, his sister, his Uncle Matt, and others. And they need to get to the cause of his anxiety. She knows part of it is the fighting between Chloë and her, but having his dad skip out when he was so young had to be in there somewhere.

So, she gets it. She needs to be home more to give her kids what they need. But to do that, she has to stop being on autopilot herself. Has to deal with her own emotions better and stop keeping doing what isn't working in the first place. She'd gotten her GED before Hunter was born, had taken a few courses at the Community College before Kyle left, but she hadn't been focused, hadn't known what she wanted, so it seemed like a waste of money. But a couple of months ago, one of her regulars at the café, a single woman who comes in for breakfast every day before work, told her how much she made as a dental hygienist with only an associates degree. She'd researched it afterward, and found that a BSDA increased the salary significantly, but she hadn't taken it any further. Laying on her daughter's bed on this strange evening with her kids statued in front of her, it seems a worthy goal. Shit, she's in debt already. What's a little more for something that'll eventually lead her somewhere and give her family some security.

She'll need to look into financial aid again, but if other people can do it, she certainly can, as bullheaded and persistent as she is. She might still have to pick up a few shifts when things get tight, but she'd be home more with the kids. And she'd show them that hard work didn't have to be a chore. It could be a path forward to something better. Not just a better job, but maybe a house of their own. And maybe it could also be part of remembering that they're a family, that they're connected and can work together for something. And that they actually love each other.

Because one thing she knows is that they *do* love each other. It's just somehow gotten all twisted and confused. But that which is twisted can untwist, and that which is confused can be made clear. All it takes is intention. That and some hard work.

Chloë

Everything's suddenly very quiet, so quiet that the echo of the slap bounces off the walls and fills her head. Her mother's face is frozen in shock, though she doesn't know which of them is more surprised. Her mother *never* hits. She'd told them she didn't wanted to be like Grammy and Pop, and promising not to hit her kids was an important first step. And she'd kept her word. Until today.

Even though she's still mad, Chloë knows she brought it on herself. Maybe even deserved it. She just gets so sick of her mother trying to control every little thing she does. Always nagging about grades, and making her clean the house and babysit her dorky brother. It's like she forgot what it was like to be a teenager. And like she forgot, too, that she hadn't always been perfect herself.

Still, Chloë feels bad about the slut comment, since she knows it's not true. Her mom never has guys over like Rachel's mother does, hardly ever even goes out with anyone. Maybe it'd be better if she did. Maybe she'd chill a bit. But her mom doesn't lie, so if she said Dad was the first, then he was the first. It isn't her mother's fault he turned out to be so useless.

Well, she isn't gonna think about him now. She's already spent too much of her life thinking about that loser. He isn't worth it. Besides, her cheek's hurting something awful. Oh, God, what if it's bruised? Bella's party's tomorrow night and she sure doesn't want to go with an ugly bruise covering half her face. It'd make a good story, but she's self-conscious enough as it is and doesn't want any extra attention.

"Though you probably won't even let me go now," she snaps as she walks past her mother...and sees Hunter frozen in the hallway, hand grabbing his hair.

"Oh, Hunter," she says, her stomach hurting even worse now. She hates it when he's upset. He might be a dork, but he's her dork and a pretty cool little kid most of the time. "It's okay," she says, even though she knows he can't hear. "We were just arguing and you really should be used to that by now, since it's all we ever do anymore."

She puts her arms around him, shocked that his head reaches almost to her shoulder. The guilt gets worse as she realizes how long it must have been since she's hugged him, really hugged him. Not that it's her fault. Not really. Sure, she's been kind of distracted lately, but all he wants to do anymore is play stupid video games. But she's the big sister and probably oughta make more of an effort.

In the bathroom, she looks in the mirror above the sink. She loves the way her makeup outlines her eyes and makes her lips look full. And purple's her favorite color, though she doesn't want her cheek turning purple to match. Her mother doesn't know anything, calling her a slut. She's not a slut. But something about that thought brings on the tears that started when her mother slapped her. Soon Chloë's sobbing and swiping at the makeup she'd applied so carefully that morning.

After washing her face, she goes downstairs to get a soda and plops on the couch. Her tears are mostly over now, and she feels calmer and ready to think back over the last few hours. Truth is, she'd been relieved when her mother came in. Well, actually she wishes she'd heard her car and had time to get Josh down to the living room, so that embarrassing scene in the bedroom never would have happened. But things with Josh had gotten so awful, she was mostly just glad her mother ended it.

It'd been great to have an older guy, someone as cute as Josh, interested in her. They'd started flirting at the mall and she didn't see any problem when he suggested bringing her home. It wasn't like she was gonna be alone with him or anything, since Hunter'd be there. But then Josh asked to see her room, and she didn't want to act like a baby and tell him her mother didn't allow her to have guys in her bedroom. Besides, she was just going to show it to him. But he'd pulled her inside and closed the door behind them. Then he'd started kissing her, and that was great. She hadn't been kissed much and only by boys her own age who sure didn't know how to kiss like Josh.

But then he'd started stroking her breasts, putting his hands under her sweater and pulling it up, saying he wanted to see her in her bra. She'd said no, but when he said, "Aw, c'mon, you sweet thing. I bet you have beautiful breasts. I just wanna see 'em, and then you can put your sweater back on and we'll go down and play a game with your brother, okay?" And so like an idiot, she'd let him take off her sweater.

And then he was sitting her down on the bed and rubbing between her legs. When she pushed his hand away, he grabbed hers and pushed it down where his hard-on was straining against his jeans, saying, "C'mon, honey. Look what you did to me. I never took you for a little cock tease. You're not a little cock tease, are you? You'll be giving me blue balls for sure if you don't help me out here."

Chloë didn't know what that even meant, but if she made his balls turn blue, it had to be pretty painful. So she started feeling guilty too, along with scared and embarrassed. But stupid her, she still wanted him to think she was cool. So next thing she knew, she had his dick in her mouth, he was moaning and pushing her head up and down so hard it hurt, and she was trying not to gag.

And then her mom came in. Thank God. She probably would have thrown up all over him if he'd come in her mouth. She knew girls at school who went down on their boyfriends all the time, but now that she'd done it, it all seemed so gross. But she understands now why she'd said that hateful, untrue thing to her mom. Because the truth was, Chloë *had* acted like a slut. She hadn't meant to, but that didn't change the facts. Josh wasn't her boyfriend, just some guy she'd known for an hour. And Mom was right, she didn't even know his name.

She couldn't imagine ever facing her mother again, let alone talking about all of it. But she knew they would. A part of her even wanted to. Chloë missed her mom. Even though they fought all the time now, it didn't used to be like that. They used to get along great, like they were best friends. But she had other best friends now, and didn't need that from her mother. And she certainly didn't want the responsibility for Hunter or for doing all the things her mother made her do around the house. She just wanted to be a kid, a girl who had a real mother, someone she could count on. Chloë knows that's not fair, since she's the one who's been pushing her mother away. Shit, she doesn't know *what* she wants, just that whatever it is, she's not getting it.

And yet there's something weird going on tonight, that's for sure.

Because even though she's still embarrassed, even ashamed, she also has this idea that it all might work out somehow. She can't imagine how, but believing it will is enough for now.

Hunter

He creeps up the stairs, careful to miss all the squeaky places. He must be totally silent. No squeaking. No speaking. No crying. Quiet as a little fawn. And on each step, he needs to quickly repeat the power words three times before his foot can move to the next stair.

He's been practicing this magic ever since he discovered the very best video game ever. He's a Healing Hands in that game, a very important character who needs to save all the good guys when they almost die. But as tricky as that is to do, it's easy compared to healing Mom and Chloë, and so he's begun adding new tricks to the magic he already has.

But they're still yelling when he gets to the landing. Their mad streaks through Chloë's doorway into the hall, and zaps him like lightning. It fills his head with that buzz he hates, and even though he's tugging his hair handles really hard, it won't stop. So he yanks harder, pulls a hunk of hair out, lets it fall to the floor and yanks again. And all the while, he keeps his spell going.

"Stop it," he thinks. "Stop it. Stop it. Stop it. Stop it. Stop it. Stop it."

His insides are like a drum now, beating in time to his words. And now he's tugging his hair to the drumbeat too, and his body's bouncing up and down with it.

"Stop it. Stop it. Stop it. Stop it. Stop it. Stop it."

And then he sees Mom swing her arm fast and hard, and though he can't see it all from where he's standing, he hears that slap. It's like an explosion of thunder—or maybe a firecracker—that makes his whole body jump.

But then they stop. The magic finally worked! They go completely quiet and still. They're deer now, too, each a doe in the forest and they've felt his magic and are stopping to listen hard. But he's still a little fawn who wants to get closer to Mama Deer and Sister Deer. So he does.

He takes a step into the room. And then another and another, until he's standing right next to them. He looks up into their faces and sees that the magic hasn't totally worked, at least not yet. It did make them stop yelling, and they're not saying mean things to each other anymore, but something's still wrong. Their bodies are stiff and their faces are red and twisted. He looks into their eyes and see there's still some mad there, but there's something else too. They're sad. No, it's something bigger than sad, something he doesn't know the word for. But he's sure of it. And he knows it's important. He just doesn't know why.

Hunter sits on the floor then, both hands in his lap, and looks up at them. He sees Mom's eyes staring right into Chloë's, and Chloë's eyes staring into Mom's. He doesn't think deer stare like that. They're too shy. Too quiet. And Chloë and Mom aren't shy and they're certainly not quiet. They're more like monkeys, mad monkeys most of the time, hopping around and screeching. Or else they're turning away like monkeys do, pretending to ignore each other. But now they're not doing either of those things. Now they're quiet and looking right in each other's eyes.

Hunter's sorry they're upset, but he's sure glad the noise stopped. He can tell that there's another magic here, a wonderful kind of big magic, a magic bigger than the house, bigger than the whole town, huger than the world. If their anger is like thunder and lightning, this big magic is like a lake of cool water. Not really water, of course, cuz that would be dumb. Plus, it would drown him since he can't swim so good. It's not water, but it's *like* water cuz it can go everywhere, and it feels soft wherever it touches, and it can put out all kinds of fires. He's soaking in it now, and it's filling him up on the inside, too. And every place it touches feels better. And the really great thing is that it turns that awful buzzing down and down, like the volume control on the remote, until there's only a soft hum in his brain that's kind of nice.

Hunter keeps looking up at their faces, trying to figure out that important thing about them looking both angry and bigger-than-sad at the same time. He stands up and slides sideways into the narrow space between them and closes his eyes. He stands as still as they are and feels the cool waters of the lake holding all three of them. He breathes it in and feels them breathing it in too.

And that's when he gets it. They don't hate each other. They love each other. A lot. They love each other so much that sometimes it gets all confused. *They* get confused. And when that happens, that water stops being the lake it is right now, and turns into a storm, with lots of thunder and lightning. Or it's a bad flood, knocking everything down as it goes.

Hunter is happy now, cuz he knows that love, just like water, can take many shapes. Yeah, it's like a shapeshifter in one of his games! Sometimes it feels wonderful like it does right now, even though Mom and Chloë are still stuck in before. But it can sometimes look like mad, even hate. It's like shapeshifters, but it's also like Halloween costumes. Mom and Chloë can look and sound pretty scary on the outside, but inside they're still themselves. And the love's still there. It's all love, even if sometimes it looks like it's not.

The happiness filling Hunter rises like bubbles in a glass of soda, until finally it bursts out of him in a giggle. He's happy to realize that Mom and Chloë love each other, even if sometimes it looks like hate.

He opens his eyes now and looks up at Mom. He's still a fawn, but he remembers he's also a Healing Hand. He reaches up and puts a hand on either side of her face. Then he fills her up with the healing magic.

"It's okay, Mom," he says out loud, knowing he doesn't need to be quiet anymore. "Chloë loves you and you love her too. It's just that love is like water and sometimes it can look like something else, but it's not. It's still love."

And then he wriggles around until he's facing Chloë. "I'm sorry Mom hit you," he says, feeling a little bit sad now that he sees her red cheek. "I don't know why she did that, but I do know she loves you. And I hope you know it too." He holds her face in his hands, too, and pours his healing magic into her just like he did with Mom.

Stepping out from between them, he says, "And I love both of you, whether you're deers or monkeys, or thunder or lightning. And all I gotta do when you fight is keep remembering that it's all love, even when it looks and sounds ugly."

And with that, he races through the bedroom door and clambers down the stairs.

Re-Pause

The fire flashes brightly before it calms once again. You are becoming more adept at managing the dislocation that comes from suddenly moving back into yourself after being so thoroughly immersed in the lives of others. You know now to let your senses lead, and so you look into the flames, listen to the sounds of fire, crickets and panpipes, and feel the rug under you supporting your weight. Air fills your lungs, and the rise and fall of chest and belly whisper "I am here. I am right here." When you are ready to speak, your eyes are gazing again into Icaro's.

"I adore that Hunter sees love as a shapeshifter. It reminds me of Sister Constance-Marie's seeing the One Love shining through a variety of guises... though I don't think she saw any of those as Halloween costumes! That metaphor works particularly well, though, when love's mask is a disturbing one. Yeah," you say with a laugh, "it's just one big masquerade ball!"

You pause for a time before continuing. "You know that I truly experience these lives, rather than just viewing them from outside. I felt Nikki's exhaustion, her sense of overwhelm, and her shock as she walked into Chloë's bedroom. And as an aside," you say with a rueful laugh, "I gotta tell ya, the image of that young man's genitals might just stay with me for awhile, thank you very much! But the guilt and shame Nikki felt after slapping her child cut deeply. Though I suppose those are the very emotions that will help her turn things around. Sometimes we need to be shocked from our complacency and into a solid commitment to do things differently."

After several moments, you continue.

"I love Nikki's realization that what is twisted can untwist, what is confused can be made clear, even though we may not be able to fathom the how of it. And I also appreciate that your magic allows everyone to believe that change *can* happen. I'd sure like to bottle up some of that and take it with me!"

With eyes full of a sweet mirth, the old man mimes unscrewing a vial, sweeping a cupped hand through the air, and pouring the trust thus collected into the waiting vessel. You marvel that you can somehow see a shimmering light move from his palm into a flickering image of a tall, slender bottle. Capping it, Icaro stretches out his arm, offering you this gift. Your fingers tingle as they wrap around a vial that feels more solid than your mind can grasp, though as with so much you've experienced here, you don't even try. Closing your eyes, you silently press the vial against your chest where a corresponding animation resonates within your heart. With each inhalation, the sensation strengthens, and with every exhalation it extends throughout your body.

At last, you open eyes that stream with grateful tears.

"Though I have been given many precious gifts during our time together, this vial of trust might be the most precious of all. I could feel it moving into me, just as I could feel something deep within moving forward to greet it."

"And what do you make of that, child?"

Silence reigns as you continue to breathe trust into your heart and feel your own heart's trust rising up to meet it. And there you find your answer.

"It seems that trust lies within my heart as well. It is as though a faith embedded there *recognized* your bottled magic and leapt up to meet it. I have been taught in so many ways to *not* trust, to expect the worst or at least always prepare for it. How different my life would be if I chose to fully embrace trust, a trust not just in the possibility, but in the likelihood that things will work out. Or better yet, that on some deep level they are *already* okay, despite surface appearances. That all I might find disturbing is simply part of the journey, an essential part of the path we're taking, individually and collectively."

Icaro beams. Silence stretches out as you continue to feel trust resonating within, and as you absorb what you have just learned. And at just the right moment, as has happened many times before, you find yourself pulled gently backward into a darkness that is both welcoming and safe. You pause here for as long as feels right before your own life begins once more to claim you.

Leia Marie

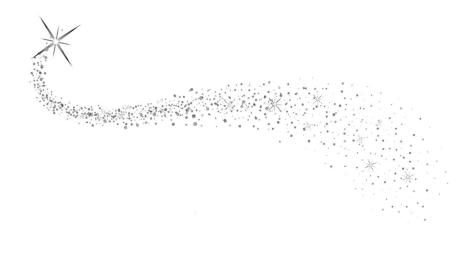

Re-Ramble...

You are traveling once again to the place that lies beyond the beyond. The silent and vast darkness calls you, and once more you know that this is not an emptiness but a fullness gathering you to it, welcoming you to its sweet embrace. You rest here until gradually the sights and sounds of the space designed just for you begin to appear. The warmth of the fire fills you as air, cool and fresh, wafts through the open doorway. The rain has resumed, but it falls gently in the night, more mist now than torrent. As has happened twice before, you perceive a change that extends beyond the weather, and you trust that it is good.

And with that thought, you are seated upon a large cushion drawn close to a low lacquered table. Across from you is an Asian woman whose advanced years are apparent in the lines etching her face and in the white strands that twine through the black of her hair. She sits without moving, conveying a deep stillness that reminds you of the statued ones you have seen in the flames. As soon as you think that thought, though, her lips curl into a gentle smile.

"No, sweet one," she responds, her voice soft and pleasing. "I simply wait, offering you space to savor these changes. I go by the name Xiuying. Please take as long as you'd like," she finishes with a delicate sweep of her hand," to drink this in."

You have no thought to see if the bed remains in the corner or if the pots above the hearth are the same as before. It is as though your vision has narrowed to a radius of mere feet: the sleek shine of the black tabletop delicately edged with golden swirls; its short curved legs resting upon an antique rug adorned with a simple design; an assortment of floor cushions in fabric the soft green of an early spring day, yet laced with flowers in full and riotous bloom.

Your eyes come to rest on Xiuying herself, dressed in a pearly tunic that shimmers in the firelight. She wears no jewelry, though her hair is swept up and held in place by a traditional hairpin inlayed with a jade of the deepest green. Her face is round, with dark eyes dipping toward high cheekbones. The serenity in this face speaks of a deep inner stillness. More than anything else, this is what endears her to you.

"I am pleased to be here with you," you say when words are ready to be spoken.

"And I am pleased to sit with you as well," she replies with a slight nod and, with quiet merriment dancing in her eyes, adds, " I trust that boredom has not joined us at this table."

"No, it has not," you smile in return. Sensing Xiuying's invitation to speak your thoughts since your last visit, you continue. "I assume you know of the precious vial of trust that Icaro gifted me when last I was here." Registering her assent, you continue. "I so often feel I must work hard to create something like trust, as though I need to make the pure and the beneficial arise out of nothing. But realizing it's *already there*, that my heart already knows how to trust, changed everything. Since it exists already, I need only drop down into it. It took the striving, the effort away. I mean, of course I still had to remember, still had to choose. But it felt more like an *allowing*, rather than any form of hard work. There was an ease to it."

You pause several long moments before speaking further. "And yet, remembering didn't always do it. Sometimes, I found that visualizing Icaro fashioning the vial and handing it to me helped bring back the felt experience. At other times, that didn't work either, and I had to content myself with the faith that trust still existed somewhere inside, whether or not I could access it."

"And what," asks Xiuying, "does that tell you?"

"I suppose," you answer, "that I am a work in progress, an evolving being who is gradually coming to a fuller awareness. I have been told that my trust in another's awakening is a gift. If I can hold that trust for others, perhaps I might hold it also for myself. Yes, I will choose to know that I cannot *un*know what I have experienced here. I will trust in my ability to trust," you grin, "and to do so more deeply."

Xiuying's smile fills you, lightening your heart even further. After a time, new words come.

"I also realized there is nothing passive about this kind of trust. The process of falling into it is receptive, yes, but not passive. As I said, it often entails a specific choice. Yet once that choice is made, I may be urged to act, but to act out of love, rather than fear or anger. There is nothing Pollyannaish about any of this. Pain cannot be denied, and there is no promise that my actions will have the outcome I desire, though choices arising from love have the best chance of creating positive ripples. If I can let love be the impetus for whatever I do, it will lend a confidence, a hope, and yes, a trust that benevolence is larger and more enduring than anything else."

A gentle puff of air sets windchimes to tinkling near the open doorway and leads to a break in your concentration. You feel no need, though, to rush back to pick up the thread of your thoughts, content instead to settle more fully into the peace of this space and the loving presence of your new companion, dear to you already. At last, you speak further.

"I've asked before if the insights realized during this time of magic will be remembered, if these individuals will really *own* them and walk them forward into an altered future. I find myself wondering that again with this new family. As a single woman, Nikki's path will be fraught, both in making her career goals a reality and in midwifing her children into adulthood. And Chloë and Hunter will continue to experience their own challenges. But likely due to that little vial of trust, I found myself accepting that this enchantment can do no more than quiet the outer racket so folks can pay attention to their insides and open to the wisdom that has likely been there in some form all along. Just like my heart responded to Icaro's vial, that wisdom has leapt up for a time to greet them. What we each, myself included, do with this opportunity is ever ours alone. It will be our creation."

Xiuying nods and smiles, and after a time you continue.

"What is known cannot be unknown, what is twisted can return to its true shape, and what is jumbled can be made clear again for us all." You pause, as you allow a new insight to emerge.

"I just then felt a sort of mental tingling, like those chimes that pealed in the breeze a little while ago, when I heard myself say the words, "what is twisted can be returned to its true shape." It seemed to call me to a new insight, one I allowed myself to drop into, rather than wrestling to claim. That insight is this: all things *want* to return to their true shape, and that true shape is love. When we live divided from love, we live in misery. But what I'm realizing now is that, in a way, we have to work hard to *keep* ourselves miserable, to keep things twisted out of their true shape. I spoke earlier about the ease of allowing, and now I see that it has an ease about it because, in dropping into trust, we are returning to our true shape."

After a pause, you continue.

"This being human is tricky business, is it not?" Seeing compassion in Xiuying's eyes, you continue. "To grow into adulthood, to raise a family, to contend with a multitude of outer demands and conflicting internal impulses. To try to balance it all when that balance must be dynamic rather than static. We must be like acrobats balancing atop a cantering horse, ever making adjustments, minor and major. And yet we make it so much harder than it needs to be. If we can begin from the love and the trust inside us and act from there, act from the bottled magic in our own hearts—and unstoppering those vials so love can flow freely, knowing it will ever be replenished—then things would go much more smoothly.

"Yes, I will trust that that which is twisted *wants* to untwist and that which is jumbled *yearns* to become clear. And what is known cannot be *un*known, though it may be forgotten for a time, even repeatedly. I will trust, too, that we each hold a magic vial of love within us, and that the dance of forgetting that vial and remembering it once more is not a detour from the path, but the path itself."

No additional words come to either of you. After a time, though, you answer Xiuying's unspoken question. And without any awareness of movement, you are again facing the hearth and the frisky flames that dance within it. Soon, though, the portal opens and you step into a new world

Maliq

Pushing back from the table, he grabs his laptop, exits the conference room, and sprints down the darkened hallway to his office. He closes the door and drops into his desk chair, sitting for a few moments gasping for air before getting up to open the window, unaware of the frozen scene on the street below. Like the caged animal he feels himself to be, Maliq paces from door to window and back again.

He'd come in early this morning to avoid them all, and was behind his closed door when they arrived. He'd been sure no one would seek him out, but for good measure had turned his status light to Busy and, but for Dhuhr salah, had spent the next several hours lost in solo work. But with the approaching deadline, there'd been no way to avoid the afternoon meeting.

And it had been every bit as bad as he'd imagined. Everyone falling silent as he walked into the room. Mandi reaching over to put her hand on his arm and, voice choked with emotion, saying how sorry she was, that she'd been upset ever since seeing it on the news this morning, and couldn't imagine what he must feel. And Maliq found that he just couldn't play the game today, that he had no interest in making everyone feel okay or pretending they were all in this together. He'd looked into Mandi's tear-filled eyes and said with a coldness that likely shocked them all, "That's right. You have no fucking idea how I feel." Thankfully, Sarah had stepped in then to pull everyone back to the agenda they'd set yesterday, and though the tension was so thick it'd take a machete to hack through it, they got to work.

Until the power went out and the white folk all froze in place. When his laptop crashed, Maliq raised his head to see them immobilized, eyes staring vacantly at their own blank screens. He'd spoken once, twice, and got no response. And so he'd gotten the hell out of there.

And now he doesn't know what to do with himself. He considers taking a walk, but he doesn't want to risk running into anyone. He picks up his cell to call Shanice, but finds he has no signal. So he paces some more...and can avoid it no longer. The fury hits full force. The killing of a Black boy, a 14-year-old beaten to death for no reason but the color of his skin. And the certainty that these kinds of things keep happening due to the tacit agreement of society at large makes Maliq want to do violence himself. Makes him want to strike out at something, anything. And so on his umpteenth circuit around the office, he kicks his desk chair with enough force to shoot it across the room, where it crashes into the wall and tips on its side, wheels spinning ineffectually in the air.

And at that very moment, the app on the phone that wouldn't let him talk to his wife sings out the call to Asr, the afternoon prayer. The Arabic words combined with the power and beauty of the muezzin's voice begin to calm Maliq's breath, slow his heartrate, and steady his mind.

When the adhan ends, he removes the small tub from beside his desk and carries it to the restroom. Maliq closes and locks the door, moves the chair close to the sink, and takes one of the towels from the tub and spreads it across the floor. He slips off his shoes and sits to remove his socks. He then stands, takes the kufi from his head, and places it on the chair. After quieting himself for a few moments longer, he speaks aloud "Bismilla".

Maliq then performs the ritual purification, especially important after his recent explosion of anger. He washes each hand three times, beginning with the right. He then rinses his mouth and his nose three times each. Using both hands, he scoops water over his face from forehead to beard as prescribed, then washes his lower arms. After rinsing his hands, Maliq shakes the excess water from them and runs fingers through his hair from front to back and cleanses each ear. He puts an inch or two of water in the washtub, places it on the towel and washes each foot three times. Though the process always settles him, it seems that the unusual stillness of this day has opened Maliq to a deeper cleansing. After intoning the ending prayer, his wudu is complete.

He pours the water from the tub into the basin and, placing the kufi over his damp hair, sits to dry his feet before putting on socks and shoes. Making sure the floor is dry and the sink clean, Maliq returns the chair to its place against the wall, leaves the restroom, and goes back to his office.

He wipes the tub dry, hangs the towels from hooks on the back of the door, and returns the pan to its place beside the desk. He then takes his prayer rug from the shelf, rolls it out facing Ka'bah, removes his shoes and steps onto the *sajjāda*. Only then, with assistance of the app to reinforce the proper pronunciation and bodily movements, does Maliq begin the prayer.

As he recites the salah silently with the imam, each word and movement resonates more fully in the strange stillness of this afternoon. Peace descends as the prayer comes to a close by taking refuge in Allah "from the punishments of the grave, from the torment of the Fire, from the trials and tribulations of life and death."

With Asr concluded, Maliq remains seated and revisits his reactions since learning of the boy's murder last night. There was certainly an element of shock, but what was many times stronger was the sheer *familiarity* of it all, something someone like Mandi was incapable of truly understanding. As the son of a Black man who was the son of Black men back through the generations, Maliq grew up knowing that *of course* Black boys and men get murdered by those in power, and often quite publicly so. And he knows too that it could just as easily have been him or his young son bludgeoned to death while others watched.

But while he recognizes anger as an understandable reaction, he knows he must continue to learn to manage it better if he's going to walk through the world with dignity and self-respect. That was one of the things that drew him to Islam 18 months ago, its insistence on dignity. He has worked hard since then, though he knows he has a long way to go. Still, the benefits reaped from his efforts thus far only deepen his resolve. As he practices the Prophet's teachings on the equality of women, his marriage improves, and their children are happier as he and Shanice bring the tenets of Islam into their parenting. And by heeding the Prophet's words that a powerful man is "the one who can control himself at the time of anger", Maliq knows he is becoming the husband and father he wants to be, the man he needs to be in order to live with himself.

And yet with the clarity of this odd afternoon, he knows that his anger will be better managed with an appropriate outlet. Another aspect of Islam that drew him was the commitment to justice that lies at its core. And as Muslims are encouraged to build a relationship with Allah by emulating His qualities, Maliq knows he is now ready to take another step forward, understands that he needs to.

He looks up at the tapestry hanging above his desk. A gift from his children, it lists the 99 Beautiful Names of Allah, each of which he is now able to read and understand in the Arabic in which it is inscribed. These are the names that call to him this afternoon: Ar-Rahim, The All Merciful; Al-Muhaymin, The Guardian; and Al-Mu'id, The Restorer. With yet another dead child added to the host of Black bodies that have piled up over the centuries, he recognizes it is time to join with others to extend the mercy of Allah to the marginalized, and to act in a very direct way as guardian and restorer of justice.

He will join the mosque's Social Justice task force. And he will also talk with Shanice about his need to find new employment. It's not that he no longer supports the mission of this organization. It is important work, good work, and they have built a solid and effective team. They work well together, each bringing strengths and a unique perspective that has led to a cohesive whole. And he respects and likes each one of them, though Mandi can drive him right up the wall sometimes. No, the change he needs to make has nothing to do with his coworkers. It's just that the events of the past 18 hours have made Maliq realize he wants to work more directly for his own community to expose and combat the effects of systemic racism. And he also knows that he never again wants to be the only African-American in a conference room on any of the days like this one to come.

Maliq stands and bows in the direction of Mecca. He steps into his shoes and rolls up his prayer rug, places it back on the shelf. He then grabs his jacket and walks quickly through his office door and down the hallway. He hurls himself down the stairs, filled with a sudden longing to get home to Shanice.

Sarah

    She feels nothing but relief when her teammates freeze in place and everything goes silent. Tension nearly always ties her in knots, but after 12 years in the Program, she can better tolerate it and has an easier time doing simply what's hers to do. Her sponsor calls it giving the Serenity Prayer its head. And today that means not being consumed by her discomfort or trying to fix things that aren't within her power to fix. And in the meeting that drew to such a strange close, it had meant embodying her role as team leader and steering the meeting back to the task at hand.

    Ignoring the elephant in the room did make her a little crazy, though. But she knew she needed to follow Maliq's lead and, if she'd read his signals right, he needed space. She couldn't fix the rest of it, but she could at least give him that much. And so she had.

    As Sarah gathers her things now, she's only dimly aware of the oddity of the afternoon. Leaving the conference room, she walks into her office and closes the door. She places her laptop on the desk, and sprawls across the old couch under the window, the one that hadn't fit in her new, tinier apartment. Closing her eyes, she breathes into her tight stomach muscles and those of her shoulders, encouraging them to relax. While that certainly calms her some, she realizes that what she really needs is fresh air and to be surrounded by green, growing things.

    As Sarah walks to her desk to get her purse from the drawer, her gaze lands on the image she'd photoshopped and framed for her office wall.

Against a background of vibrant color, she'd paraphrased the words of Parker Palmer: "Aim for effectiveness. Live in faithfulness." It was something she often needed to be reminded of in this work. As Palmer put it, if the only measure of success is whether or not you're being effective in bringing about needed change, you'll easily become discouraged and be tempted to give up. But if you instead use faithfulness as your measure—if you're being faithful to the gifts you've been given and the vision you hold—you'll be able to keep going through the inevitable setbacks and with spirit intact. Another expression of the Prayer that forms the backbone of her recovery.

Sarah slings her purse over her shoulder, grabs her jacket, and leaving the office, takes the stairs to street level. Once outside, she heads toward the Park, only vaguely registering the unmoving cars and pedestrians frozen in place. But what she *does* notice is the silence of this afternoon in a city that is never silent. To Sarah, it is a balm, one that soothes as it fills her. She loves her life here. The excitement, the art, the diversity, the sheer vibrating energy of the place is quite different from the white-bread suburb of her childhood. But still, a little quiet is welcomed, particularly on a day like today.

Sarah reaches the Park and as she walks briskly along its curving pathways, she replays the events of the past few hours. She'd sent a brief email to Maliq first thing this morning after seeing his closed door. "No words, Maliq," it said. "Just wanted you to know I'm thinking of you." And that really was all there was to say. She knew she couldn't soften his reactions or make him feel better about any of it. Yet that faithfulness thing had her needing to acknowledge his pain, even though she could only guess at what it must feel like. Because one thing Sarah knows is that Maliq wouldn't view this murder as an isolated event, separate from all the others or the rest his life experiences. And growing up as a Black man in America is something she knows nothing whatsoever about. Sure, she can call up a slew of statistics, but outward facts don't say a thing about lived experience or how those facts resonate inside. Yeah, Sarah knows something about what she doesn't know.

Unlike Mandi. It was Mandi's reaction that had been the hardest. She'd totally misread the signals Maliq had been sending off, all day and when he walked into the conference room. But as Sarah thinks about it now, it doesn't seem that Mandi misread those signals at all. She didn't bother to look for them in the first place. Of course her heart was in the right place. She didn't hold any ill will. But Mandi's behavior showed that her more immediate concern was her own distress. Maliq's experience got lost in the shuffle.

Except Maliq refused to allow that. Of course he'd only let out a small portion of what was probably going on inside, but he'd staked claim to his own ground. And Mandi likely felt unfairly treated. Attacked, despite the fact that no one had bashed a club into *her* head. Sarah knows she'll need to reach out to Mandi at some point, maybe tomorrow. She may not be able to help Maliq, but just like men need to school other men in exposing and turning around misogyny, she knows that it's her place as a white woman to help other white women see the subtler ways privilege shows itself. And right now that'd be helping Mandi see that her interaction, however well-intended, was more about her than Maliq. And assuming she was still smarting from his response, Mandi'd need to be reminded of who this man has shown himself to be over the years they've worked together.

Sarah finds a bench with a clear view of the colors that are beginning to appear in the west, and revisits what she hopes will be her very last relapse. Maliq had knocked on her office door to share the disappointing results of a call with a School Board member. She'd invited him in without thinking, saw the look on his face when he registered she was drunk. His eyes held hers and something she saw in them stopped the stream of excuses she had always at the ready. Not one iota of judgement or blame, but a calm acceptance instead and what felt like compassion. Like he'd known pain and could recognize it when he saw it.

"Hard day, huh?" he said. "How 'bout we get you home now?"

And though she'd protested, he'd helped her collect her things, walked with her through the reception area, casually telling Marti they were leaving early and would see her in the morning. He didn't make a big deal out of any of it, as he steered her into the elevator, walked her to the curb, hailed a cab. When she stumbled getting into the back seat, he'd simply climbed in with her, prompted her to give the cabbie her address, and sat quietly without small talk, lecture, or encouragement. She thought her mortification complete when she couldn't get the key into the lock of her apartment door and he'd had to do it for her.

But she'd been wrong. She'd only been circling around mortification before she saw through his eyes the mess that was her living room: an empty wine bottle on the couch and two others on the rug, newspapers and articles of clothing draped over furniture and strewn across the floor. But even that was nothing compared to the shame she dove into after coming on to him. He'd just put his hands on her shoulders and gently nudged her back a step, saying, "Now Sarah, we don't wanna be doing that, now do we? Of course we don't. You have someone you want me to call?"

She doesn't remember much after that until waking in the middle of the night to a pounding headache and a vile taste in her mouth. And the shame. Luckily it was a Saturday and she didn't have to go to the office. She'd met with her sponsor that same day, and had begun again the 90-meetings-in-90-days thing. That was 4 years ago now, and she hoped to never again take sobriety for granted.

Just as she'd like never to take for granted any of the many gifts she'd been given. She'd gone through the Steps several times now, but recently the 12th step has been nudging at her. *"Having had a spiritual awakening as the result of these steps, we tried to carry this message to alcoholics, and to practice these principles in all of our affairs."* Sarah certainly tries to practice AA's tenets, continuing to share at her regular Saturday meeting and having sponsored a few women along the way. And of course, she tries to bring AA's perspective into all her work and personal relationships. But she knows now it's time to take that Step into new territory.

Her Church has been batting around the idea of a study group, but the Pastor's holding out for someone to spearhead it. And while something inside her jumped at the possibility, Sarah hasn't volunteered yet. She'd researched some online resources, though, and hearing Krista Tippett's interview with Resmaa Menakem and Robin DiAngelo got her thinking that a great place for a group to begin would be reading DiAngelo's book *White Fragility: Why It's So Hard For White People To Talk About Racism*. And Sarah knows now that it's time. She is ready.

With the sunset colors gone now, Sarah heads home. As she walks toward the main road, she recognizes how right this decision feels. Heck, she might even invite Mandi, though she doubts she'd attend. The one time Sarah spoke about her Church's progressive stance, Mandi made clear that Christianity not only didn't have anything to offer her, but that she couldn't forgive its efforts to wipe out the spiritual practices of other cultures, particularly those of indigenous people. Sarah's only response after a rueful "Guilty as charged", was to point out that those actions were taken in opposition to Christ's teachings and were, in fact, blasphemous. Mandi had not been swayed.

And that was fine. Sarah would write up her proposal and talk with the Pastor. And she would reach out to Mandi about today's meeting and invite her to the study group. What happened after that was not hers to worry about. The Serenity Prayer in action.

Reaching the main road, Sarah strides toward home.

Mandi

Gracious Goddess, but she's relieved when everything comes to a halt. Looking up to see the others frozen is all the encouragement she needs to get the heck outta there, and the tears she'd been holding back erupt as soon as she closes her office door.

She'd only wanted to offer support, to let Maliq know she cared about him. But the way he'd looked at her! She knew he was upset—of course, he would be—but it was like he blamed *her* for what happened. Like it was *her* fault. And even though she knows she should cut him some slack, give him time to adjust to another reminder that racism is alive and well in this country, it still hurts. A lot. And it seems so unfair.

Mandi knows this kind of thing bothers her more than it would most people, but she's never been able to slough things off easily. She's always been just really sensitive. It's like she's wide open to the suffering of the world. It just wooshes in and fills her up. And when anger is aimed directly at her, like Maliq did this afternoon, that goes right in too, and it just crushes her.

But even with tears streaming down her cheeks, she gets it. This hadn't been the first time she'd gotten an angry reaction when she was only trying to be supportive. During their last year in college, her best friend, Lisa, had gotten so furious with her that she'd stormed out of the room they'd shared and hadn't returned for hours. But not before she said the words Mandi needed to hear and would never forget.

"Stop it! Stop it!" she'd screamed. "This is about *me*, not you! You make *everything* about you, and it's not fair! Every time I'm falling apart, *you* start crying, and I feel like I gotta stop and take care of you. This is *my* freak out," she said, slapping her chest, "*mine*, not yours."

They'd made it through that, and Mandi'd worked hard ever since to tone down her reactions. But the murder last night was just so awful that she hadn't been able to stop herself and it all just spewed out. She'll apologize to Maliq, but something in the energy of this strange afternoon makes Mandi realize that she needs to take care of herself first. Otherwise, she'll likely just do the same thing all over again. She's *that* full.

So she forages through her huge shoulder bag until she finds the small bottle of essential oil she takes with her everywhere, a blend of lavender, bergamot, rose, and ylang ylang mixed with avocado oil. The calming begins as soon as she unscrews the lid and the scent wafts out. She puts a dab at the pulse points on the inside of each wrist, behind her ears, and in the hollow just above her collarbone. With her breath deepening, Mandi swivels her chair toward the south-facing window. It doesn't offer much of a view, but the collection of prisms she's hung from silk ribbons of varying lengths and colors cheers her, even though it's too late in the day for the sun to splash rainbows across her walls. Plus, she likes the symbolism of looking through an opening onto a larger expanse. That's what she needs on a day like today.

But as she closes her eyes, she again sees the footage from the morning's news. There were at least three cell recordings online, with the best video taken from an apartment across the street with an unobstructed view. The evidence was right there, including identifiable shots of the two men who did this, as well as another who kept witnesses from intervening. She's glad it was recorded for the world to see, but the raw hate was devastating to watch, as was the complete absence of compassion for the pain of another human being. And seeing the life beaten out of that boy's body...well, there are no words big enough to hold that.

And Mandi's tears begin anew. This is what always happens when she tries to do something like this. The upset just rises up like a tsunami and takes her under. She's tempted to give up again, to get busy doing something else—or better yet, dig into that candy bar in her desk drawer—to avoid feeling this, but she knows that will only make it all worse. Not only will she carry the feelings around with her for the next few days, but she'll be mad at herself for again cheating on a diet. No, she needs to find another way to manage it all. The world's just so painful, people getting hurt and hurting others, but she needs to find a way to live with it, because it's not likely to stop any time soon.

She suddenly remembers a guided meditation they did in her Women's Group last year, the one in which she'd met her spirit guide, Bennú. She hadn't gotten a strong visual, just sensed that Bennú was female, powerful and very, very old. Mandi had intended to communicate with her in meditations since, but she'd given up after a few attempts. Well, that was because she'd stopped meditating altogether. Again. It's a big problem, this difficulty sticking with anything. Well, anything good anyway. She'd stuck with Brian about five years longer than she should have. True, she'd ended things with Jesse a whole lot sooner, but she never should have hooked up with him in the first place, so she's not sure that even counts.

But on this weird afternoon, Mandi realizes she's just not interested in beating up on herself or tearing into that chocolate bar. Instead, she opens her eyes and focuses on one prism, the multifaceted round one hanging from a purple ribbon in the center of the window. She notices the way the light hits its various facets as she consciously breathes in the soothing aroma of the oils. And she imagines Bennú standing right behind her, hands resting lightly on her shoulders.

Another wave of tears hits then, but it feels safer now. Survivable. As does closing her eyes and letting those images of Roscoe Little's murder play out again. She again hears the sound of the club hitting the boy's head. Again sees the other man kicking him in the back. Again, the frantic reaction of two people in the crowd gathering on the street corner. And Mandi knows that some variation of this scene—those with power abusing other living beings—is happening at this very moment in many places around the world.

And her heart breaks with the pain of it all. And the sheer waste of precious life force energy being turned toward hate, being used to create harm. Because if there's one thing Mandi does know, it's that this energy is more conducive to Love, more in sync with Love, comes from a Love that wants to be passed on as more Love.

And something about that thought in the stillness of this odd day grabs Mandi and won't let go. As the images and sounds of the murder begin to dissipate, Love calls even more strongly. Mandi feels it reaching for her, claiming her and sending a palpable inpouring of Love through body and soul. And as a little "Oh!" bursts from her lips, her eyes pop open as a new realization drops into her awareness fully formed.

"If I can be wide-open to pain, " she whispers, "then I can also be wide-open to Love." And with each breath, Mandi lets that Love fill her and grow stronger, until she feels it expanding beyond the confines of her body, spreading beyond any awareness she has of herself as separate from the rest of life. She is swept into a Love so huge that it encompasses everything, so enormous that it *is* everything.

And another insight flows into her now, as she recognizes that this Love is not only grand and huge and magical, but it is also the most commonplace of things. Her eyes close again, and she sees this Love playing throughout the world—parents raising children and doing their best to keep them safe and put food on the table, elderly women feeding birds and children playing with animals, people smiling at strangers and choosing kindness, communities coming together for the greater good.

And Mandi knows it is the ability to recognize the omnipresence of Love that will allow her to not collapse into despair or turn away from the harm some people perpetrate against others. Because she sees that all of the heartache in the world comes from an inability to feel what she now feels, and acting instead out of an emaciated and limited view of life.

"So I promise you, Bennú," Mandi whispers, "I will do my best to be wide-open to Love. I won't ignore the suffering in the world, and will continue to do what I can to make things better. But I don't want to give my precious energy to despair any longer. There's enough of that already in the world."

But she senses an uneasiness right there behind that vow, and she lets it find her.

"I'm afraid I'll not only fail—cuz of course I will, again and again—but I'm afraid I won't stick with it, that I'll give up, just like I give up on so many other good things."

And again, a limited view breaks open into one larger and far more accurate.

"That's just a story I've been telling myself, isn't it?" she says, laughing and wiping tears from her cheeks. "Of course I don't always follow through, don't always get it right. But the truth is, oftentimes I do. I finished college, spent 3 years in the job I had after graduation, and I've been in this one for 5 years. Lisa and I have been friends for over 10 years, and I've been going to my Women's Group for 3 years now, never missing a meeting unless I'm sick. And I've kept in contact with my family, even though they drive me crazy. I already *do* stick with things, and just want to, need to, do it more consistently."

And that tiny shift of perspective shifts so much. Mandi's glass has always been *at least* half full, and often far more full than half. Like it is right now.

"My cup runneth over, Bennú" Mandi whispers, opening her eyes again. "And maybe it always does, even when it doesn't feel that way. I'm not sure, but I do know that this Love is always there. So even when my cup *feels* totally empty, I'll try not to give into despair. Instead, I'll try to open to the right thing, Love, and let myself be filled up again."

And with that, Mandi stands and stretches before grabbing her bag and jacket, and heading for home.

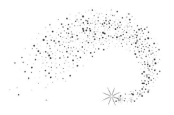

Jacob

He registers the silence. He'd only been half listening, as is usually the case in these meetings when he needs to be tuned in just enough to know when an IT question is asked, or to offer help when they're struggling with something he could streamline for them in a matter of minutes. That leaves plenty of brain space for other things. Today, his fingers have been working under the table on the latest MoYu cube, a present from Liam for his birthday, one he's lubed so the inevitable clicking is quieted as much as possible so as not to annoy his coworkers. He's just solved it again when the lights go out.

Raising his head, he sees the others immobilized, and then notices his laptop's black screen. He tries unsuccessfully to reboot and, walking around the room, finds the other computers in a similar state. Usually, Jacob would feel pressure to get things back up and running, but today he only takes out his cell, finds it dead as well, and decides to work on it all later. He slides his laptop under his arm, grabs his Mountain Dew and the MoYu, and returns to his office.

His is the only one without a window—they call it The Jacob Cave—so it's black as night. Not that it matters. Jacob doesn't need light to walk the path to his desk in the far corner. Sarah keeps on him about ordering more shelves to better organize what to her looks like a confused jumble, but Jacob knows exactly where everything is and has no problem now making his way around boxes of video equipment—tripods and shoulder mounts, lighting kits, mics and a variety of cables—or avoiding the one bookcase angled out from the wall that holds the rest of it—four cams, a collection of lenses, some old how-to manuals, and a portion of the videos they've made over the last few years.

Reaching his desk, he puts down his laptop, drops the cube in the righthand drawer, and is particularly attentive to where he places the Dew, figuring he could do without a repeat of the repair efforts caused by Mandi having dumped an entire venti latte on her laptop last year. Jacob's desk is downright tidy compared to the rest of the office, holding only the triple monitor, the DVD drive, two caddies for office supplies, and his only personal item: a picture of his sister and nephew.

He sits now alone in the dark silence of this afternoon, and realizes it's not much different than other afternoons in the past few months. Or mornings and evenings for that matter. Depression has been a companion for nearly two decades now. Last year his psychiatrist suggested ECT, but though Jacob knows it's been fine-tuned to great success since its early horror days, he's just not ready to take that step.

True, depression killed his father and paternal grandmother, as well as who knows how many others who died, either by overt acts or well-planned "accidents", before suicide was something that could even be discussed, let alone documented for future generations. Still, Jacob knows he'll never do it himself.

That choice was made for him several years ago. His sister didn't believe in keeping silent about things that mattered, so when Liam asked how his grandfather had died, she'd told him the truth. But even though it'd happened years before Liam's birth, Jacob was stunned at the depth of the boy's reaction and the ripples it brought into the years since. Jacob had been there for that first conversation, and saw Liam trying to make sense of such a thing.

"But why didn't you try to cheer him up?" the 8-year-old had asked. "You coulda told him that if he's not alive, he wouldn't be able to eat ice cream or get Christmas presents or do any of the fun stuff."

"Those are great ideas, Liam," Gina had answered, "but we couldn't tell him about those things because we didn't know he was gonna hurt himself. He didn't tell anyone."

"Not *anyone*?!!" Liam asked, eyes wide, voice incredulous. "How come?"

"Well, we didn't talk about things like that growing up," Gina answered. "We didn't talk the way you and I do."

"Well, that's just stupid!" Liam said. "It probably woulda made him feel better."

"Yes, it might have." Gina agreed.

That's when the doorbell rang. Liam had rushed to get the pizza from the delivery lady, and carefully carried it to the coffee table before expertly working the controls that streamed the next Harry Potter movie in the queue. Gina said Liam didn't have much more to say when she tucked him in that night, but Jacob knew his nephew well enough to know he'd be thinking about it all the same. But he wasn't ready for him to bring it up a few months later when it was just the two of them.

"So about Grampa," he said out of the blue. "Do you think I coulda talked him out of dying if he'd waited until I was born?"

"I don't know, Liam," Jacob answered. "Maybe."

"I bet I could've!" was all he'd said.

A few weeks later, Jacob was staying at the house to give Gina a weekend away. The little toughie had taken a fall off his bike and scraped his knee bad enough to make him cry. While they were bandaging him up on the back porch, Liam asked, again without warning, "How come he didn't love me enough to wait until he met me?"

Though Jacob felt way out of his league—why the heck didn't the kid ask his mother these things?!!—he did the best he could.

"You're talking about Grampa, right?" After the boy nodded, Jacob continued. "It's not that he didn't love you, Liam. He didn't even know you were going to be born, though I sure wish he'd waited for you. But there's this weird thing about the kind of sadness Grampa had. It makes it hard to believe anything good will ever happen again, that you'll ever feel better, no matter what you do and no matter what anyone says. So it makes you want to just give up."

"Do you think I'll ever get so sad *I'll* wanna give up?"

"I sure hope not. But if you do get that sad, you have to promise you'll talk to me or your mom or someone else, okay? Because I'd miss you something awful if you weren't here."

"I promise," Liam said solemnly, those big brown eyes looking directly into Jacob's. "And you have to promise that you won't leave me either, cuz I'd miss you something awful, too."

And even though Jacob's pause couldn't have lasted more than a few seconds, it felt as though the significance of those moments couldn't possibly be held within such a short period of time. He knew even then that this was one of those before and after moments, a line that divides "I might" from "I never will."

"I promise," Jacob replied. And though those words were spoken softly, they seemed to ring with a formality and a gravity that felt like a promise to the God he no longer believed in, but needed to obey anyway. Maybe this is what God was to him now, the trusting eyes of a young boy, full of love, a boy whose life would be irrevocably altered if Jacob went back on his promise. And he knew too that this trusting little boy would always live inside the man Liam would become, so he couldn't lie to himself that waiting until Liam was grown would make it okay, because he knew it never would.

That was 6 years ago now, and Jacob has learned to manage things better since then. His psychiatrist just started him on a new med combo, which might be starting to help. He meets regularly with his therapist, increasing the appointments when things worsen, spacing them out when his depression clears for a bit which, thankfully, it sometimes does. While he's not sure exactly why therapy works, he suspects it has to do with simply being witnessed. Sure, they've worked to find things that soften the bad times—aerobic exercise, intervening when the critical self-talk begins, involving himself with others, like the work they do here with teens at risk. But it seems that what helps most is having someone he can speak the truth to, without worrying she's going to freak out. That and remembering the promise he made to his nephew.

So he keeps the picture of Liam and Gina on his desk here, and has placed one in every room of his apartment. And he looks at them whenever he needs a reminder of what matters, as well as his promise to stay alive. But on this strange day, Jacob finds that promise growing wings. While Gina was already included in it, his pledge expands now to hold his coworkers and all the kids they've interviewed as he held the camera. If he wants those boys and girls to stay alive, with all the challenges they've experienced already and the others that will come to them in the future, it's only fair for him to do the same.

His thoughts double back to the tension in the meeting this afternoon. He sees again Maliq's face as he walks into the room and those of his other coworkers, but those images are joined now by the school photo of Roscoe Little shown on the news last night. And Jacob's original vow to stay alive takes on a deeper meaning. If what has helped him is being witnessed, perhaps he ought to consciously act as witness for others, no matter their particular brand of pain.

And now the film he sees in the utter darkness of his office streams through frame after frame of those in pain, people being beaten or raped, those running for cover as bombs drop from the sky, those starving or diseased. The pain of the frightened, the lonely, the despairing, and those who redirect their pain into a hate that amplifies the agony of the world.

Jacob begins to breathe in the pain of them all, and he breathes out compassion. Breathes pain in, and breathes out comfort. Pain coming in, and on the outbreath he sends a steady awareness of the kinship between them. "You are not alone," he whispers to them in his head. "I see you. I feel you. I am here, and we are linked."

Even though his pain is not theirs, pain is pain is pain, and he will not turn away. And he will not abandon them by exiting himself. While his promise might always wear Liam's 8-year-old face, he knows now this is about more than just Liam. He might not be able to make any huge change in the condition of the world, but he can witness. And he can honor. And he can stay.

Another Pause

You return to your body and relish again the step-by-step process that brings you back fully to this nurturing space after your time within the lives of others. You see flames. Hear gentle rain. Feel cushion. Breathe air woven through with smells of woodsmoke and a lovely scent you cannot name. And when you are ready, you practice the good soul-care you have learned, welcoming your reactions and bathing each in your loving attention. Soon you recognize something new reaching for you, and you wait until words rise up once more.

"It is so very instructive to see the shift that happens when people connect to something true. No, that's not quite right," you say, pausing for a few moments to grasp the distinction. "It is not something I *see*, and the word instructive doesn't fully capture my meaning. I *felt* the shift inside me as it occurred inside each of these four people. It is true that I experienced the horror as the videos of Roscoe's murder played out again in Mandi's mind, but I also experienced her joy as she opened herself to the omnipresence of Love, and Maliq's deep resolve as the path before him became clear. And in my odd role as companion-spectator, I found myself steadier upon my return to you here."

You pause for several heartbeats until something new appears.

"Your enchantment allows space, a time out of time, for these individuals to drop into that place of knowingness that is always and ever there. And in accompanying so many of them through that process, I am allowed to visit that place myself, and to do so again and again. I don't think I'll ever again be able to doubt its existence or its continual availability. I *know* it is there now, not just sometimes, but always."

You pause, dropping down into that flow again. After many slow breaths, another thought finds expression.

"And with what has unfolded in your flames this time, I realize again the truth of the Dalai Lama's words that good religion gives good heart. The spirituality of these four people varied considerably in the specifics, but felt so very similar in their essence. And Jacob, though he does not see himself as religious at all, was a regular little bodhisattva," you say with a smile. "It was a profound gift he offered."

"Yes," Xiuying replies. "Just as your trust in another's ability to heal funds that ability, feeling kinship funds an awareness that connection exists, even when it cannot be objectively seen. Jacob found his way into a practice that some of your kind have called tonglen, while others might see it as a form of loving-kindness meditation or agape love. Many, like Jacob, come to this type of practice on their own and with no need to label it at all. Did not one of your bards speak of a rose smelling lovely no matter its name? Love is lovely, no matter the stamp your mind places upon it."

"So it seems that Rumi was right again," you say with another smile. "There are many ways to kneel and kiss the ground, a multitude of pathways to Love."

You let all of this percolate as you drop down into that stream and float there for several heartbeats. You sense something new wanting to rise up, something about the pain of the world. But you do not feel ready to go there just yet. You check in, and find that it is fine to wait a bit longer to give it voice.

"It is not only fine," Xiuying replies, though you did not speak. "It is beautiful to wait when waiting feels right. Your culture reveres pressing on, does it not?" You laugh and nod, and she continues. "Balance is a precious thing. The natural world models it for you in the dance of day and night, in the spin of the seasons, in the harmonious relationship between all things. Perhaps following its lead would be wise."

"Oh, I know it is wise," you say, with another laugh, "but it's not always easy to do. It's a challenge even to recognize when I'm *not* doing it. I suppose it's more evidence that I'm a work in progress. Yep, the journey of evolving consciousness makes itself known once again!"

Xiuying's laugh is like the tingling of the chimes outside the door. Silence returns, but for the boisterous dance of flames. Soon, though, all begins to fade as you are pulled again into the deeper silence of that enveloping and utterly protective darkness. You rest here until you step once more into your own world.

Ambling Anew...

The sweet darkness is quite familiar to you now. Indeed you have chosen to come here a time or two on your own without completing the journey to your dear guides' wonder-filled abode. Now, though, you rest for brief moments only before continuing on. Soon you are again at the low table, Xiuying in a sea green tunic sitting motionless across from you. After a few heartbeats, she gestures to the items laid out for a traditional Chinese tea: a small gaiwan elegantly trimmed with a design of pale green leaves, two tiny matching cups, a cannister, and two pitchers, one of steaming water, the other empty.

"I thought we would start this visit with tea," she says. The serenity that has endeared Xiuying to you is apparent in each of her movements now: as she pours hot water into the gaiwan, lets it warm for a few seconds before transferring the liquid into each cup, and emptying the spent water into the waiting pitcher; as she sprinkles tea from the cannister into the gaiwan, covers it for a few moments, removes the lid to inhale the aroma of the leaves, and invites you to do the same; as she pours steaming water again into the pot, covers the gaiwan briefly before draining it into the cups and emptying them in turn into the waiting pitcher; and as she adds additional hot water, and replaces the lid, letting the tea leaves steep.

"Fresh spring water has purified and warmed both gaiwan and cups," Xiuying explains in her soft voice. "The tea has been washed and given time to expand, awakening its subtle aromas. And the water is now being infused with a flavor I hope you will find pleasing. These same leaves will then be steeped several times more to bring us additional pleasure."

Xiuying speaks truly, and as the process silently unfolds, you feel you are drinking tea for the very first time. Savoring the range of delicate flavors that awaken your tongue, you know the difference between a beverage consumed in this reverential manner, and one swallowed hurriedly or with attention elsewhere. When the ceremony is complete, the same care is given to wiping the items clean and returning them to a lidded bamboo basket. Xiuying then returns to stillness.

"You mentioned earlier my culture's tendency to press on," you speak at last. "Well, I have just experienced the opposite of pressing on. And that reminds me of the balance we discussed on my last visit. I did not speak directly of Roscoe Little's murder. It was not because I was unaffected. Actually, it was because I was so affected that it seemed better to wait. I see now that I was balancing my need to express with my need to sit with what I had seen. I am ready now to speak."

The Old One waits unmovingly as you pause for several breaths.

"Joined with Mandi as she did her own brand of good self-care, I too experienced a range of emotions as the video of Roscoe's death played out and as she opened to Love. But I was left with an existential quandary. It has to do with the pain of the world. I'm not talking about the inescapable pain, like the fact that death and loss are woven into the substance of our lives. I accept that as just part of this EarthWalk. It is the *escapable* kind of pain I'm struggling with, the kind that doesn't need to be. The way we treat one another, the devastation we inflict on other life forms and the Earth itself. Can you help me make sense of that?"

"I am not sure," Xiuying replies, gentle eyes holding yours, "but I will try. First, please tell me more."

"Well," you respond, "children being abused and murdered, bombs dropping, rape and pillage occurring across the planet, precious species extinct or heading in that direction. And then there are the systems that support these things, institutional structures that allow horrors to continue unabated, either through direct practices or by turning a blind eye. I know, of course, that there will be times when fear turns into rage or our unconscious impulses are acted out on others. But there seems to be a *tolerance* for the rest of it, an acceptance of cruelty and oppression that allows them to continue when much could be done to turn them around. The adage, "Where there's a will, there's a way," says it well. And when there is no sustained will, these things not only continue unabated, but might even increase as they appear condoned."

Logs shift in the grate, and your question presents itself.

"Does evil exist? And are some people truly bad?"

Xiuying looks at you with her sweet smile and eyes filled with compassion, but she does not speak.

"Okay," you say, with a smile of your own, "not a big fan of this soft incursions only rule!" Silence returns as you consider your own question.

"I suppose my answer goes back to the underground stream metaphor. If it is true that there is an essential *goodness* existing in the cosmos, nothing that rises out of that can be truly and irredeemably evil, and that would include individual humans. And yet, Icaro and I discussed how our actions can certainly *appear* evil, offering base impulses safe passage out into the world and amplifying those qualities in others."

You fall silent again. After a time, Xiuying speaks.

"In your discussions with Icaro, I believe you referred to the Yin-Yang world in which humans live. I wonder how this ancient concept might assist as you grapple with the concept of evil."

Many heartbeats pass as you consider the question.

"The world is divided into active and receptive principles," you say at last. "The Yang of action is essential to express the needs and wishes of the individual, to create new structures in the world, and to alter what needs altering. And Yin receptivity is vital to accept and appreciate what is, to respect the rights of others and the collective itself, and to allow movement of a different sort, an internal rather than an outward one. And yet what seems crucial is that these two forces be held in balance, a dynamic balance that allows them to adjust to the changing particulars of any situation while maintaining a harmony between them."

"Yes," Xiuying agrees when you fall silent once again. "And what would be the result should one of these forces go unchecked, unbalanced by the other for an extended period of time?"

"Well, if Yin was on its own, not a lot would get done," you laugh. "Yin's receptivity would become passivity. We'd be *too* internal without the energizing force of Yang. And if Yang were given free rein, unchecked by Yin, we would..." you pause as insight arrives, "have what we see in the world today. Violence and degradation can only occur when the active principle is not infused with compassion for others, when the desires of the individual are not harmonized by the needs of the whole. So the evil I see is what unopposed Yang looks like. Yang becomes too outward without needed reflection, forceful without sufficient tenderness, self-serving without recognizing the impact of its actions on other individuals and the collective."

After a time, Xiuying adds, "And that is why many of your kind are now recognizing it is time to strengthen the principle of Yin. Some refer to this as the return of the Divine Feminine."

"Yes," you nod. "I find it immensely helpful to conceptualize it in this way. We must respond to evil, and yet this view reminds me that battling an unbalanced Yang with a similar type of imbalance—with anger or aggression—will ultimately be counterproductive. As history has shown time and again, violence begets more violence. So we need to commit to infusing any action we take with the qualities of Yin. But how do we respond best to deaths like Roscoe Little's? How do we address in a wholesome way the various -isms out there and the institutions that support them? How do we bring it all back into harmony?"

"That, indeed, is the challenge of your time," Xiuying acknowledges, "and we cannot specify the details of your way forward any more than has already been shared with you."

And you hear again Zosia's voice as you looked into the hearth that first time: "Prophets and teachers had been sent, myths generated and passed down, and ream upon ream of sacred writings amassed. The people were indeed moved by the messages of the Wise Ones, but often forgot or never let those words root deeply into the soil of their being. And purest wisdom not deeply anchored and well-tended, swirls away with the first rising wind."

"So," you say, after a pause of many heartbeats, "we need to let those teachings root now, tend them consistently, and find ways to apply them in these lived lives of ours."

And with that, your words are spent, and you drop into the tranquility that radiates from Xiuying, ripple upon ripple. And at the perfect time, you find yourself again facing the flames as they rollick and shimmy until a new set of lives unfold within them and you are drawn in.

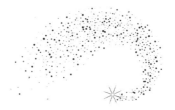

Henry

He's stretched out on the floor when the silence comes. Geography book opened to the full-color maps in the back, he's using a ruler to measure the distance between the places listed on Mr. Amberlan's latest worksheet. He loves geography, and has a collection of maps from all over. Sure, he knows he can find stuff online, but when he's got an actual map spread out on the floor, he can be like Raven soaring above, seeing it all. Topo maps are the best. The squiggly lines become canyons and mesas, rivers and mountain peaks, and he can easily fill in the grasslands, stands of piñon and juniper, elk trails and all the rest.

The sudden quiet makes Henry look up from his book. He has a clear view into the kitchen and can see his mother standing at the counter. She is singing no longer, and her hand is stilled in the act of grating cheese. Másání sits in her chair by the window, eyes closed and probably sleeping, since she says the dialysis is an *ani'hii*, a thief who runs off with her energy.

But this silence is much bigger than a quiet house. Henry walks to the window and sees the street crowded with cars as usual, but they're stopped in place now, engines hushed. The people on the sidewalk are like living sculptures, not walking or talking or anything. He doesn't get it, but he's not worried. As long as he's near Másání and his mom, he knows things are okay. Plus, he can sense that whatever has stopped time is good, very good. Though he hungers to understand things, Henry is also content with not knowing. He moves willingly into this strange and sweet stillness and lets it hold him.

Henry tucks the blanket around Másání's legs before sitting at her feet, his favorite spot in the whole world. He rests his back against the chair, and gently leans in until he's snug against her legs. Though he's careful not to wake her, he knows that if he did, she would just smile and place a hand on top of his head. She might even tell one of the old stories, the ones he never tires of hearing.

But in the quiet of this afternoon, she sleeps on. The sun is dropping into the west, and its rays slant across Henry's legs and spill onto the rug. He watches as they slowly creep across the room, lighting up his geography book, climbing up the edge of the couch. The twitter of birds that has been a background chorus for this movement of light gives way now to one bird's voice. Henry recognizes its song and knows the junco has landed on the bush beneath the window.

And he remembers the nest he found last summer. It was in a crevice in the tumble of sandstone rocks near Másání's *hooghan*. When he was much younger, an uncle had helped him make his slow and careful way to the top of the rocks, and he'd run home laughing and excitedly announced that he'd climbed a mountain. Henry had been planning to climb it again on this day, but he'd caught a flutter of movement off to the left and had slowly backed away. He'd then walked up the hillside to a place where he could observe without worrying the birds. And he'd returned each day to watch as the female sat and the male sang, as both fed their babies when they hatched, and as the young juncos learned to fly.

Thinking of those birds now and the sandstone rocks that were their first home, Henry longs for his own first home. He's happy enough in the city, and school's all right. He likes to learn and since he's respectful and does his work, the teachers treat him okay. But he always feels a bit odd in the cafeteria and on the bus. It's not that he gets picked on. It's more like he just doesn't fit. But it's different back home. Whether he's running with his cousins, learning from the uncles, or helping Másání, he knows he belongs. *That* is the place where his laugh bursts free. *That* is his home.

And each time he returns there, after they unpack the car and put things away, he walks out to the place near the firepit where he can see Turquoise Mountain, Tsoodził in the language of his people. And sometimes, Másání walks up beside him and tells again the story of his naming.

"When you were born, you didn't make a sound, though your eyes were open wide and you saw everything. After you and your *shimá* were cleaned up and she had drifted into sleep, I wrapped you in two blankets against the chill of the night, and brought you here so the land would know you. And I raised you up like this," the mother of his grandmother says, an imaginary newborn held in arms reaching high, "and I showed you to Sky and to Ooljéé́', and to the many Stars. And then I held you facing out like this, so you could see," she says, bringing her arms down to hold the *a'wéé'* he had been upright against her chest.

Másání turns then in a slow circle, the boychild Henry moving with them. "We greeted and honored *ha'a'aah*, the east...We greeted and honored *shádi'ááh*, the south...We greeted and honored *e'e'aah*, the west...and when we turned toward *náhookos*, the north, a cloud suddenly moved aside, and Ooljéé', the Moon, shown brightly on Tsoodził. And it was then that you made a sound, your very first sound. And I knew, though in truth the dreams had already told me. But still I did not say a word to anyone."

At this point in her story, Másání usually reaches out to take Henry's hand. "I brought you here the next day, and in all the days and nights to follow. I told you the stories of the Diyin Dine'é. I introduced you to the birds and the animals, the rain and the snow. The wind knew you, too. And each time we came, we turned the circle and we honored and greeted the directions, *ha'a'aah*, *shádi'ááh*, *e'e'aah* and *náhookos*."

"You were not yet three months old when it happened. As we turned toward Tsoodził that night, you laughed. And it was not a small laugh either. You laughed big." At this point in the story, standing next to Másání and facing Tsoodził, Henry often laughs again, while Másání smiles in her quiet way before continuing.

"You know that when an *a'wéé'* laughs, it is a sign that the child is ready to fully join its earthly family. This is to be celebrated. Since you were with me when you laughed, the laughing party, the *A'wee Chi'deedloh*, was held here. But I made sure that everyone knew that you had not laughed for me. Your first laugh was for Tsoodził. But even after the *hataalii* heard your true name, for us you have always been Ashkii Anádlohí, our Little Laughing Boy."

The last time Másání told this story, two months ago when the ground had been covered with snow, she'd finished by saying, "But you will be a man soon, and you will be our Little Ashkii Anádlohí no longer. Then you will be Hastiin Anádlohí."

Henry turned into her arms then, eyes suddenly wet. "But I don't ever want to stop being your Little Ashkii Anádlohí," he thought. And though he hadn't said the words aloud, Másání heard them anyway. She held him close and said, "It is the way of things. Ooljéé' does not remain a crescent forever. She grows into her fullness, just as you, Little Ashkii, will grow into yours. But in some way you will always be my Little Ashkii Anádlohí." And that made Henry smile.

As he smiles now in the enchanted quiet of this late afternoon and in the city where he lives much of the year, Henry stands and looks to the colors lighting the western sky. The junco has quieted now and all is still. Though not visible from the window, Henry knows Tsoodził is there. And this knowing strengthens him, brings him peace. Henry is a patient boy, content to wait for his return home, content to wait for what will unfold, content with not knowing what that will be.

And it is as if he is an *a'wee* again, held in Másání's arms. Looking toward Tsoodził now, joy rises up, and again Henry laughs. And his laugh is big.

Selva

She sings on, pleased by the silencing of traffic noise. When the cheese is grated, she returns the block to the fridge, intending to remove the container of cooked pork and the anaheims for roasting. When she looks into the living room, though, and sees both grandmother and son stilled, she senses that dinner will be delayed tonight and leaves them on the shelf. She lifts the lid from the cooler by the back door to see that Másání has mixed the dough for the *náneeskaadi*. As relieved as she is that her grandmother had enough energy for that task, she's hoping she won't insist on cooking on the grill, since the day has grown cold again. Of course, tortillas and peppers taste better that way, but sometimes a skillet and a stovetop are good enough.

Walking in to join her family, she sits on the couch and props up her feet. It's been a hard day. The hospital is always bustling, but a grizzly four-car pileup on the highway added to the pressure today. And as usual Dr. Gordon took his stress out on anyone in the vicinity. Today that had mostly been her. Selva never speaks back to him, as she's seen the others do. She's been taught that it's rude to draw attention to the bad behavior of another. Plus, she respects his skill. He's a gifted surgeon and she has learned much during the two years they've worked together. Still, she's glad he's taken the position at Keck and will be leaving at the end of the month.

In the odd hush of this afternoon, though, Selva knows this is not the only change on its way. Her gaze comes to rest on Másání asleep in her chair, face turned toward the window. It is the face she has loved since before she could remember, and while she knows it must have been altered by the years, she cannot see the change. It is deeply lined, but it has always been deeply lined. Her hair has grown thin of late, but it is the same color, a startling white contrasting with coppery skin further darkened by years of sun. It is a face that has always meant comfort for Selva. Másání has always been the steady force in her life.

As she was when Keith moved out, just before Selva was to begin an NP program specializing in surgical science. She hadn't wanted to give that up, nor had her grandmother expected her to, though she did suggest that Henry come home to live with her. Thankfully she hadn't insisted, because Selva wouldn't have been able to refuse. And so Másání had once again done what was needed and made the move herself. And Selva knows there is joy in tending her great-grandson and schooling him in the old ways, delight in the special bond between them that has only grown stronger with the years. They travel back to the Rez as often as possible, and Henry spends all his school holidays with family there, but Selva knows that the days in the city are a hardship for her grandmother. She is simply not made for city life.

Selva knows the effect of stress on chronic health conditions, and fears that the move has shortened Másání's life. But as her grandmother says when Selva brings it up, "My life has been longer than most, Little Shundeen, and it will end when it ends no matter where I live." And though she talks of it seldom, once she added, "I remember the pain of leaving my own mother when I was young and I would not want that for Henry."

Selva's gaze moves then to Henry, her little laughing boy whose laugh is often muted these days. He's lying on his stomach, head bowed over ruler and book, legs bent at the knees and frozen in mid-swing. Like Másání, his true life is back home. Selva doesn't know what the future holds for him, but she does know her son is made for wide-open spaces and is sure he has a role to play in that world.

She has spoken of it often with Másání and the uncles. They have all seen how the cousins defer to him, even some of the older ones. But Selva knows this reaches wider than kin. His teachers have spoken of it for years. At the last conference, one said. "Your son is quiet and doesn't speak often, but when he does, the other students listen." And another wrote on the online portal, "Henry is respected by his peers, and they often come to him as a mediator."

As Selva sits in the calming stillness of this late afternoon, she considers the vague uneasiness she has felt these last few months. She'd assumed it was from the tension at work, but that edginess begins to speak truly to her now. Yes, work is stressful and people like Dr. Gordon only add to it. But she knows in this moment that this is not what wakes her in the night or clenches the muscles of her shoulders. It is time to return. It is time to return Másání to her *hooghan*, her place home, so she can live the days remaining to her there. It is time to return Ashkii Anádlohí to his cousins and his uncles, to the place where his heart resides and his laugh rings out, to the place where he can move into his own future.

And Selva recognizes something else. It is time for her, too, time to move away from the lights and the noise of the city. She'd stayed after her degree and certification were complete to increase her knowledge and skill. And though she knows there is always more to absorb, she recognizes that she has learned enough, and what she needs to learn now can be found anywhere. She has periodically checked for openings with the IHS, but it is now time to do more. It is time to apply. And she wonders why she has waited so long.

Yes, change is coming, and it is time to greet it. She stands and bends down to stroke her son's hair, "Little Ashkii Anádlohí," she whispers, "we're going home." She looks at the beloved face of her grandmother. "*Shimá* of my *shimá*, we're going home," she whispers, bending to kiss her head. Selva walks then to the window and gazes out toward the west. "We're going home," she whispers. "We're going home."

Másání

Opening her eyes to the sunlight, she wonders what has called her back. She turns to see Little Ashkii Anádlohí doing his homework on the floor. She looks into the kitchen, and sees Shundeen is home and preparing dinner. And though she gives little thought as to why they are both stilled and it is suddenly so quiet, she settles down into the goodness as her thoughts return to the dream.

They have been coming more frequently, these dreams of the ancestors. In this one, her *shimá yázhí*, the sister of her mother, was teaching her to grind corn. It was a true dream, unfolding just as it had happened in the long-ago time of her childhood.

"We crack the kernels like this," Shimá Yázhí says as she works, "pressing them hard between the grinder and the stone. The grinder is the sky and the stone the earth, for Father Sky and Mother Earth are both needed for the corn flour we eat. They are both *in* the corn flour we eat. Remember this always, Little Ahéénibaa'."

As she continues grinding, Shimá Yázhí tells the story in the dream just as she had told it under the weak winter sun in waking life many years ago.

"Fox and lizard were walking down the road together," she begins, "and they were speaking again of the silly antics of small duck who, as you know, was always up to something. This time was no exception."

"You will *not* believe what he's done now," lizard said.

"Oh, I think I will believe whatever you say," fox replied, chuckling already though the tale had not yet been told. "You always speak truth, and we both know small duck is a wacky duck for sure. What has he done this time?"

"Well," lizard said, "he has decided to pretend he is not a duck at all. First, he found a puddle to wet his feathers in. And then he rolled in the dirt to make them tan."

"And why did he do that?" fox asked, bushy tail quivering with curiosity. "What was he up to?"

"I'm getting to that," lizard said. "Next, he walked to the field near the river and began digging in the clay with his big webbed feet. Soil was flying everywhere!"

"Oh, no!" laughed fox. "Don't tell me he..."

"Well, I won't tell you if you keep butting in," lizard interrupted, though she was laughing herself. "As I'm sure you know, webbed feet are no good for moving dirt on dry land, so he could not dig a true burrow. But soon, he turned around, put his bottom down into the hole so only his head was showing, and began to make the squeaks and chirps of a prairie dog. Or tried to. They came out sounding like quacks and nothing more!"

"Hahahaha!" fox said, doing a few quick rolls in the grass as he laughed. "And I bet he didn't look at all like a prairie dog either!"

"You got that right!" lizard agreed. "He looked like a muddy duck sitting in a hole! But he didn't care. He was having fun!"

When their giggles subsided, lizard continued. "And later that day, he had another kooky idea. His feathers were still brown from his morning as a prairie dog, and he wanted to keep that color for this new scheme. But he needed other colors too, so he took ash from a cookfire and painted his belly and rump white. And then he found some black dirt and very carefully added dark markings to his face."

"Now how did he do that?" fox asked, suddenly skeptical. "His legs are quite short and his big floppy feet could never have managed all this."

"You have a good point," lizard acknowledged, "and I have no answer for you. I tell this to you as warbler told it to me. Perhaps wee mouse or frisky ferret assisted, I am not sure. But may I continue?"

"Oh, yes," fox encouraged, "please do!"

"Well, to make the look complete, small duck needed something more. He needed sticks."

"Sticks?" asked a perplexed fox.

"I tell you true," nodded lizard. "He searched until he found two sticks of just the right size and shape. And I don't know how he attached them to his head—again, perhaps he had help—but when he was done, a stick rose up from each side of his head, and he began then to lift his legs all delicate-like. And you're never going to guess what he was then."

"It is true," fox replied. "I cannot guess."

"A pronghorn!" howled lizard.

"A pronghorn?!!" fox roared, rolling again across the grass. "A short, plump, two-footed, feathered pronghorn with sticks glued to his head!"

"Yes," laughed lizard, trying a little roll of her own. "And you know small duck. He was enjoying every minute of it!"

It was at this point that the strange but benevolent silence had awakened Másání from her dream. But as she sits in her chair in the city, she remembers the rest of small duck's shenanigans, just as she remembered them during her years spent away from everything she knew, everything she loved, everything that gave her life meaning.

For it was soon after the day she ground corn with Shimá Yázhí that the men came and forced Ahéénibaa' and her brother onto a bus with other Navajo children. After several long hours of travel, her first in a loud and smelly vehicle, they arrived at a building far larger than any she'd seen before. The children were stripped in the yard and their hair cut before they were washed roughly with a harsh soap and sprayed down with hoses. Their clothing was burned and they were made to wear uniforms of a rough material that itched and chafed against the skin. Only then were they taken inside to what was called the dining hall, and given unrecognizable food with a taste that was bitter on the tongue.

As the weeks and months unfolded, Ahéénibaa' became accustomed to the pattern of the days, but never to their meaning. The children were punished harshly when they spoke their own language or when they violated any of the many incomprehensible rules of the place. Sitting in hard desks laid out in hard rows, they had formal schooling at mid-morning. The laundry or kitchen, though, were where Ahéénibaa' and the other girls spent most of their time, doing what was needed to keep a place as large and crowded as this running. Such work also readied them for being hired out to serve in the homes of white families, which began for Ahéénibaa' in her second summer there.

At times Másání has wondered how she'd survived it. But she always knew. She was Ahéénibaa', which roughly translates into English as She

Who Fights in a Circle. She was a warrior, but she'd learned early on that she could not fight the matrons directly. They were too large and their control absolute. After her first attempts met with beatings or bewildering punishments, such as kneeling for hours with arms held high, Ahéénibaa' learned to fight back carefully. Sideways. In a circular fashion. She was a warrior who would not give up or give in. And she was a warrior who would not forget.

And so she remembered. As she went about her tasks, Ahéénibaa' spoke silently of her family and of the hills, of the scent of piñon and juniper, and of food that held Father Sky and Mother Earth within it. And in the dark of night, she huddled with the other girls whispering aloud the language of their birth, sharing the stories each had been told. Those of small duck were a favorite, and though they were not quite as funny when told in this place, the girls loved him all the same. Small duck never once forgot he was really a duck, and that gave them the courage to never forget as well. They needed only to pretend.

And so Ahéénibaa' did. When she sat at her desk and parroted back the answers the teachers expected, she pretended. When she appeared docile and attentive and said, "Yes, ma'am," when they called her Judith, she pretended. And when her mouth spoke the words of the Christian prayers in the dark, solemn and stale-smelling chapel, she pretended. As she hung out the laundry, though, she kissed Mother Earth with her feet through the tight skin of the shoes she was made to wear, and she felt Father Sky stretching above. And as she sat in the crowded dining hall, she sought the eyes of her brother and, holding his gaze, thought hard, "I remember you. You are Hashké Dilwo'ii. We will not, either of us, forget."

The sun is setting when Másání's mind returns from those long-ago days. The pain of that time is no longer sharp, though it has woven its way through her, giving her both great endurance and a bone-deep weariness. The weariness has increased of late, though in the silence of this strange afternoon, that truth opens onto another.

Yes, she is old, and age and dialysis are *ani'hii* who steal her energy. But the listlessness that comes with this fatigue feels familiar, feels like what she felt when she was a child so far from home. She recognizes within herself now a similar longing for return. And she knows she can stay in the city no longer. It is time to go home.

After growing into her fullness, Ooljéé' begins to wane, and Másání knows she is no different. Surely Moon not only accepts this process, but looks forward to disappearing from the sky altogether as she again visits with her Sun. Másání longs for that same release, and the ancestors are appearing in her dreams to tell her it won't be long now. It is nearly time for her to travel the yellow corn pollen path, and she needs to prepare. And to prepare, she needs the hills and the sky and the quiet of her *hooghan*.

Másání looks to the window and feels a quiet joy at the thought that her days in the city are few. But turning toward Ashkii Anádlohí, she feels sadness as well. She will not live to see him become a man. Yet she knows that while she can never tell him all the stories, she has told him enough. And perhaps when her voice wearies further, he will give them back to her again.

Because in the stillness of this afternoon, she knows she will take him with her. He has learned what he needed to learn from the city, but this is not his place any more than it is hers. His spirit needs the large spaces of home, undivided by fences or cluttered with powerlines, pavement and noise. Ashkii Anádlohí needs the freedom to roam, and a steadier access to the uncles who are teaching him what it means to be a man. And the *hataalii* need to be near, so they can determine if her dreams about his future are true.

Her eyes move now to Shundeen at the kitchen counter. She is proud of what her granddaughter has accomplished. She has seen the respect with which she is treated when Shundeen accompanies her to dialysis and other medical appointments. But city life is difficult. She was named Shundeen, for she was the Sunshine Girl from the very beginning. But that light has grown dim of late. Yes, Shundeen will also return home. It is time.

They will speak of it later, but for now Másání feels only a great peace. They are going home. They are going home.

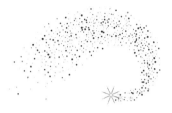

One Last Pause

The flames in the hearth are simply fire once more, magical as fire ever is, but no longer drawing you into the lives of others. Your attention settles on the expansion and contraction of your lungs as they fill with air and as it is released. The full range of sensory information streams your way and you attend to it, seeing the objects surrounding you, receiving the smells of woodsmoke and the sweetness on the air wafting through the open doorway, the sound of drizzle upon the roof.

"I return to myself with much greater ease now than I did at first," you say. "I have learned it is best to ground myself in sensory impressions, rather than speaking quickly of what I have experienced as I accompanied these people through their lives. And I realize the importance of this practice, this coming back to the present moment, being with what is. And I know it is not simply a technique for use here with you, but a way of living that will offer something in each situation of my own life, particularly when I feel a bit off kilter."

"Yes," Xiuying nods, "you have just described mindfulness practice, though as we have discussed, meditation comes to your kind in many forms."

"Perhaps our task," you reply nodding, "is to find the types that work best for us. For example, I have a friend who can't abide sitting meditation, but seems to inhabit the same place during her morning runs. And it seems that some types of meditation could fit better to a certain situation or mood. But regardless of the particulars, I have learned through your flames that dropping into quietude is often the first step to finding one's way forward."

As the hearth sends wave upon wave of warmth to surround and hold you, you are ready again to practice the good soul-care you have been learning here. For while you fully entered Henry's delight in seeing the family of juncos and hearing again the story of his naming, you also fully entered the experience of young Ahéénibaa' as she found herself suddenly dropped onto the foreign soil of harshness. The pain bit hard, and you realize it was but an inkling of what she must have felt *for years*.

As you have learned, you pause and await the arrival of emotions, allowing them whatever time they need to rise up. And when they do, you receive them and welcome them just as they are, without barricading yourself or attempting to change or explain them away. And you bathe each in love, a love that soothes as it accepts, holds as it comforts. As has happened before, your emotions ebb and flow, intensifying and diminishing, each weaving through all the others, separated only by the words you choose to give them: terror, anguish, horror, fury, despair, outrage, admiration, fierce protectiveness, exhaustion, wonder.

And yet, as is the way of such things, at some point pain's sting lessens, and you find you can feel more fully Henry's delight as his laugh rolls out across the fields of his home. You can feel, too, Shundeen's and Másání's quiet joy as they claim readiness to return home themselves. These lighter elements begin to thread now through the pain as the weaving grows, a unified whole spun of many strands, none removed, none ignored, each respected and offering itself up to the overall creation. Only after every reaction has been received with welcome, bathed in love, and fitted one to the other do you open your eyes.

"Such a beautiful practice," you say, wiping tears from your cheeks. "Another way of coming more fully into the now. I hope I will remember to use it throughout my life." Xiuying winks, and you laugh. "Yes, I know. I will again offer myself the gift of trusting that what I have known cannot be unknown. I can trust not only that it is a part of me now, but that learning that mechanism of return is part of the path itself. So yes, I will likely forget this, as I will forget other lessons taught me here. And yes, I will remember again. And I can also trust that, over time, I will come to remember more quickly, more fully, more reflexively."

And with that, you drop into stillness. You look into the bottomless eyes of your dear companion, committing to memory the tender benevolence you find there...as her face begins to waver...as the sights and sounds, smells and feel of this place recede...as you are again welcomed into a darkness that nurtures as it holds...and as you rest there until your own life rises up once more. And you take with you into that life this tender benevolence, holding it close, offering it freely.

A Final Amble...

The nourishing darkness holds you once again as you ready yourself to step into the cherished space of your wise companions. Breathing in the delicious stillness of this waiting place, you let the details of your own life drop away for a short while, knowing they will be there to be picked back up upon your return. Once more you claim your right to pretend-play as you sense your way into what is to come. In a few breaths or in many, the shape of the hearth appears, as do the sounds of rain pummeling roof and pane and a fierce wind blowing in the night. It is many long moments before you turn to see that it is Nyah with whom you sit.

"Well, hello!" you exclaim, a smile spreading across your face. "It is lovely to see you again."

"Yes, it is lovely to see you as well, my child. Though truly, have you not known I was ever near?"

"I suppose I have," you reply, though you hadn't been fully aware of it. "Still, it is good to be with you in *this* way again."

After a time you continue.

"You likely know I have been grappling with the existence of evil in the world, and I was shown another of its many faces in what was done to Ahéénibaa' and the other children. I assume those responsible for the residential schools thought that ripping children away from their families in order to eradicate indigenous culture was a good thing. But even though they didn't see themselves as doing evil, it doesn't change the fact that what they did was brutal and inhumane. And I know that children have been subjected to cruelty throughout history, with atrocities happening currently in many places around the world. But I was *there* with Ahéénibaa'. Right there. And your ensorcelled hearth didn't allow the distance my intellect usually affords me or the filters my own culture provides. I felt for a short while what she had to endure for many long years. I believe I will be forever changed by that experience. I hope I will be forever changed by it."

Before continuing, you take a sip of the warmth in the mug you find in your hand.

"Sometimes I despair of our ever learning to do things differently. But then I remember the underground stream ever available for us to tap into. Yes, that's it! It's like we each have a taproot, a strong, enduring and indestructible part of the human apparatus we are born with. Its purpose is to reach down into that flow and draw up the nourishment to sustain us and bring us to the fullest expression of our humanity. And not in some abstract way either, but within the particulars of our very own lives. Of course, we'll still make mistakes since, as we've discussed before, erring is how we learn. But if we regularly drink of the nutrients from that stream, we'll be better able to act out of its love and better able to return to it when we stray. And that just has to keep the errors that we *do* make smaller and more easily and quickly corrected."

Logs shift in the hearth as many heartbeats pass. "Humility is a good thing," you continue. "I'm not talking about self-abasement, or believing ourselves weak or powerless. All of these people have shown me the importance of engaging fully with life and choosing to act as we're called. That takes a healthy sense of self. By humility, I mean the willingness to question our motives, and to judge our actions against a higher wisdom to see how they measure up. That would go far to ensuring that we do not allow evil an entry into the world. As I was reminded when last I sat with Xiuying, saints and sages have been with us always and have appeared in various guises and forms across many cultures. It's not that we haven't been told. It's that we haven't listened, not deeply. We have not done the hard work of applying those teachings within the nitty gritty of our own lives."

"So it's an all-or-nothing thing, is it?" Nyah suggests, though her eyes are teasing.

"Yeah," you respond, "I did make it sound that way. I do think that most of us *intend* to live well, loving our neighbors and trying to do the right thing."

You become aware of your own taproot now, and reach deeply through it before continuing. "I do humankind a disservice when I let our errors loom larger than our strengths. I have learned that my belief in another's ability to grow and to heal is a gift, and so I wonder if the same holds true for the collective. Perhaps remembering the good we are capable of and much of the time enact will fund that ability." You pause until a decision made brings a smile to your face. "Yes, I will choose to believe that is so. There is much good in the world, and I will place my energy and my trust there."

"Marvelous," Nyah says, with a joyful clap. And when you only smile in return, she continues. "Dear one, our being together in this way will soon be drawing to a close, and there are but a few more journeys for us to take together. Given what we have just discussed, I'm guessing you might like to travel into some of that good now?"

"Yes," you enthusiastically agree, even as you find yourself facing the hearth again, "I'd like that very much."

And the flames shoot high, curling and swaying before settling once again.

The Holy Ones

As images come to the hearth, you quickly realize this journey will be different than the others. Rather than moving deeply into the lives of a few individuals and spending time there, you enter instead a montage, as you are dropped into one scenario before being swiftly moved into another... and another...and yet again another still. And as this occurs, Nyah's voice provides an ongoing narration.

"I'm sure you are aware of the great acts of heroism that occur during times of crisis," she intones, as the hearth carries you into scene after scene of turmoil. Here, medical personnel work as the ground shakes with the explosion of nearby bombs. There, an officer rushes to pull a driver from a car as smoke billows from beneath its hood. In the aftermath of a flood, people arrive by boat to rescue the stranded, while others hand out sandwiches in overcrowded shelters.

"In times such as these," her voice continues as more images of human courage and kindness roll by, "that underground stream of which you speak swells and rises more fully into human awareness. The Oneness that ever exists bleeds through the surface differences that so often ensnare and, despite personal risk, you act out of that deeper, more expansive and truer perspective.

"But such crises are proportionately rare," she continues, as a new tone comes to the scenes into which the hearth now carries you. "In the day-to-day world of humankind, *these* experiences are much more common." And you join now with a father helping his daughter with homework, then become one with an exhausted mother bouncing a crying baby on her hip while she adds vegetables to a pot on the stove. You walk into a factory for a grueling nightshift because your kids need shoes, before you find yourself wiping the ass of an incontinent patient in an Alzheimer's unit. With a teenage girl, you protect a younger child from bullies, and you help a young fellow right a drunken man who has fallen on the sidewalk. People of all genders, skin tones, and ages fly by in the flames. Teachers and attorneys, business owners and accountants, actors and mechanics. Rich and poor, physically robust and frail. You join with person after person as each carries on, trying simply to do the next right thing and doing so out of love.

"So while calamities do occur in your world," Nyah speaks on as the play of images moves even more quickly," so do actions such as these, and they are the more common. These individuals are everywhere, as Mandi recognized during her own enchantment. They are the daily champions of Love, heroes all. Don't forget them or participate in the lie that what they offer is irrelevant."

This rapid play of images continues for some time, each person and situation as unique as they are universal. Another shift of mood then comes to the hearth as the rapid sequence of scenes slows as the shimmer intensifies.

"We move once again now directly into the magic the Guardians devised. I'd like to show you a few additional faces, those for whom the sudden stillness of this enchantment changes little."

And you once again find yourself in the neighborhood where Jessica and Mugsy began their walk-run. You see the bearded man place his now-silent hedge trimmer on the ground and straighten up, a smile of delight upon his face. As you breathe in the stillness with him, you somehow know that this enchantment has merely intensified his usual joy through eliminating the background static. And in the mysteriously wonderful way the hearth allows, you feel that joy yourself.

You return to the convent, though you are now in the kitchen with Agnes who has been cooking for the Sisters since her retirement from the elementary school five years ago. She has come back from her own home to prep for tomorrow's meals and, when the magic arrives, she has just finished mixing the yeast batter for breakfast pancakes. Her usual smile deepens as she covers the bowl with a cloth and begins singing a hymn. You find yourself humming along.

Now you are in the hallway of Ann's workplace, outside the office of her colleague Rājīv. As you see him lean back in the chair and close his eyes, you are drawn into the peace that radiates around him, again knowing that it is merely an amplification of his usual serene state.

You're in the pub now where Nikki works parttime. Danny's whistling *Love So Soft* as he wipes down the bar, swiping the rag around the immobile arms of patrons leaning on its walnut surface. Soon though, he tosses the rag in the sink, moves out from behind the bar, and dances with abandon, body loose, arms pumping, hips gyrating. He belts out the words to the song, and somehow you're dancing and singing with him.

Until you arrive in the reception area of the teen assistance program where Maliq, Sarah, Mandi and Jacob work. Marti's watering the schefflera in the corner, but stops and places the watering can on the desk. She inhales deeply, and you can feel the intensification of the natural glow that emanates around her.

The scene changes again, as the magic envelopes the home of Emma, Meghan and Richard. Someone dressed in the rugged attire of a workingman exits an outbuilding tucked under the towering oaks and hidden from the house by carefully maintained shrubbery. You know Raul as the crew leader for the properties in the neighborhood, which gives him the chance to stop by frequently. You know, too, that while he may busy himself in tidying up the already organized gardening supplies, his true intention is to direct Light into the anguish that is this family's life. He looks up now to the house on the hill, and as you drop into his experience of the enchantment, you find a constant and pervading compassion overlaying a quiet calm.

And you are now with a man you know to be Henry's uncle, in a wide-open outdoor place. On horseback when the enchantment begins, he reigns in his midnight bay stallion and leaps to the ground, boots kicking up dust. Removing his hat, he remains still for a few heartbeats before making a slow turn to the directions. Then he sits upon Mother Earth, Father Sky embracing from above.

Trees surround you now in the Park across from the apartment building where Aingeal, Sakiya and James live. Their neighbor from Apartment 3C is feeding the birds. Gretchen's arm drops to her side and she throws back her head. Looking up through the branches into the deepening blue of the late-day sky, the merriment in her eyes grows brighter. She laughs aloud, and you laugh with her.

The pace of images quickens once again as others flash in the hearth. Here, a man in a business suit walks a city street lined with tall buildings and unmoving pedestrians. There, a teacher drinks in the silence surrounding her now-stilled first graders. A burly construction worker lays down his silent jackhammer, removes his goggles and earbuds, and looks to the sky. A man dressed in the universal garb of the homeless pauses not a second, continuing to bless the statue-still passersby from the high steps of a library. A letter carrier slows in her rounds and looks up too. The driver of a delivery van steps to the pavement, and begins weaving his way through the unmoving vehicles that fill the roadway, his usual smile growing wider. A serene woman walks alone down a forest path as the natural world continues its blooming all around her. One after another, these images fly by, each individual linked to the others by the joyful peace they radiate, a peace you somehow know is theirs always.

Finally, the images fade, and the fire becomes mere flames again. You feel rather lightheaded, and Nyah encourages you to drink of the mug, promising its brew will anchor you. And the beverage does help. You sip and you breathe and you ground yourself in the here after having traveled so far.

Widening The Aperture

You sit for a time, settling back into yourself. When the words that find you are ready to be spoken, you are again facing Nyah.

"Well, my main reaction is a huge WOW!" you say with a laugh. "It was like being whirled inside a giant kaleidoscope, and the quickness of the movement was dizzying at times. That is not, though, my main takeaway," you continue after a brief pause, your voice whisper-soft. "Profound awe has claimed me. I often say that the world is full of goodness, that love is stronger than hate, but truly I had no idea. Not really. It feels now that I've only been giving lip service to the idea. But here, I *felt* it. I was *enveloped* in that goodness. And an experiential sense always makes a stronger impression than something known with the mind alone. Yes, that's it. I now know with my whole being just how strong and true that goodness is."

After a time, you find another realization wanting to be voiced. "I was quite taken with those for whom the enchantment merely diminished the background noise. Well, perhaps it also boosted their shine, I don't know, but they seemed to live largely connected to that source from which Love and Light spring. Yet every person I have met in the hearth from the very beginning of my time here was able to access that as well. Maybe not fully, and maybe they won't be able to hold onto it, at least not as strongly, when life revs up again. What has been given me, though, is a visceral sense of the intrinsic goodness that lies within ALL of us, and the certainty that we are each connected to a Source from which we can draw even more."

Nyah's eyes hold yours and there is something within her gaze that validates this awareness you have just articulated. You sit together for a long while, listening to the sounds of storm and the crackle of fire. Finally, with a smile and a nod, she speaks.

"We have one last journey to take together, child, and it is possible that this trip will be the most disorienting of all. To make you as comfortable as possible during this passage, all with whom you have spent time in this room will accompany you."

As she falls silent, a quiver of energy dances across your skin, foretelling a new expression of the uncanny. Nyah then rises from her chair with such fluidity and grace that she seems to ascend directly from the Earth itself. She stands motionless as her dark skin begins to shimmer. The outline of her body grows less distinct, oscillating now in a rhythm of expansion and contraction. You briefly glimpse Xiuying's features, and then watch as she steps from Nyah's left side. In each hand she holds a long ribbon of green silk. She sways in place for a few moments before leaping and twirling around her sister, ribbons unfurling and swirling as she goes. She is beautiful and she is ageless. Dance complete, Xiuying comes to deep stillness again. Her eyes meet yours, and she smiles and bows in greeting.

You have a chance to offer only a brief smile in return before your eyes are drawn back to Nyah, whose body continues to glow and to pulse. The sound of Peruvian pipes fills the space now, as another form becomes visible within hers. After several moments, Icaro emerges to stand at Nyah's right side. He holds an arc of bamboo tubes of varying lengths tied together with brightly woven straps. It is his breath now that makes them sing. When the tune ends, he becomes as still and as solid as Andean stone, though his smile is sunlight shining in a mountain sky.

You smile yourself before your gaze returns to Nyah. Zosia quivers into view now, becoming fully substantial as she steps out to join the others. Spine straight and unbowed by the years, she is taller than the others by far, and embodies such vitality that you wonder again how you could ever have thought her frail. Regal is the word that comes to you now, and though her eyes shine as warmly as ever, there is an elegance and a dignity about her that makes your breath catch even as you smile a greeting in return.

Nyah's edges solidify once again, though her radiant shine continues. As your eyes move from one dear companion to another, you notice it is not just Nyah who glows. They all have that same luster. And something else occurs to you as well.

"I have often sensed more than simple kinship between you," you whisper. "Though your outer forms vary and something unique shines in each pair of eyes, it is as though you are one, arising from a similar wisdom or essence or something that varies only in its expression. Am I perceiving true? And please tell me I haven't just said something stupid or offensive," you finish, suddenly unsure.

Nyah's throaty laugh calms you. "Don't you worry, child. You have offended no one here, though in truth we do not offend easily. We are, indeed, facets of the same crystal. One Light shines through us all."

"As is true for all living things," adds Xiuying. "One Light, many forms."

"And I have learned," you comment into the silence that follows, "that seeing beyond outer appearances is one of the essential tasks for humankind during the EarthWalk we have undertaken. I am pleased that I sensed it with you all, and am trying to employ that same awareness throughout my life, so that I may recognize the One shining through the guise of the many."

"And perhaps," Zosia speaks after a brief pause, "this final excursion will aid in that goal. We will surround you now," she continues, as your companions move closer. They form a circle around you, and remain silent for many breaths. It is as though they sense the tingling that runs across your skin, the sweet shiver that began as one became four, but grew more palpable as they stepped close.

"Breathe," Icaro whispers into your ear. "All is well."

Of course you know it is, but the reassurance calms you anyway. After several more breaths that steady you further, Xiuying speaks.

"Soon and with your consent, we will each place our hands upon you. You will likely feel an increase in sensation at that time, though we trust you will find it rather pleasant. Please take all the time you need to adjust. There is never cause to rush things such as this. When you signal you are ready, your final pilgrimage will begin. May we touch you now?"

You take a deep breath and release it, feeling both kindness and great power surrounding you. At last you nod. Slowly and gently, four pairs of hands come to rest upon head, shoulders, back, and arms. You had thought you'd felt tingling before, but that was nothing compared to what you now feel. The spark of a thousand candles fills you, as your edges grow porous to receive even more. Xiuying is correct. Though the sensation gives new meaning to the word intense, it is also wondrous, like the most loving embrace you've ever experienced amplified a hundredfold. It is also an embrace that awakens further the love at your own core, a love that leaps up in welcome and in return.

You take several breaths as you become accustomed to this energetic shift, feeling no need to hurry. Finally, though, you recognize it is time. Surrounded and filled with such love, you know you will be carried safely into whatever comes next. You nod and say, "I am ready."

"This will likely be easier if you close your eyes, dear one," Nyah says in a voice that soothes as it thrills. "We will hold you in our Circle as we rise."

You close your eyes. In a moment, you have a sense of upward movement. The hands of the Wise Ones press in on all sides, gently but firmly anchoring you within this Circle as that movement gains speed. You feel now the night air against your skin, and hear sounds of storm, though your body is touched by neither rain nor sleet. These sounds soon dim before disappearing altogether, and you realize you are traveling now through the higher reaches of the atmosphere. And then air itself is left behind, and the thought occurs to you that you may not be able to breathe. But before that thought can bloom into fear, Zosia speaks from behind saying, "All is well. You are safe with us."

The momentum accelerates even further within a silence so all-encompassing that sound is forgotten. But then something like sound does come to you, something you have no way of comprehending, for it is not a sound heard by your ears. Neither is it a sound heard with the body, though that description comes closest to your experience. It is a palpable thrumming that travels over and through you, filling every nook and each cranny of what you have identified as yourself, though that concept seems now to have lost all meaning.

"It is the music of the spheres, the sound of pure energy unbound," Icaro explains, though his voice now comes to you in the same way in which you hear that strangely beautiful music, not with earthly ears but as vibration, a part of the weaving that holds you, that fills you, that expands you out of all earlier confines.

"We shall soon reach our destination," Nyah's voice adds, taking its place within that weave as the speed of your ascent slows...and slows...and further slows. At last, you feel yourself stationary, though that concept has no more meaning than does the notion of sound or an individual self. You know only that you have arrived.

"You may open your eyes when you are ready," someone speaks, though you can no longer distinguish individual voices. You wait but a moment before raising your lids.

The vastness of space is spread out before you, an expanse larger than your mind can fathom. Dark beyond any previous understanding of the word, still it is lit by the light of an untold number of stars stretching out before you. You think briefly of Ann, a laugh bubbling up as you imagine the indescribable joy she would feel to be here. "I will appreciate it for us both," you think, before that thought dissolves. As your Circle begins a slow turn, you see yet more stars, with brighter lights amid the darkness. You know these as the nearby planets of our own solar system, before that thought leaves you as well.

As your rotation continues, our own bright star comes into view, an intense brilliance within the inkiness of space. You behold its fiery surface and the corona radiating beyond its edges. As you continue to turn and even though you're a distance away, you recognize Venus. And with one last fraction of movement, there she is. The Earth herself

Half her surface is dark, but the other is glowing in the Sun's rays. A slender layer of atmosphere surrounds her, the caress of the life-sustaining gasses you so recently moved through. Though your own continent is on the dark side of her body, others are visible, as are oceans of startling blue. Clouds spin in a few swirling storms, some with lightning bursts, but your view to her surface is largely unobstructed. And she is dazzling beyond measure, a beauty as exquisite as it is precious.

"We will adjust your vision now," someone speaks into your mind, "so you can see how she looks energetically."

Across the surface of the Earth and extending beyond it, you suddenly see a dancing, swirling vitality, ever moving, strengthening and waning, coalescing here and dispersing there. The certainty that she is a being alive, making adjustments large and small as conditions alter, is a truth that arrives fully formed. You think briefly of Kayla and her understanding that forests have an intelligence that human brains are not shaped to recognize.

"How much greater must be the intelligence of the Earth herself," you think, "and how similarly impossible for us to truly comprehend. She is magnificent." And that thought also evaporates.

"And here," a voice speaks after moments pass, "is what the enchantment brings."

Bursts of light, one after another, begin to appear now across the surface of the planet. They glow in bright patches on her lit side, while on her darkened surface they are candles kindling in the night. Yet as you watch enraptured, more is revealed. As each brightness flares, it links to other sparks. The Light grows ever more luminous, the vitality of individual lights and of the Earth itself enhanced.

Additional sparks, each a person awakening, continue to ignite and join with that greater Light...brightness encouraging brightness, radiance begetting more radiance, luster becoming more luminous. And though you are unaware of it, your own light has responded in the same way, having grown more vivid and dazzling. You receive it all. Open to it all. Love it all.

You have no idea how long you bask in the Light before a voice calls you back. "It is nearly time for our descent. Again, we suggest you close your eyes to ease your passage, but please be assured that you will not be able to unsee what you have been shown. It is a part of you now."

For a while longer, your eyes behold the precious Earth, and you vow to love her more fully and more fiercely than ever before, and to demonstrate that love in ways large and small. And as you see her lit now by the light of an untold numbers of souls, you commit more deeply to being one of those flames yourself, knowing that the light you carry in your heart and shine into the world matters. After one last drink of this wonder, you close your eyes and nod.

And you find that indeed it is true. You cannot unsee what you have seen, for the glowing Light remains visible behind your eyelids. As your descent begins, you know that Light is a part of you now, as is the awareness that it connects the one to the many, the individual to the whole, the one to the One. Your movement gains momentum, then begins to slow again as you feel sweet air against your skin, further slowing as the sounds of storm come once more to your earthly ears. At last, you are standing in the chamber of the Wise Ones once again.

Leave-Taking

You open your eyes and draw a few shaky breaths. You become aware that the four pairs of hands that accompanied you on your journey to the stars continue to rest gently but firmly upon you now that you have returned. Their touch steadies you as you stand together before the hearth. When the time is right, your companions bring you to a chair and lower you into it. The pressure of hands lifts, though the warmth of their imprint remains. Your eyes close of their own accord.

Though time ever seems an odd notion in this place, you need longer than usual to absorb this last experience. You feel it continuing to weave more deeply inside, reshaping and transforming you as it moves. At last, though, you open your eyes to find your beloved companions seated in a crescent before you, Icaro and Xiuying on the floor, Zosia and Nyah upon chairs. You hold the gaze of one after another for many long moments. Silence stretches on, and you are content to marinate in it. Finally, though, you speak.

"Words cannot do justice to what I have just seen. And yet," you say with a laugh, "I want to find them anyway. Such a weird human trait."

Nyah raises one eyebrow in question.

"Or maybe," you reply in answer, "words are our attempt to understand and to share that understanding with others. So maybe they are a good thing, as long as we remember they are merely fingers pointing and not the Moon itself."

Nyah nods and smiles. After a time, you continue.

"Earlier, I noted that awareness rising from direct experience is far more meaningful than one claimed with the mind alone. Well, this last voyage was an odyssey for sure, one that has radically altered all my previous understandings. I was shown a tapestry, a living, breathing tapestry that is intricate, exquisitely beautiful, and ever-evolving."

"Can you say more?" Icaro urges when you fall silent again.

"That tapestry is already there AND we are creating it, too, as we each add our own stitches to the whole, stitches that affect other threads."

"Yes," nods Xiuying, "This is a secret widely shared. This tapestry of Light and of Love was not created for this enchantment. It has ever and always been there. And it evolves."

"And," adds Nyah, "when a being awakens more fully to it, when any heart grows larger and glows more brightly, the whole shines more vividly as well."

You nod. A log settles in the hearth as the wind howls and sleet pings against panes.

"Tell us more," Zosia encourages. "What else have you learned, not only in this most recent foray, but from your first arrival in this cottage we fashioned just for you?"

"Well," you laugh, "that oughta be easy to sum up!" Yet the love that shines through these four wise and beautiful faces strengthens your desire to make the attempt. Reminding yourself that you are not trying to capture the Moon, you continue.

"First, I'd say that my talk of an underground stream was much too narrow. I see now that Love is not only always present and accessible, but that it is all there is. It is everywhere and much too huge to be held within a notion such as a streambed. I see, too, that this energy is sacred beyond measure. It is the raw material, the very substance that makes up all things. What the enchantment has done is return us to something we never left at all. It is not something we *can* leave since it is everywhere and as close as our own hearts. When any one of us awakens, either with outside help such as your enchantment provides or simply through the events that unfold within our day-to-day lives, we are merely returning to an awareness of what has always been."

You breathe deeply until the next theme emerges.

"That unbelievably complex and enormous whole is holy, pulsing with Love and with Light. And yet that whole is made of individual strands, which are also sacred. Those threads include all life forms, each one holy in its own right *and* as it interweaves with others for good or for ill."

Another pause.

"Okay, this is a bit trickier to grasp. That sacredness is the raw energy we are given. And yet as humans we can distort that energy or we can enhance it. We can use it to harm or to heal, twisting it into all manner of ugly and atrocious expressions, or amplifying it and adding our own unique spin before sending it out into the world. This gift of Light and of Love is not an end in itself. It is alive and it is evolving as well. What we create from it is our own personal contribution to the whole. It is ever our choice what that addition will be."

Time elapses as logs settle in the grate, and you breathe with The Wise Ones. Finally, more words arrive.

"I've met so many people in your flames, each life unique. I know now in a new way, in a deeper way, that our personal stories are not irrelevant. They are holy beyond measure, since they are the vehicles of our awakening. Our sorrows and our joys, our struggles and our delights are the threads that make up our personal tapestries. Creating a thing of beauty there is where our main work lies. And yet our small lives do have a larger significance. The work we do there, the *awakening* we do there, creates portals that allow more Love and Light to flow in, not just in our own individual sphere, but in the much larger one I was shown during this last journey. And because we are so interconnected, when any one of us awakens even a bit more, it encourages the awakening of the whole.

"And your enchantment makes quite clear," you conclude, "that we awaken best when we allow ourselves to come into the stillness that ever awaits us and allows greater access to the Love and wisdom that is always there."

"Not bad, child," Nyah beams. Soon, she continues. "And here is a question we have for you. Earlier, you met enlightened ones in our flames. You were quite taken by them, I believe."

"Oh, I loved joining with them for the time I was allowed," you nod enthusiastically. "And I loved being reminded that Light workers always walk among us, for the most part working their magic very unobtrusively."

"So, dear one," Xiuying asks, "here is our question. Will you join them? Will you consciously take your place as the Light Worker you were designed to be and truly already are?"

Stunned by the question, you wait several breaths before replying.

"Of course, my first reaction is that I am not enlightened. And then I realize I am seeing enlightenment as a either-or thing. Most of us have had at least moments of clarity, times when we sense a greater pattern to our lives and recognize the importance of Love. But you have asked if I'm ready to do that more consciously, to embody that role more fully, to declare it as my own. In truth, I made that pledge already when I was among the stars. Yet I know a vow is strengthened when given voice."

Eyes closing, you fall silent for a time. As you prepare to speak your next words, you feel a gathering of energy in your belly, a tingling running across your skin. Finally you open your eyes and meet the gaze of each of your beloved guides.

"Yes," you say at last, "I vow to be a worker of the Light. And I will go one better," you add with a smile. "I vow to *dance* with the Light, to leap and spin and frolic with it, to be one flame among a multitude of others gamboling about within the hearth of Life itself."

Your oath is met with a round of applause and much laughter.

"We have one last set of images to show you now," Icaro speaks when silence returns and you find yourself again facing the hearth. The movement of the flames there grows wild before settling once again as images unfold.

Lana is painting in her garage studio, and Jack holds a baby bird on his lap. Ella and Wangtang are standing atop a mountain with Ginger, Lily, and Rio, while Jessica and Mugsy weave through the soccer field. Ann lies under a gleaming night sky, while Eric sits in meditation and Phil listens to birdsong streaming through an open window. Emma smiles at Sunshine, while her father looks up at the house on the hill and her mother plans her next move. Kayla and Mia commune with little Sophia, each in her own way, while in another facet of this enchantment, Antonio spoons with his wife. Sister Constance-Marie sits in chapel, marveling at the Love that has always been her companion, pooling around her and welling within.

Aingeal readies herself for a home in Ireland, as Sakiya puts away her journal, and James dries his eyes and turns toward his wife after many months away. Nikki places her arms around each child, while in another part of the tapestry her children hug her and each other. Maliq is eager to reach Shanice, Mandi and Sarah shine more brightly, and Jacob sits in his darkened office soothing the suffering of the world. Henry, Selva, and Másáni all rejoice as their time in the city nears its end.

You recognize each one as friend and companion in awakening. But the last face you see causes your heart to race in the cave of your chest. For looking back at you now from within the flames is your own face.

"Breathe, my dear," Xiuying whispers in your ear. "All is as it should be."

"Indeed, it is," agrees Nyah, "for being here with us has been your own enchantment."

"It has been our delight to be this soft incursion for you," Icaro says softly. "This incursion, though, is now complete."

"Let its gifts root," adds Zosia, "and let them grow in the rich soil of your being and twine themselves through the specifics of your own life. It is there that these understandings will bloom and emit their rich scent."

"In that way," Nyah concludes, "just as you saw from your place among the stars, your light will shine ever more brightly, encouraging a more robust glow in others. You will be then a soft incursion, both for yourself and in the lives of all you meet."

You sit for a time, letting the words of your companions settle. Finally, you speak.

"You said once that this place is always available to me. Is it true that I can return at any point?"

Love washes over you in waves as Zosia, Nyah, Icaro and Xiuying nod and smile. It is Zosia, though, who speaks first.

"Of course you can, child. The form will be different, as this part of your odyssey is concluded. But ever and always, as is true for precious souls everywhere, this realm is available to you."

"Simply become still and open to Love," Nyah adds, "and you shall arrive."

Icaro speaks now. "And once you enter again this time out of time, if something has distressed you, let it rise up. Remain still and listen for the guidance that will surely come, if not immediately, then over time."

"And if instead," Xiuying offers, "you simply seek the rest and replenishment woven through this place, drink it deeply into your core. There it will meet the spark that is your own sliver of that larger Light and cause it to glow more brightly."

"And this is truth, dear one," Nyah finishes. "Our enchantment was not enchantment at all, but awakening. For when you joined with others in the hearth and when you visited with us in this chamber and among the stars, what rose up was true, a reality you now are better able to live."

Silence returns. Soon, though, the Wise Ones stand and once again form a circle around you. Four sets of arms reach out, and four sets of hands sweep lightly through the air surrounding your body, setting in motion another round of pulsating energy. A deeper peace comes to you, one that softens the sorrow of this leave-taking and your uncertainty of how you will live the teachings that have been given you.

"We bless you, dear one," Xiuying begins. "In all that you are, in all that you do, we bless you."

"We trust in your unfolding," Nyah continues. "Your glow is strong and we see that vibrancy increasing as you live what you have been shown here."

"Pause often," Icaro adds, "and trust that assistance is ever available to you in whatever form you need."

"And never doubt in the presence and the power of Love," finishes Zosia. "Drink of it often and always, knowing that it shall ever be replenished."

The Wise Ones stand for a bit longer, holding you in an energetic embrace, filling you with their love, their recognition, and their trust in your unfolding. And then their outer forms begin to waver, though your connection does not diminish. The structure of the room itself dims, as do the furnishings it contains. The last thing you see before that warm and inviting darkness swirls about you is the hearth that opened you to such magic, a hearth you may not have seen in this lifetime, but have always known. Soon, though, it too dissolves. You remain within the embrace of that nurturing darkness for as long as you want and as long you need, before your own life, precious thread within a glorious whole, rises up in welcome once again.

Post-Amble...

Hello again, my friend. As I type these words, sunlight streams through south-facing windows, just as it did when those first words came onto the page so many months ago. A second Imbolc has passed, and we stand now on the cusp of the Spring Equinox. An auspicious time to complete the writing of a book and begin the process of launching it into the world, yes?

I thank you for joining me here, sweet reader, and for allowing me to place images before your eyes, suggest thoughts for your mind, and put words upon your tongue. It is my hope that this has been your enchantment, one that woke you more fully to the larger, truer reality that you have always known. It certainly has been so for me in the writing of it.

All of these many words have been my fingers pointing, and I do not claim them as the Moon itself. How, after all, could anyone capture the Moon? It delights me to no end that you might take the words that have come through me, breathe your own life into them, and send them out into the world with value added. Such is the way of this cosmic relay dance we have undertaken. Together we will continue to make something magical, a wonder that is expanding even now in ever-widening circles.

In every difficult moment and each joyous one as well, my wish is that you never question the sacredness of your own story, that assistance is ever available, and that you are connected in a substantive way to a whole so magnificent as to be truly indescribable. May you open more fully to the Mystery by whatever name you give it, and may you find there a magic uniquely your own. And may you choose Love, dear one, knowing that Love has already chosen you.

My companion in awakening, be the incursion. For yourself and for others, be the incursion. And as you dance with the Light, may blessings galore fall upon you. And may you forever be enchanted, and may that enchantment be true.

The End

A Few Parting Words From Leia

Enchanted, A Tale Of Remembrance now comes to a close, and I get to thank you, dear companion, for accompanying me on this leg of my journey. The writing of this book was a rich, profound, and life-changing experience. One of the many surprises along the way was recognizing that it was time to revamp my self-image. As an introvert whose career primarily focused on transformational work with individuals, I never saw myself expanding into such a public sphere. And yet, here I am. It hasn't always been comfortable or easy, but it has always felt exactly right. It required that I dig deep, clarify my vision, and remove blocks to letting myself shine out. So the process of writing *Enchanted* truly did become my own enchantment, one that propelled me in unexpected directions and called forth new facets of my being.

Another surprise was discovering just how much is involved in bringing a book into the world. Most of the last year has been spent learning about the field of publishing and discerning the best approach for a book that was not simply fish or fowl, but rather a delectable stew of self-help, fantasy, and spiritual exploration. Self-publishing showed itself as the most fitting avenue to birth this creation...which, of course, opened a whole new round of decisions and tasks. Since you have arrived here, obviously those were successful.

In order for *Enchanted* to continue on its unique path, I ask for your help. Potential readers rely largely on customer reviews for deciding which books to buy, and I would very much appreciate your writing your own review. Short, long or somewhere in between, your words could very likely result in a greater audience for the themes explored in this book. Now how's that for an introvert coming out of her shell and asking for what she wants?!! If you feel so inclined, simply go to Amazon's *Enchanted, A Tale of Remembrance* page, and scroll down to click on the Write A Customer Review button. It's really quite easy.

Whatever decision you make, I appreciate the investment of your precious time, energy, and purchase price to read *Enchanted*. You can find more about future offerings and sign up for my emailing list by visiting my website, https://www.in-awe.net.

Thank you, my friend. Thank you for reading *Enchanted*. Thank you for adding its messages to those you've received from other sources, including your own sweet soul. Thank for all that you are and all that you do in the world. Thank you, dear reader, thank you.

Leia

Leia Marie

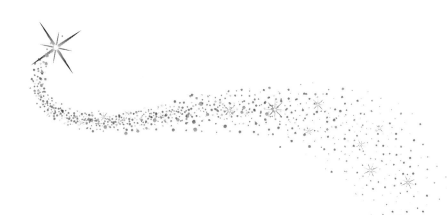

Gratitudes

Affection and heartfelt thanks stream out to all who have had a part in the creation of *Enchanted, A Tale of Remembrance*...

To family and friends who lovingly and consistently watered the seeds that grew to be this book, as well as those who read the manuscript in its entirety or in portions, I thank you. These include most notably Kelli, Marilyn, Jay, Cindy, Nancy, Ksenya, Tracy, Robin, Martha, Judy, Connie, BeeJ, Diana, Maggie, Ann, Itza, Monica. And special thanks to Loretta Sword for first offering me access to a larger audience through *The Pueblo Chieftain's* Faith & Religion section, where some of the seeds for *Enchanted* were planted; to Bonita for encouraging me to let go of old stories to shine as I was meant to; and to my husband for whom there are no words large enough to hold my love.

To the many precious and trusting souls who have shared their tender places as we worked together over the years, I thank you. You taught me so very much about the art of living and astonished me with your courage and the brilliance of your healing. I cannot, of course, name you here, but you know who you are. I hope you recognize how deeply your gifts have woven their way through me... and through this book as well.

To the extraordinarily talented, steady, and supremely generous

Mel McCann, I thank you. You not only created a cover that portrays the essence of this book's message, but you helped me negotiate the world of technology and publishing. This book may have come into the world without your astute guidance, but it would not have been as beautiful and I surely wouldn't have survived the birthing process nearly as well.

To cultures not my own that I imaginatively entered in the writing of this book, I thank you. I hope my respect shines through any inaccuracies held within my words.

And to that indescribable Mystery that whispers always to us, calling us to a greater flowering even when, perhaps especially when, we cannot hear your voice, I thank you.

Gratitude overflows for the privilege of walking our individual paths together. Namasté, my loves. Namasté.

Turn the page

for a sneak peek

at

the exciting new Children's book

The Great Forest...and Beyond
by Leia Marie

due to publish very soon!!!

A delightful romp through magical realms,
it also encourages positive values, environmental stewardship,
and a deep awareness of the interconnection at the heart of life.

Appropriate for kids ages 5 through 12,
it also will delight those of any age
with a childlike sense of Adventure.

Read on...

Leia Marie

Chapter One
An Invitation

Once upon a time in a land far, far away and in a time of great magic and adventure, there lived a family whose name was Greenwood. In addition to Mama and Poppi Greenwood, there were three children who called the fields and the near edge of the Great Forest home. Ginger, the oldest child, was nine years old, Liliana had just turned seven, and young Rio was almost six.

The children spent part of each day helping their parents with all the daily tasks of a life lived in those faraway times. There were chickens to feed, eggs to collect, Clarissa to milk, butter to churn, and berries to pick for eating raw or making into jam. Every Spring the children helped plant seeds in the large garden, and each child tended a section of baby plants until they rose up strong and healthy to bear the blossoms and vegetables that the family would eat through the long, cold winter.

But even though the children did much to help the family survive and grow strong, it was not simply a life of work. They learned new things each day, from how to read time in the stars that revolved in the skies above, to predicting the weather from the smell of the breeze. Together, they could make a shelter out of branches, build a fire to warm themselves, and cook a meal from the plants that grew wild at the Forest's edge. Mama and Poppi had taught each child their letters, and though Ginger could read the fastest since she'd been practicing a long time, even little Rio could read simple books and write short notes.

And, oh, how the children played! There were no telephones in this world, no TVs or video games, no movies theatres or malls, and so the children made their own fun day after day. They invented grand games of

The Great Forest...and Beyond

make-believe and made friends with the animals that roamed wild and free through the meadows that surrounded the house. And since there were no cars, they needn't look both ways before racing across the worn path down the hill from their house. Yes, it was a pretty fine life.

One day as the children were playing one of their favorite games—calling animals from the woods by imitating their calls—there came a sound from the skies above unlike any they had ever heard before. All three looked up at once and as the sound grew louder, they recognized it as the shrill cry of a great bird who was only now becoming visible with their human eyes for it flew so high.

As they watched, the bird circled down, and down some more, until the children could make out its ruby feathers and the hook of its great purple beak. When it was still higher than the tallest tree in the woods, Lily, who had the best vision of them all, called out, "Hey, look, it's holding something in its feet!"

At that very moment, the great bird stretched its talons wide and let the object drop. As the golden tube fell to the ground, the bird screeched once more, rose fast, and flew back in the direction it had come.

Ginger reached the spot where the cylinder hit the ground just as the bird faded from view.

"What do you think it is?" asked Rio, who arrived at Ginger's side as she picked up the golden tube.

"I don't know," Ginger answered, holding the object carefully.

Lily, who had watched the bird disappear into the heavens, ran up and began jumping up and down excitedly, squealing, "Open it, Ginger! Open it! I bet it's a Call. I just *know* it is!"

And that is what all of them wished for more than anything else, because in this magical world children expected Calls To Great Adventure. Most kids had already received one by the time they were Ginger's age. In fact, in this land you were not considered grown-up until you had had *three* Adventures.

But the trick about Adventures, of course, was that even the bravest and most enthusiastic child needed to wait to be called...you couldn't just decide to have one on your own. So Ginger, Lily, and Rio had waited, sometimes not very patiently, for their call. Lily, for one, did not want to wait any longer.

The three kids examined the tube. Its golden material was a bit like paper and a bit like cloth. At one end, a thin thread dangled.

Leia Marie

"Pull it and see what happens," Rio suggested.

"Okay, here goes," said Ginger, gently pulling the thread.

Well, that little tug set about a great spinning and unraveling such that the cylinder hopped out of Ginger's hands and bounced wildly across the ground. Within a few seconds, the tube was nothing but a pile of curled thread shining like the sun against the green grass.

A page of what looked to be very old and very brittle paper lay rolled up beside it. With Lily and Rio looking over her shoulder, Ginger sat on the grass, smoothed the paper across her lap, and read aloud:

Needed:

Three Adventurous Children

For

An Undertaking

Of Great Importance

Must Be Kind

Must Be Curious

Must Be Brave

All Interested Children

Meet At The Edge Of The Great Forest

At Dawn Tomorrow

Ready To Travel Far

"I knew it!" cried Lily, jumping up and down and clapping her hands. "We're going on an Adventure! We're going on an Adventure!" With a bouncing Rio adding his own excited shouts, they raised quite a racket.

The Great Forest...and Beyond

"Well, that depends if Mama and Poppi give us permission," cautioned Ginger, holding the Invitation with care as she stood up. "And we may have to convince them that Rio is old enough to go."

As the oldest, she thought it her duty to calm her excitable siblings... but inside, Ginger was jumping up and down, too. She just did it in a quieter way.

"I am *too* old enough!" Rio said, angry at the thought of being left behind. "The bird dropped the Invitation to *all* of us, didn't it? I'm invited too, and I'm going!"

"Well, let's go ask Mama and Poppi!" Ginger yelled, and the kids raced to the house.

Since it was nearly lunchtime, they burst in the back door to find their parents in the kitchen putting food on the table.

"Well what's gotten into the three of you?" asked Poppi, looking at their faces flushed with excitement.

All three children began talking at once, so that Poppi and Mama couldn't make out a thing they said.

"Hush now!" Mama called out over the noise. "Ginger, what's this about?"

"A really big bird dropped this to us when we were playing in the field," Ginger said, holding out the Invitation.

Mama and Poppi looked at one another, and each saw the truth in the other's eyes. It was finally time for their children to set off on an Adventure of their own.

Poppi took the Invitation and read it aloud, "Needed: Three adventurous children for an undertaking of great importance. Must be kind. Must be curious. Must be brave. All interested children meet at the edge of the Great Forest at dawn tomorrow ready to travel far."

"Kind, curious, and brave certainly sounds like our children," smiled Mama. "Do you think they're ready, Husband?

"I imagine so," replied Poppi, "but we need to discuss the situation calmly and thoughtfully."

"Let us sit down to eat then," Mama suggested. "You three can then tell us more about how you came by this Invitation, and we will decide what is to be done."

Leia Marie

And that is exactly what they did. By the time Rio licked the last of Clarissa's cream from his gingerbread bowl, it was decided. The three children would go to the edge of the Great Forest at dawn tomorrow, ready for a great Adventure.

About the Author

Leia Marie has been a psychotherapist and spiritual mentor for over 40 years, and an essayist, retreat facilitator, and ceremonial guide for nearly two decades. Her passion for all things transformational began in her early teens, with those first forays into various wisdom traditions deepening with the years and finding expression in her personal life and through a career of accompanying others in breakthrough moments of healing and deep change. This love continues now with *Enchanted, A Tale of Remembrance*, her first full-length work, with other soul-inspiring creations already underway. Leia lives amid the splendor of the American Rockies with her dear husband of many decades. When she's not absorbed by the sheer wonder of the Cosmos or falling flat on her face proving yet again she's a work-in-progress, Leia is marveling at the beauty of the natural world, writing, reading fantasy fiction, and/or cherishing deep connection with other exquisite work-in-progress souls. Oh, and laughing! She does love to laugh!

Leia invites you to visit her website www.in-awe.net, and follow her on FaceBook at https://www.facebook.com/awewithleiamarie and Instagram at https://www.instagram.com/leiamarie1234/

Made in United States
North Haven, CT
25 March 2023